TWO NEWCOMERS STEPPED INTO THE ROOM. . . .

An Elosian male and a Romulan female.

"Ah," the Elosian premier said, "I believe the others have arrived."

"Captain Picard," Daithin continued. "This is my chief of staff, Larkin, who was responsible for making the arrangements to bring you here."

Picard only glanced at the Elosian premier in response, and if the world leader said anything else, he missed it. At that moment, all of his attention was focused on the woman walking into the room and toward him.

All he could see was the blond hair.

"Why, Captain Picard, so good to see you again," Commander Sela said.

Look for STAR TREK Fiction from Pocket Books

Star Trek: The Original Series

Federation
Sarek
Best Destiny
Shadows on the Sun
Probe
Prime Directive
The Lost Years
Star Trek VI: The Undiscovered Country
Star Trek V: The Final Frontier
Star Trek IV: The Voyage Home
Spock's World
Enterprise
Strangers from the Sky
Final Frontier

#1   Star Trek: The Motion Picture
#2   The Entropy Effect
#3   The Klingon Gambit
#4   The Covenant of the Crown
#5   The Prometheus Design
#6   The Abode of Life
#7   Star Trek II: The Wrath of Khan
#8   Black Fire
#9   Triangle
#10 Web of the Romulans
#11 Yesterday's Son
#12 Mutiny on the Enterprise
#13 The Wounded Sky
#14 The Trellisane Confrontation
#15 Corona
#16 The Final Reflection
#17 Star Trek III: The Search for Spock
#18 My Enemy, My Ally
#19 The Tears of the Singers
#20 The Vulcan Academy Murders
#21 Uhura's Song
#22 Shadow Lord
#23 Ishmael
#24 Killing Time
#25 Dwellers in the Crucible
#26 Pawns and Symbols
#27 Mindshadow
#28 Crisis on Centaurus
#29 Dreadnought!

#30 Demons
#31 Battlestations!
#32 Chain of Attack
#33 Deep Domain
#34 Dreams of the Raven
#35 The Romulan Way
#36 How Much for Just the Planet?
#37 Bloodthirst
#38 The IDIC Epidemic
#39 Time for Yesterday
#40 Timetrap
#41 The Three-Minute Universe
#42 Memory Prime
#43 The Final Nexus
#44 Vulcan's Glory
#45 Double, Double
#46 The Cry of the Onlies
#47 The Kobayashi Maru
#48 Rules of Engagement
#49 The Pandora Principle
#50 Doctor's Orders
#51 Enemy Unseen
#52 Home Is the Hunter
#53 Ghost Walker
#54 A Flag Full of Stars
#55 Renegade
#56 Legacy
#57 The Rift
#58 Faces of Fire
#59 The Disinherited
#60 Ice Trap
#61 Sanctuary
#62 Death Count
#63 Shell Game
#64 The Starship Trap
#65 Windows on a Lost World
#66 From the Depths
#67 The Great Starship Race
#68 Firestorm
#69 The Patrian Transgression
#70 Traitor Winds
#71 Crossroad
#72 The Better Man
#73 Recovery

Star Trek: The Next Generation

Star Trek Generations
All Good Things . . .
Q-Squared
Dark Mirror
Descent
The Devil's Heart
Imzadi
Relics
Reunion
Unification
Metamorphosis
Vendetta
Encounter at Farpoint

#1   Ghost Ship
#2   The Peacekeepers
#3   The Children of Hamlin
#4   Survivors
#5   Strike Zone
#6   Power Hungry
#7   Masks
#8   The Captains' Honor
#9   A Call to Darkness
#10   A Rock and a Hard Place
#11   Gulliver's Fugitives

#12   Doomsday World
#13   The Eyes of the Beholders
#14   Exiles
#15   Fortune's Light
#16   Contamination
#17   Boogeymen
#18   Q-in-Law
#19   Perchance to Dream
#20   Spartacus
#21   Chains of Command
#22   Imbalance
#23   War Drums
#24   Nightshade
#25   Grounded
#26   The Romulan Prize
#27   Guises of the Mind
#28   Here There Be Dragons
#29   Sins of Commission
#30   Debtors' Planet
#31   Foreign Foes
#32   Requiem
#33   Balance of Power
#34   Blaze of Glory
#35   Romulan Stratagem

Star Trek: Deep Space Nine

Warped
The Search

#1   Emissary
#2   The Siege
#3   Bloodletter
#4   The Big Game

#5   Fallen Heroes
#6   Betrayal
#7   Warchild
#8   Antimatter
#9   Proud Helios
#10   Valhalla

Star Trek: Voyager

#1   The Caretaker
#2   The Escape

STAR TREK
THE NEXT GENERATION®

THE ROMULAN STRATAGEM

ROBERT GREENBERGER

POCKET BOOKS

New York   London   Toronto   Sydney   Tokyo   Singapore

An *Original* Publication of POCKET BOOKS

POCKET BOOKS, a division of Simon & Schuster
1230 Avenue of the Americas, New York, NY 10020

This book is published by Pocket Books, a division of
Simon & Schuster Inc., under exclusive license from
Paramount Pictures.

ISBN: 0-671-87997-9

First Pocket Books printing May 1995

10 9 8 7 6 5 4 3 2 1

POCKET and colophon are registered trademarks of
Simon & Schuster Inc.

Printed in the U.S.A.

For Edwin L. Greenberger, who encouraged me to dream and helped teach me how to write.

Author's Notes

This one was a long time in coming. For the better part of the last decade I have always thought that I had a *Star Trek* story in me and have made a few attempts at fiction through my delightful collaborations on *Doomsday World* and *The Disinherited*. Now's the chance for me to put up or shut up and write a novel.

There have been few creations in this century that have spurred the imaginations of so many people. *Star Trek* and Superman are two of them and I have been a proud part of both for more than a decade now. Both fire the imaginations of fans and fellow professionals alike. Both have also survived the sometimes painful transition from one medium to the next. And both are about ideals, something the rest of us can strive toward. During the twenty-fifth anniversary hoopla, I spoke with more than a few reporters on the subject of *Star Trek*'s longevity, and it's really come down to the fact that Gene Roddenberry found something to say at a time when people were ready to hear it. He spoke about peace and prosperity when the world was divided by cultural revolutions and an unpopular war.

He said that we would survive the ecological time bomb, and racial hatred was to be put aside. Gene never said it was going to be a painless transition (just look at the glimpses he had given us between 1966 and the twenty-third century) but we *would* make it. Such optimism certainly struck a chord within me, and I've signed on to help us get there one way or another.

I would not have got this far without the help and friendship of many people, and this is my chance to thank them all at once.

Dave Stern was the first Pocket Books editor to have faith in my skills and to give me a chance to contribute ideas that have grown into other novels and to allow me in on the collaborations even though I had no prose experience.

Current Pocket Books editor and *Star Trek* guru Kevin Ryan has continued to display that kind of faith and has read the outline to this novel far more times than either of us can count or choose to remember. His patience with me has been exemplary, and even if he won't return calls as fast as I (or any other novelist) would like, he has been there for me.

Howard Weinstein, one of the earliest prolific *Star Trek* novelists, has been my close frieind for nearly twenty years now, and he has finally gotten his wish and seen me sweat out a novel. His unwavering support has been deeply appreciated.

My boss at DC Comics, Terri Cunningham, has suffered through many *Star Trek* trials and tribulations (never say the word *stardate* around her). Her encouragement and friendship meant that I actually got to take the time off and complete this. Thanks also to my long-suffering assistant, Liz Seward, who so ably covered for me at DC Comics while I stayed home to be a writer.

Over the years I have appeared at many *Star Trek*

conventions, none was more fun than Shore Leave in Baltimore. I have made many terrific friends through the appearances I've made once or twice a year. Here's my chance to tip the hat of thanks toward Lance, Kathy, Dave, Mary, Bob, Julie, Steve, Renee, T. Alan, Eric, George, Debbie, and the many incarnations of the STAT committees that have seen fit to invite me.

The biggest thanks must go to Michael Jan Friedman who somehow found the time to read, critique, and help me polish the basic story before it became a novel. Remarkably, he found the time to help out a fledgling writer when he had deadline upon deadline hanging over his head, and a family that liked to see him come up for air a few times a month. His rock-solid support and friendship meant that this novel finally got done.

Finally, there has been no bigger supporter than my wife Deb. She has sat through far too many dinner discussions that turned more toward *Star Trek* than anything else. She has also accompanied me to the shows, reminding me that there is a bigger world to be a part of, and her love and devotion has enabled me to keep *Star Trek* a part of my life but constantly reminded me that there are many other pleasures as well. Two of them, Katie and Robbie, have also been very supportive. As this was written, Katie usually camped out on a beanbag chair in the office and read comic strip collections just to keep me company. Robbie thought it was neat Dad was writing a *Star Trek* novel but wanted to know why it wasn't done already. Families are one of the greatest inventions in the history of mankind, and I'm quite proud and thankful for mine.

Robert Greenberger
Connecticut, 1994

Historian's Note

This adventure takes place several months after the sixth-season episode "Face of the Enemy."

Prologue

FADING STARLIGHT seeped through the small window in the alcove of the bedroom. The dim light fought the room's darkness, enabling Daithin to slip into his chosen uniform of the day without disturbing his still-slumbering wife. She had earned her long morning's nap after years of getting up and preparing him and their children for one kind of battle or another. Rough hands, starting to stiffen with age, stuffed pant legs into boots, and the man marveled—for the thousandth time—just how quiet and peaceful and utterly impossible life had become. Each time he awakened and didn't hear the sound of mortar fire or water slapping against the side of a boat as it crept into harbor under cover of fog, Daithin was surprised.

Silently, thick fingers filled his tiny belt pouches with bits and pieces of his orderly life. Daithin was not sure how he felt about the coming day. He had slept well, remarkable enough given the importance of the events to come, and was curiously at peace with himself despite the aches that were his constant companions—unwanted souvenirs of war. No surprise, though—he had spent months preparing for this moment, one he was sure would forever enshrine his name and his family's in Eloh's history books.

Creeping slowly toward his wife, he leaned over and kissed her gently on the forehead, receiving a satisfied sigh in return. As she turned over he left the room and with measured, practiced steps made his way down the hall, past the children's wing. Children, he mused. They were still his children, although one was destined to marry in half a year and the other was completing her studies half a world away.

Shandra, living amongst the Dar. He shook his head in wonder. Twenty years ago, she would have been studying how to kill them. Now, they were teaching her how to help their world survive. It truly was the age of miracles.

Her room was empty now, as was Danith's, silent monuments to his wife's success in raising them despite the odds. Daithin considered himself fortunate, having two fine offspring—alive, no less—at the tail end of the bitterest, bloodiest chapter in his planet's history.

At least, he hoped it was the tail end.

He entered the kitchen, where a small carafe had already filled up with *kintare*. The tart smell brought a smile to his lips and reminded him of the pride his wife took in raising the fruit from which the hot drink was made. Her abilities with natural things—plants, animals, children—were a constant source of amazement and pride to Daithin.

He sipped his drink, enjoying the thick taste and the silence. Events were building to a crescendo now: within the span of a fortnight, Eloh would be irrevocably changed. And so would his life. It was time for him to rest. Over the span of seven decades he had seen far too much battle, killed far too many innocent people, made far too many decisions based on instinct and whim rather than a balanced knowledge of the facts. Daithin had grown wiser over those years of decision making but those first infant years still weighed heavily on him. He constantly reconsidered actions, sifting facts and situations over and over again in his memory, hoping to find some better way to resolve a given conflict. Often he had managed to find different solutions, but then he was lost in wondering if they were *better* ones.

The drink finished and starlight rapidly giving way to a bright dawn, Daithin rose from his seat, dusted some stray lint off his sleeve, and strode out of his home.

Waln, as always, was standing out in the street waiting for him.

Daithin looked his friend over, and smiled. "You look good today, Governor," he began, a hint of frost coming from his breath.

"And you look terrible," the older man snapped. "That uniform is too tight on you."

"My wife's cooking," Daithin replied, patting his stomach and letting out a chuckle. "Come now, Waln—why are you being so snappish?"

"Do you have to ask?" Waln said. He barely looked over at his old friend as they began walking. "You know how I feel. We're not ready for this! None of us is. The Cooperative Defense Projects are going to be stalled for another month at least, and you can bet the Dar won't let any construction begin until they receive assurances about their existing weaponry, and the conductor general is not going to start disarmament until he receives assurances that his office will be free from any legislative interference, and . . ."

Waln continued his usual litany of complaints about the Unified Government's failings as the two men strolled past home after home, most with windows shuttered and lights still out. People in government usually rose much later, he knew, and he was initially considered a bit odd for the early days he put in. A legacy of his life as a soldier.

"—So it's ridiculously early to consider putting any further strain on these alliances. The governors all agree with me, you realize, and—"

Daithin shook his head. "That's not how they voted, Waln. You know that."

"Well, you know how I voted." Waln looked down and kept walking. "They'll bite our hands off."

"My, you're in rare form this morning," Daithin replied, trying to keep the mood light. They had had this same debate almost every morning for the last week.

Waln was having none of it, though. "I do not for the life of me understand your urgency," he said. "We argued and debated for months at a stretch, and then one day you announced we would have a vote. You never pushed through a vote before in your life. Why now?"

Daithin stopped in his tracks and turned to Waln. In that instant, he saw not his lifelong friend, the soldier who had fought by his side for a quarter century, the general who had been among the first to declare his support for the Unified Government, but a tired, scared old man, afraid of any further change in a lifetime that had already seen the world turned upside down. And in that moment, Daithin had a sudden urge to grab his friend's shoulders and shake him, and tell him the truth.

Why did I press this decision? Daithin wanted to say. *Because the Grand Alliance is on the verge of falling apart, Waln! Neither you nor any of the other governors have learned to set aside your clan interests* and put Eloh's first. And if the disarmament issue doesn't push us all back into civil war, something else will. This is the only thing that can possibly save us!

But there's another reason, old friend, maybe the most important of all.

Because I'm going to die soon—and I want to make sure my world, and my son, and my daughter, and all the others I care about—survive.

Daithin said none of that, though. Instead, he simply smiled and clapped Waln on the shoulder.

"You trusted me to know when the time was right to make peace with the Dar," he said. "And I was right about that, wasn't I? Trust me now, Waln. It was as important to make this decision—now, at this very time."

Waln looked up at him and shook his head.

"I do trust you, Daithin—but with all my heart, I believe that the decision you have forced upon us now is wrong. Catastrophically wrong." Waln paused a moment, and looked his friend in the eye. "I am not alone in believing this, you know."

"I know," Daithin replied. "But it is your opposition that wounds me the most."

"I do not intend to wound you, Daithin. Only to serve my world—my people—as I see best." His tone was uncharacteristically grave and made Daithin acutely uncomfortable.

The two walked on in silence, until they finally came to the parliament. The building was set off from all others by a vast ring of greenery that added pomp and circumstance to the structure. Morning sunlight was reflecting off windows both clear and frosted, twinkling as if it bid the duo greeting.

A half-dozen guards stood flanking the main entrance. Daithin's heart skipped a beat. Something was wrong.

As he watched, a younger man in civilian clothing detached himself from the soldiers and strode briskly forward to meet them. Daithin relaxed slightly as he recognized his chief aide, Larkin.

"Good morning, Governor," Larkin said to Waln. Then he turned and gave his full attention to Daithin. "Premier—they're early. They will achieve orbit within the hour. Our first meeting with them will follow an hour after that." Larkin's eyes glittered. "In less than two hours, sir, you will be making direct contact with people from a distant star. It's remarkable."

Daithin smiled. It was good to see someone else excited about what the day would bring. "I promise you, Waln," he began, turning to his friend, "you will have no cause to regret today's events. I—"

He stopped talking, because the governor had already stalked away and was even now entering Parliament.

"Something wrong, sir?" Larkin asked.

Daithin shook his head. "The governor is not thrilled about our visitors, Larkin."

"You know what they say, sir," his aide replied. "The future waits for no man."

Larkin's earnestness made Daithin smile. "Well, Larkin," Daithin said, taking his first step toward the parliament building, "the future will have to wait just a little while for me—at least until I've had another cup of *kintare.*"

"Yes, sir," Larkin said, falling into place beside him. The younger man took out a sheaf of paper from the folder he was carrying and began to read from it. "You should know that the leaders of the trade council have agreed to attend the evening session with our visitors, so I've moved that session to the Main Assembly, and arranged dinner for an additional fifty people with the staff. I've also arranged tours of the purification facility, the council sessions, and the youth league. Your first meeting . . ."

As Larkin reviewed the day's schedule, Daithin felt himself begin to relax and the unpleasant aftertaste of his argument with Waln fade away. The governor will see I'm right, he told himself, once he meets with our visitors.

And if Waln didn't like today's guests, well then— perhaps tomorrow's would be more to his liking.

Chapter One

SCREAMING.

That was the first thing Ensign Ro Laren heard as the lift doors opened. Then the smell hit her. Smoke.

"Computer," she began, hitting the hallway at a dead run. "Identify source of fire. Locate."

There was no response. As she had feared. The fire must have damaged the audio interface. Damn. It would take her precious seconds to find the fire on her own. She hoped those seconds weren't too costly.

Ro had been heading to her quarters when the lift she was in had been brought to an abrupt halt by the ship's computer systems on this floor. To allow her to render assistance, she surmised—and to allow others a chance to escape the fire.

She turned a corner and blinked. The hall before her was filling rapidly with smoke. The screaming here was louder, more insistent.

Children, she realized suddenly. The fire was in one of the *Enterprise*'s classrooms. The one right before her.

She forced the door open, and stepped into chaos.

9

It was an electrical fire, she saw instantly. Sparks escaped from behind the wall paneling with little hisses and pops. Children shrieked and ran away from the wall, scurrying around the corridor, at first unsure where to turn. The blown circuits continued to create their own cacophony, trying to make themselves heard over the children. Their teacher pushed them back, making calming noises in the back of his throat.

"This way!" Ro shouted. "This way out!"

The children nearest her looked up and began moving toward her—too slowly. They were still too scared—and too young—to react intelligently. She needed help.

With swift strides Ro moved toward their teacher, an unremarkable man of about fifty with a slight stoop to his shoulders, who was standing before the computer display on the far wall. The fire had originated from there, she saw instantly. Short circuit.

"Sir, please move out of the way so I can shut this console down." Even as she spoke, her eyes were scanning the wall for a fire suppression device. There. "I need your help in getting the children out."

The man looked up, glanced at her a second, and then—incredibly—returned his attention to the computer display before him.

"I almost have the circuits rerouted," he said. "A minute more and I'll be able to stop the malfunction from spreading."

"We don't have time for that now," Ro said urgently. She reached behind the wall panel next to her for the fire suppression device, grabbed it, and moved next to the console. "Sir," she repeated. "Please—step aside."

"One minute more," the man said, sweat pouring down his brow. "I'll have it."

This was insane. The fire was less dangerous than

she had initially thought, but it was bad enough. And every second it continued, the potential for a catastrophe existed. She had no time to argue.

With her free hand she grabbed the back of the man's shirt and ripped him away from the computer interface. He landed hard against the far wall, the thud a quiet sound compared to the spreading fire.

Ro snapped off the safety lock on the fire suppression device, and a second later a stream of foam poured forth. The console shut down—and moments later the fire was out. Within minutes uniformed engineers had arrived to handle the situation. They thanked Ro for her work and then ignored her.

By the time she reached her cabin, she'd turned her mind to the thousand and one other things she had to do aboard the starship.

She honestly never expected to hear anything else about the fire.

"You certainly have a way with people," William Riker said as the observation lounge's door swooshed closed behind her. The first officer, tall and broad, leaned over the chair at the head of the table, near the doorway.

"Thank you, Commander," Ro said. "Do you mean in general, or do you have a specific person in mind?"

"Gregori Andropov," Riker said.

Ro frowned. "I don't know the man."

"You nearly tossed him through a bulkhead yesterday, Ensign," Riker continued.

"Oh," she said. "The teacher."

"That's right—the teacher." Riker shook his head. "Ensign, what are we going to do with you?"

Ro frowned again. Ever since she signed on board nearly two years earlier, she knew her stubborn independence had found her in one confrontation after another with the senior command staff. Ro also knew that circumstances had dictated that she totally trust these people with her life, and they had never failed that trust. Therefore, she always submitted to these meetings even though it meant doing her level best to keep her famed temper in check. She kept herself in profile to Riker, watching the streaked stars drift by as the proud starship traveled through warp space.

"Sir," she began. "We had a major circuit failure on that deck, and if I hadn't moved him out of the way—fast—we could have had a catastrophe! What was I supposed to do? Wait and politely ask for him to shuffle away?"

"No, but he's a civilian, not trained to react the way you and I are, and you have to keep that in mind, Ensign! There are over a thousand people aboard this ship; that means over one thousand possible reactions to any given situation, and as an officer, you must be ready to act or react accordingly. Charging through him like a moose certainly doesn't earn you anyone's respect, and it only heightens tension between the civilian side and Starfleet."

Ro continued to stand ramrod straight and paused before speaking again, forcing herself to act like the officer she was.

"I suppose so, sir," she replied. "I suppose my actions could have been a little less—emphatic."

"You suppose?" Riker asked.

Despite herself, Ro glared at him. "Yes, sir. My actions could have been a little different and the end result would have remained the same: the circuit fire would have been contained."

"I'm glad to hear you say that, Ensign," Riker said. He began to move toward her and she watched the practiced ease of his gait. Everything he did as first officer was merely rehearsal for when he would gain a long-deserved command of his own. She admired the dedication Riker brought to his job, and in some ways found him a kindred spirit. Their chief difference was that he had long ago learned to rechannel his passions so they would not interfere with his job. Ro sometimes feared this was something beyond her grasp.

"I can't fault your dedication to duty," Riker said. "But your approach . . . now that's something we have to work on."

"Again," she muttered, under her breath.

"Again," he echoed and then let go one of his patented smiles. "Ensign, I think I have just the solution so this kind of a problem will not happen again. We have quite a number of civilians living aboard this ship, not all of them with direct ties to Starfleet. Just as you're not sure how to act around them, they may not know how to act around you. When we left Starbase 211 two days ago, fourteen new families transferred aboard. I'm assigning you to escort one of these new families around for three or four days. Get used to their point of view, their understanding of how we operate. They can also get your perspective on being part of Starfleet. I think both sides would benefit."

Ro's jaw dropped. "Commander, I'm not a tour guide! I didn't come aboard the *Enterprise* just so families can see me as a role model. I'm a Starfleet officer, and my place—"

"Your place, Ensign, is where it best serves this ship," Riker snapped. "Your schedule will be adjusted to accommodate your new role as orientation officer and yes, role model it may well be. I think, and I'm sure Captain Picard will agree, that you could use a little more experience with the civilian element aboard this ship. I'll have your orders posted to the computer." Riker took a deep breath and then said, "Dismissed."

Ro spun on her heel and stormed out of the observation lounge, thoroughly unhappy. She almost ran headlong into Geordi La Forge on her way out. The *Enterprise*'s chief engineer stepped aside to let her pass.

"Had another one of those chats, did you?" he asked Riker as the door slid shut behind her.

The commander sighed wearily and smiled. "I'm going to make an officer out of her one of these days or die trying."

As La Forge slipped into his accustomed seat, he smiled. "I'm betting on you dying. In fact, the odds are in my favor."

Riker looked surprised at the comment. "Odds?"

"Yeah, Lance Woods in research has been taking bets on you two for months. I figure I can retire on my winnings."

The first officer laughed and settled into his own seat, and glanced toward the doors. Expectant, he wished he could will people in so the meeting could begin. No matter what their next mission was, it had to be better than their current mapping assignment.

Within minutes, Dr. Beverly Crusher, Counselor Deanna Troi, and the Klingon Security Chief Lieutenant Worf all joined him and Geordi in the observation lounge. Despite the casual manner in which they greeted each other Riker could detect the undercurrent of expectancy in the room. He pictured the Captain, sitting in his ready room, on the opposite side of the bridge, counting off the minutes before he could make a dramatic entrance.

Instead, to his disappointment, Riker watched the doors quietly *swoosh* open and admit the captain, deep in conversation with Data, the ship's android second officer.

"Not everything is as it seems, Mister Data," Jean-Luc Picard commented as they walked through the doorway. "You certainly have learned that during your time aboard the *Enterprise.*"

"Of course, Captain," Data responded as he took his place at the polished table. "I was merely pointing out that Stelin of Vulcan's writings address themselves to the clarity of logical deduction."

"I do not question that," the captain said, taking his place at the table's head. "But we have dealt with situations where logical deduction has left us with wrong answers."

"Only because all the information was not available at the time," Data countered.

"Wouldn't you say that Arthur Conan Doyle wrote on much the same topic in his own way?" Picard suggested.

Data paused briefly, his expression indicating he was considering this new thread of thought. "Yes, sir. I believe it was Doyle who first put forth the idea that when all else proves unlikely, then the only thing left is the impossible."

Picard shook his head and replied, "Poe."

"Who, sir?" Riker asked, jumping in. Picard looked in the opposite direction of Data and seemed just then to realize that his other senior officers were already assembled, quietly watching the discussion.

"Edgar Allen Poe, Number One," Picard said with a small smile. "I recall reading his detective works during a survey course at the Academy. Not at all my style."

"Are you well read on detective fiction, sir?" Data asked. "I had thought you concentrated only on Dixon Hill."

15

Picard grinned. "Actually, this course gave me an opportunity to sample the works of major writers and characters in that genre. They did not include Dixon Hill, whom I discovered on my own."

"I didn't realize Poe wrote a detective character," Riker said.

"Poe is credited with inventing the genre, Commander. I recommend you review his works."

"I'll do that, sir," Riker replied. "Time permitting, of course."

"Of course," Picard said. "Now then—shall we begin?" The captain straightened his red duty jacket and folded his hands before him. The act was unconscious—but it was also a cue to Riker, attuned to his captain's mannerisms from their years of service together, that the matter about to be discussed was a serious one indeed. The first officer adjusted himself in his chair and gave Captain Picard his full attention.

"We have been given a wonderful opportunity by Starfleet to pave the way for full diplomatic relations with a new world," he began. With the touch of a button, a view screen behind Picard came to life and displayed a star chart with one solar system highlighted in a crimson frame.

"This is Eloh—a world that has just gone through several decades of civil war and is finally united under one government," he explained. "Their world lies in the buffer space between the Klingon and Romulan Empires. To date they have not been visited by any other extraterrestrial race, but their communications equipment has alerted them to our presence. Now that they can concentrate on matters beyond survival, it has become apparent to their leaders that sooner or later, they will be involved with one empire or the other."

"And they've chosen sooner," Riker said. "Rather

than get gobbled up on someone else's schedule, they want to set the agenda."

"Exactly," Picard nodded. "As you will see from this chart, by having Eloh as a Federation protectorate, we will be closer than ever to having a direct influence on Romulan affairs. The theory is that prolonged contact with our way of life will only have a positive impact on Federation/Romulan relations."

At the end of the table, Worf leaned forward and spoke. "We would also be able to legally place an observation post in their system. An early-warning device, in case of a planned Romulan attack."

"We would," Picard agreed. "Our job here is to make the first contact in person, establish the necessary ties, and prepare for a full diplomatic mission to follow. As I understand it, the Federation Diplomatic Office has already equipped them with universal translators and our systems now have their language stored. At our present course, we will be in their system within hours. I estimate we'll be spending close to a week here, getting to know as much as possible about the Elohsians."

"What have we learned about them to date?" Riker asked.

"The *U.S.S. Cochrane* did a preliminary survey about three years ago—strictly instrumental probes, nothing intrusive. Technlogically, they're at a level roughly equivalent to late twentieth-century Earth." The captain paused. "Here's the tricky part. Starfleet wants us to keep technological matters to a minimum at present. The planet has two options: form an allegiance with us or ask to be left alone. If they choose the latter, the less they know about us, the better. If we are to proceed together, then the formal diplomatic team can bring them up to date later. I hope I'm clear on this point."

The small group of officers then proceeded to discuss matters involving the Romulans, the Klingons, and galactic politics as it might pertain to the new planet. Riker delighted in these sessions since it gave everyone a chance to understand the mission and display their own concerns. He was able to absorb their feelings and questions, usually finding one or two things to consider that he himself had not previously thought about. It was the captain's practice to allow such discussion to take its own course until the topic was exhausted. This time, they had barely gotten started when an all-too-familiar klaxon sounded and a flashing red light went off in the lounge.

Riker was on his feet and heading toward the bridge before he was even aware of it—just a step behind Captain Picard.

"Status," Picard said, taking his seat in the center of the bridge. But Riker didn't even need to hear the duty officer's reply to know what the problem was.

It was staring him in the face, right there on the forward viewscreen.

"Romulan warbird, sir," Lieutenant D'Sora announced from behind them, at the tactical display. "Now in orbit around the planet Eloh."

Chapter Two

LIEUTENANT JENNA D'SORA sidestepped to allow Worf his customary place behind the tactical station.

"Tell me about that ship," Riker said as he rounded the sloping walkway that led to the center command section. He couldn't sit down—not until he knew exactly what was happening.

"From this distance scans are imprecise," Commander Data replied. His pale golden hands flew briefly across the Ops panel. "Detecting no subspace communications or weapons activity of any sort."

"Ship is an older style warbird, B-type, similar to the ones we encountered near Angel One," Worf declared. "Sensors show the hull is damaged, most likely in a recent battle. Repairs have not yet occurred." He looked up at Riker with a satisfied expression. "No threat to the *Enterprise.*"

Riker nodded. Now he could sit—and did so, in his accustomed seat in the center horseshoe, to Captain Picard's right.

"Mr. Data—how long till we reach Eloh?" Picard asked.

Data barely paused before answering, "Eleven hours, thirteen minutes at present speed."

Picard nodded. Tomorrow morning, right on schedule.

The android glanced down at his console again. "Sir, my instruments show no traces of the kind of residual energy associated with recent weapons activity."

"Our last contact with the Elohsians was yesterday evening, so nothing's happened since then," Picard said. He frowned and turned to Riker. "Opinion?"

Riker thought a moment. "Mr. Data—check that ship for radio-band frequency transmissions."

Picard smiled, and nodded. "Of course. Twentieth-century technology—"

"—Twentieth-century equipment," Riker finished. "They won't have subspace capability yet."

"One moment, Commander," Data said, hands flying over his sensor panel, reconfiguring it for the task at hand. "No distress signals—however, I am picking up extensive communications between the warbird and the Elohsian government."

"Informational exchanges, sir," Worf said from the tactical station behind them. "Cultural, historical—"

"I think you can cancel the red alert, Captain," Troi said from her seat to Picard's left. "It's clear the Romulans are the Elohsian's guests."

Riker got it instantly. "They've invited all the neighbors."

The implication did not sit well with Picard but he admitted to himself that it did fit the facts. Signaling to Worf to cancel the red alert, he finished the thought his officers had left unspoken. "Just as we have been summoned to present the Federation's case, they may well also have invited the Romulans to make the same . . . pitch."

"The Elohsians would willingly join with the Romulan Empire?" Worf was astounded. "That would be . . . suicidal."

"We know that," Riker said. "They may not."

"With all due respect, Commander," Data said, turning in his seat. "I must disagree. Federation records from the early twenty-third century refer to several cultures which not only survived but prospered under Romulan stewardship."

"None of which we've heard from recently," Picard said, cutting in. "Still, there must be something attractive about the Empire to them."

"I'm wondering why they didn't tell us we'd be undergoing this kind of . . . competition," Riker said.

Picard nodded, asking himself the same question. To find the answer to that, though, he'd have to know a lot more about the Elohsians and their culture. He'd skimmed the *Cochrane*'s initial reports, giving all but the last twenty-five years of Eloh's history short shrift. He wanted to correct that error now—in his ready room, with a nice hot cup of tea.

He stared at the screen, trying to guess which prick of light might be Eloh's sun. He wondered, too, at the choice of an older warbird to represent the Romulans. An older ship also meant the planet was desirable to the Empire but not supremely important. And it also almost certainly meant he wouldn't be seeing Admiral Tomulak again—a thought that caused a momentary smile to crease his face.

The captain stood, straightening his short jacket and gray shirt. "Number One, continue sensor scans on the planet and the warbird. Notify me immediately if the situation changes. Once we arrive, we'll assume orbit and confirm our appointment with their premier. Until then, I'll be in my ready room."

"Aye, sir," Riker said, sliding into the center seat.

As he left the bridge, Picard overheard with satisfaction his first officer reminding all command personnel to give the mission briefings a thorough going-over.

No matter what they came up against on Eloh, Picard felt certain his crew would be prepared.

This was ridiculous, Ro Laren thought, gripping the data padd tightly in one hand as she swiftly rounded the corner of the deck. The *Enterprise* was on an important first-contact mission now—as a bridge officer, she had access to the mission briefing—Romulans were involved, and here she was getting ready to lead a guided tour of the starship.

Commander Riker was out of his mind. Time enough to work on improving her relationship with the ship's civilian population once the crisis was over. She'd gone to Riker this morning, expecting him to see the logic in her argument and restore her to active duty.

"You have your orders, Ensign," was all he'd said. "Dismissed."

Just like that. She still couldn't believe it. And now she was in some backwater part of the ship she'd never even seen before. This part of the saucer section was normally reserved for officers' families and other civilian personnel. She had no family, of course, or friends that were civilians.

Which was lucky, she supposed. Because she didn't like it here. The corridor had an undisciplined look to it—each doorway was individually decorated, to indicate the occupant and planet of origin, which she didn't object to at all in theory. But in practice, she found most of the decorations just a little bit gaudy for her taste.

She checked her data padd and realized with a start that she had arrived at her destination.

She stopped before the door and noted the calligraphy announcing the family name and the small holographic projection of Earth. Taking a deep breath, she tapped the door buzzer.

The doors slid open to reveal a young boy—no, a teenager, she decided—who looked rather surprised to be face-to-face with a member of the command crew.

"Uh, hi," he stammered. One hand ran through his long sandy brown hair and another tried quickly to tuck his gold-striped shirt back into his dark brown pants.

Ro glared at him. From the youth's attitude, he probably thought he was in trouble.

"I am Ensign Ro Laren," she began formally. "I have been assigned to be your family's orientation officer."

"Uh-huh," he said, stammering again. "I'm James Kelly. My family's not here right now. Sorry. But you can come in if you want."

Ro rolled her eyes. She had no desire to see this boy's home. She was supposed to show *him* the *Enterprise*. This job was clearly going to be a complete waste of her time. Nonetheless . . .

Commander Riker had given her a responsibility, and Bajorans always regarded responsibilities gravely.

"I will see your quarters," Ro said, taking a step forward.

James stepped back, allowing Ro to enter. She looked around, trying to get a sense of the family. It was hard. The main room was largely filled with boxes marked Personal Belongings that had not yet been unpacked.

"My mom's working a shift in the cargo bay and Dad's teaching a fifth-grade group," James said.

"I see," Ro nodded.

There was an awkward silence. Ro had no idea what she should say next. Neither, clearly, did James. He alternated between staring at her and then looking away abruptly.

"You have a lovely home," Ro offered.

"Thank you, Ensign Laren," James said, his voice cracking.

"Ro. It is Ensign Ro," she informed him coldly. She then realized that the civilian crew would not need to be versed in the ways of Bajoran address.

"Sorry," came the reply. "Yes, Ensign Ro."

Ro looked again at her padd. "My time is committed to your family for the remainder of beta shift," she said. "I could begin with your ship orientation, if you wish."

"You would orient me?" James gulped. A huge grin crossed his face. "Wow . . . that would be great."

Ro nodded, unsure of why James was so excited. Perhaps his enthusiasm would help the tour go faster, she told herself.

"We will begin in engineering," she said matter-of-factly. "This is the heart of the starship, powered by a matter-antimatter reactor which . . ."

James fell into step beside her, positively radiant.

Picard stepped up on the transporter platform next to Commander Data and Counselor Troi, who were already in position.

"Any parting words of wisdom, Number One?" the captain asked.

Riker, standing at the transporter console, shook his head.

"Same ones as before, sir. I wish you'd let me go in

your place. Or at least take Lieutenant Worf. I don't like having you down there without security—especially with the Romulans on the planet."

Picard smiled. They'd been over this ground already. "My orders have me representing the Federation, and I must be there for that first meeting."

"Your orders, sir, did not take into account that Romulans would be present."

"No, they did not," Picard said evenly. "However, the Romulans would be making a very poor case for themselves were they to open fire the minute I materialize on Eloh. No, I think they will be on good behavior."

"Then all I can do is wish you good luck, sir," Riker responded. "Energize."

Picard, Data, and Troi materialized in the anteroom of the parliamentary chambers. As soon as Picard could adjust his vision, a second or two after the transporter began rematerializing his atoms on Eloh, he spotted a small delegation. One thing was immediately clear about the Elohsians.

They were tall. Very, very tall.

Humanoid in appearance, of the delegation of a half-dozen dignitaries before them, none was shorter than two meters. And at that moment, none of them was smiling. It made for a very foreboding first impression, and Picard wondered briefly what lies the Romulans had already told them about the Federation.

He stepped forward. "I am Captain Jean-Luc Picard of the United Federation of Planets. This is Commander Data and Counselor Troi."

The Elohsian in the center of the group—a man somewhat stouter and older-looking than the others—took a step forward and gestured with his left fist over his heart.

"Welcome to Eloh," he said. "I am Daithin, premier of the United Parliament." Daithin's clothing was dark purple with gold and silver ornamentation and silver piping in intricate designs along the sleeves and pants. The shoes were half-boots, brightly polished and tipped in a copper-colored metal. The premier wore nothing resembling a weapon or communications device except the Federation-sent universal translator, Picard noted, but the man had eyes that showed experience and a face that had weathered many a battle. Small, violent red scars remained around his broad forehead, set off against the dark skin. While the clothing was all dark, none of the outfits worn by the six Elohsians matched, so Picard ruled out any military meaning to the clothing.

Daithin took a step back and opened both arms, the gesture sweeping enough to take in all five people in his delegation. "These are my advisors, and you will meet them all in due time." Daithin smiled. "But first, allow me to offer you some refreshments."

Picard and his officers followed Daithin into a small anteroom off the main chamber. He studied his host as food and beverages were served, careful to follow Daithin's lead. And as he studied the premier, Picard watched Daithin and the other Elohsians studying himself and his crew. Measuring each other up.

No sense in small talk, Picard thought. He decided to ask the question that was on his mind.

"Premier," he said. "Can you tell me what a Romulan warbird is doing in orbit around your world?"

Daithin looked at Picard for a moment and then smiled slightly, showing white and straight teeth. "Of course, Captain Picard, of course. We naturally invited the Romulans to meet with us as well. After all, the parliament must study both our neighboring Empires before choosing which one to ally ourselves with."

"Of course," Picard agreed. "I was just surprised since we were not informed of this in advance."

"Nor did we inform the Romulans about you." Daithin smiled. "In fact, I just finished discussing the matter with their leader. Come, let me make the necessary introductions so we may confirm an agenda and a schedule." Daithin spun on his heel and turned away from the Federation group. Picard appreciated brevity as much as the next man, but he suddenly got the feeling he had just witnessed Daithin's normal modus operandi. Explanations around here, it seemed, would not be easy to come by.

Exchanging glances with his officers, Picard led the small group behind Daithin's party. The anteroom was not exactly small, and it led into a corridor which ended with a set of double doors, also ornately carved in steel.

As the doors opened, Picard studied the construction of the parliamentary chamber. The room was made of a smooth, rounded material. No wood was in evidence nor was the structure metallic. Instead, it seemed made of other materials, all seamlessly fitted together and in complementary colors. Whereas their clothing was dark with bright highlights, the room was neutral with bright turquoise trim. The ceiling seemed to be about twenty feet high with skylights every few feet, allowing bright filtered light to fill the chamber. Stained glass windows stood on either side of the large dais that was at the front of the room. On both sides of the dais were row after row of small tables and chairs. At a quick glance, Picard estimated that the ruling parliament had eight seats on the dais, and another forty or fifty seats finished the room. Small lamps glowed needlessly, illuminating empty desks and giving off distracting shadows below Picard's field of vision.

Those interested him far less, though, than the half-dozen Romulans near one of the windows. They appeared to be deep in conversation, oblivious to the arrival of the Federation party.

"My Romulan friends, I want you to meet your Federation counterparts," Daithin began as he worked his way toward the dais. At his words, the Romulans all turned toward the doors and watched the Federation officers approach.

Daithin used simple hand gestures to introduce each officer from the warbird. The clear leader of the group was a tall, older officer named Plactus. Each Romulan in turn merely stared at the *Enterprise* officers. Only Plactus, introduced as a subcommander, nodded something resembling a welcome.

"It is an honor to meet you, Captain Picard," Plactus said.

"Oh?" Picard tried to read the subcommander's expression, but it was impassive and his eyes were shadowed.

"You and your ship are, of course, well known among my people."

Picard replied tightly, "I'm sorry we cannot say the same for you and your crew."

"These men are under my command, yes, but I am not the leading representative from my government."

"I see, and then your commander is . . . ?" Picard found this interesting. If they had a commander, where was he and why would he not be with the rest of the delegation?

"Occupied."

Picard started to prompt Plactus for additional information, but then noted out of the corner of his eye that Daithin was watching the exchange with deep interest. It wouldn't do to seem too preoccupied with the Romulans. He was here to impress the Elohsians with what the Federation had to offer them, not with their feud.

He was trying to find a safe topic of conversation with Daithin when he heard voices approaching from the corridor. As the heavy wooden door swung back, he could hear a woman's voice saying, ". . . there is much more to our technology, and we can happily show you during your tour tomorrow."

Suddenly something clicked in Picard's subconscious. He knew that voice, but from where. . . . His brain began rifling its private files, trying to match the voice to a name. He began to stand a little taller, suddenly on alert.

The two newcomers stepped into the room. A man and a woman. An Elohsian male, and a Romulan female.

"Ah," the man said, "I believe the others have arrived."

"Captain Picard," Daithin said. "This is my chief of staff, Larkin, who was responsible for making the arrangements to bring you here. Your—liason, I believe the word is—am I correct?"

Picard only glanced at the premier in response, and if the world leader said anything else, he missed it. At that moment he was not at all concerned with Larkin. All his attention was focused on the woman walking into the room.

All he could see was the blond hair.

A split second later he tore his attention away from her. Daithin, Picard finally forced himself to note, was continuing to watch the exchange with great interest. He tried to remind himself that every word, action, and expression would carry great weight with the Elohsians present. The premier walked toward the two commanders, gesturing in an attempt to make introductions. "You said you were unfamiliar with this crew, Captain Picard, so let me . . ."

"Why, Captain Picard, so good to see you again," Sela said. Her manner was imperious as always. Her demeanor was cool and inflexible—although she did manage a smile in the direction of Premier Daithin.

"There is no need for introductions here, Premier," she continued. "Captain Picard and I know each other very well." Her tone belied the apparent warmth of her words.

"Commander Sela," Picard said steadily. He nodded his head toward her, still staring. As always, her unmistakable resemblance to the *Enterprise*'s original security chief, Tasha Yar, gave him pause. Sela claimed to be Yar's daughter—a Yar from an alternate time line, whom fate had delivered into the Romulans' hands. But whereas Yar had a vulnerable quality to her features, there was nothing weak about Sela. The hard, set mouth and fierce blue eyes blazed as she took Picard's measure. She was dressed in standard Romulan command garb, complete with bulky shoulders, and adorned with weaponry.

Tasha Yar's daughter? Picard still found that difficult to believe—even more so after their initial encounter, when Sela told him that she herself was responsible for ending her mother's life.

"My father had offered her everything," she had told him aboard the *Enterprise* more than a year earlier. "He had given her a home, a daughter. How did she repay him? With betrayal. They executed her. Everything in me that was human . . . died with my mother that day. All that is left . . . is Romulan. Never doubt that.''

Her actions in their two previous encounters had more than convinced Picard of that, but he continued to wonder if her story were true or the brainwashing of a fanatical empire willing to do anything—even destroy someone's life—to further its goals.

Daithin raised a hand. "Captain Picard, Commander Sela—over the next few days, our parliamentary council will speak with you together and separately. We want you to know more about us, and in exchange I hope that I or my people will have the opportunity to see what your ships are like, perhaps speak with your crew?"

Sela jumped in first. "Of course, Premier. However, there will be some areas that will remain off-limits."

"We pride ourselves on a content crew, and speaking with them should show you that," Picard began. "Our ship will be more than happy to host a visiting delegation. Sad to say, like our Romulan counterparts, we, too, have certain areas that we need to steer clear of.''

"Perfectly, perfectly understandable," Daithin agreed. With that said, he turned back to his small cadre of Elohsians and had a few quiet words.

"One final fact you all need to know," Daithin began. "While we were a people divided by war for so long, we remained united under a shared belief system. *Nelvana Del,* our holiest of holidays, begins in seven days' time, and our parliament must conclude its business of the season for everyone to return to their families. We can, therefore, only afford you four days. Our parliamentary members will poll their constituents and then vote on the fifth. Does that pose a problem for either of you?" He eagerly watched the reactions.

"No problem for the Federation, Premier," Picard said without hesitation.

"Of course, not, Premier," Sela snapped.

Daithin smiled again.

"Very well, then," the Premier said. "I look forward to seeing you both shortly."

Picard glared at Sela, and slapped the communicator insignia on his chest.

"Picard to *Enterprise.* Three to beam up."

She glared right back at him.

The competition had begun.

". . . The matter replicators take the frozen, sterilized raw stock and rebuild a pattern through a phase transition chamber and form whatever the menu called for through the replicator distribution net." Ro finished gesturing toward the mess room on deck 32. She had given James Kelly the most detailed tour of a starship she could imagine giving. The ensign had strained herself to give the teen every bit of information he could possibly ask for. Short of giving away Starfleet security codes, Ro wasn't sure if there was another shred of information to provide.

To her astonishment, James Kelly did not seem bored by even the most arcane piece of information. Instead, he hung on to her every word, staring keenly at circuit boards, isolinear chip arrangements, and transport board configurations. The botanical gardens were as interesting to him as the supply lockers.

Clearly, something was wrong with the boy.

"Who determines the menu?" James asked.

She sighed and continued walking through the room, avoiding the two tables filled with engineers just completing their dinner. She had done a lot of sighing these last few hours. "The crew can program the system for any meal they want. Our data banks are filled with thousands of menus from across the Federation."

"Do people cook here? My dad cooks," James said, stopping to gape at the remains of some alien bird bones left over from a meal at one table.

Ro nodded. "Some of the crew use cooking as a hobby. Commander Riker, for example."

Kelly whistled. "So, you spend a lot of time with Commander Riker?"

"When I am not attending to my duties with civilian crew, I am usually at the conn station aboard the bridge. Often I have served with Commander Riker."

"On away missions, too?"

"We have served quite well together," Ro answered. She disliked having to think about her complex relationship with Riker and decided the boy's questions were too personal. After all, Kelly had been on the ship for a handful of days and missed the time the entire crew was given a neurologic shock that left people playing out different roles from normal—including that of Ro and Riker as lovers. Ro barely liked to discuss her life with Picard or Guinan, and she certainly wasn't about to let this youth pry information from her. She abruptly turned away from him.

"I think we had best return you to your quarters. It's after sixteen hundred hours and your parents must be waiting for you. There may be just enough time to meet them before I have to return to duty."

James rushed to keep up with her pace. It was obvious to her that his endless enthusiasm meant he had energy to burn, and she had failed at extinguishing his desires. She remained unsure of what fueled his interests and enthusiasm.

"Aren't we going to visit the bridge?" he asked.

"No," she said. "It is a place of business, and distractions take away from maximum efficiency."

They had arrived at a turbolift. She stood aside to let James enter before her.

"Oh, no," he said, bowing. "Ladies first."

Ro eyed him strangely as she stepped inside.

"The bridge can't always be busy," James said. "Maybe there's another time we could get together and you could show it to me."

Suddenly Ro had had enough. Didn't this child know anything?

"The bridge is not, I repeat *not,* a tourist attraction!" Ro snapped. "It is a place where trained Starfleet officers do their jobs—important jobs, where they accomplish things other than uselessly wandering the ship! Halt!" she barked out. The turbolift came to a stop.

"I am getting out here," she said brusquely to James. "The lift will take you back to your quarters. Please make my apologies to your parents. Good afternoon."

Her last glimpse of Kelly was of the youth looking after her forlornly as the turbolift doors shut behind her.

This had not gone at all well, she realized.

Sela was first off the transporter platform when the materialization was complete. Plactus was on her heels and the two strode without speaking through the hard, metal corridors until they found a lift, which swiftly delivered them to the bridge.

"Status," she snapped before the doors were fully open.

The duty officer stood tall, looked straight ahead and gave a terse report. "*Enterprise* is maintaining geosynchronous orbit. Their weapons remain deactivated, although they have been performing sensor sweeps of the planet."

"Transporter activity?" Plactus asked taking his accustomed station to the left of the lift doors.

"Landing party beam–down and beam–up, Subcommander."

"You are relieved. I will complete the watch," Sela said as she moved toward the command chair. Settling herself in, she put her chin on her right hand and stared at the viewscreen. The main viewer showed the *Enterprise,* large, gleaming, and oh so close. She pictured herself gripping it in her left hand, crushing the hull like tissue paper, and watching the one thousand crew members burn upon entry into Eloh's atmosphere.

"So, Picard and I get to match wits again," she said quietly. Her voice cut through the quiet, tense atmosphere on the bridge like a warning klaxon. Of course, she had expected *Enterprise.* Intelligence reports had predicted the Federation would send their flagship and the warbird's sensors had detected the vessel hours earlier. From that moment onward, she'd had her officers monitoring *Enterprise*'s every move. She had no doubt that word of her unusual orders had quickly spread through the ship and those officers whose careers were now inextricably intertwined with hers had certainly discovered by now that Sela had an old score to settle with this particular vessel.

More than just an old score, she reminded herself, glancing around the bridge at her crew. How far she had fallen, and how fast. From her place at the Praetor's right hand, at the center of the Empire's decision–making nexus, to command of a single run–down ship on the far fringes of Romulan territory. And Picard, more than any other, was to blame.

And here was a chance to even that score—just a little.

Sela glanced around the bridge at her crew, locking eyes with each of her officers in turn as she spoke.

"The stakes in this mission are nothing less than the world beneath us. We must do the praetor proud. A job done well will see our names, and the name of this ship, sung in the halls of the senate—and all our careers made."

"Plactus," she snapped.

"Commander." The older officer stepped forward to stand at her side.

"Let me see that agenda Daithin gave us," she said. "I want to make sure we are prepared for everything."

Plactus nodded and handed her the data tablet.

As she studied it, Sela allowed herself to visualize the instant that she knew was to come—the instant when she would snatch this world away from Picard. She lived for that moment.

Chapter Three

MORNING ON ELOH was sunny and warm. The breeze felt good on Geordi La Forge's skin. This would be the perfect planet for shore leave, he decided. If only we had more than a week.

Geordi was riding in the back seat of an Elohsian "sojourner"—a ground transport vehicle similar to Federation land skimmers. This one was battery-powered, wheel-driven and, his VISOR told him, ran efficiently and emitted few harmful gases.

In the seat beside him, he noted that Deanna Troi was also enjoying the ride and the sights of this small continent. The two of them had beamed down at the crack of dawn and, after getting an overview of their planned schedule, had been flown from the main continent of Regor to Carinth Dar. There, they'd been met by their appointed guide, Ilena.

Ilena, like all the Elohsians, towered a good foot above Geordi and Troi. She wore a dark one-piece jumpsuit, with brilliant blue trim around her neck. Her translator was affixed there like a brooch. Her size had made her a little intimidating at first, but during the ride they'd gotten to know each other better. Geordi was surprised at her age—on Earth, she would have just been graduating Starfleet Academy—but she was a friendly, expansive young girl, willing to answer just about any question. An hour into the drive, they had seen quite a bit of the shoreline and the deep, green-blue sea beyond.

Ilena craned her neck around and looked over at Geordi. "We're about five minutes away from the computer facility. The core is an amazing sight," she said proudly.

Geordi leaned forward. He thought maybe he'd misheard her, and asked, "Your entire world works off one computer system?"

Now it was Ilena's turn for a quick, surprised look at La Forge. "Why—yes," she said. "Ever since the war ended, we have all been connected to the main computer system—to promote unity. We use fiber-optic cables under the ocean and microwave relays to connect everyone. There's even talk of a satellite system for more comprehensive coverage."

"That's very impressive," Troi said.

Politically, maybe, Geordi thought. But from an engineering perspective, putting all your eggs in one basket was just inviting disaster.

"I assume you have back-ups," he prompted.

"Yes, on Dos Dar," she said. "Here on Carinth we have the main computer and most important school; on Regor we have worldwide commerce markets and the parliament; on Delpine Dar we have farming and food manufacturing; Dos Dar has the desalinization plant, which is vital for our growing population; and on Hyanth we have our major manufacturing and sciences. It all makes a good kind of sense, don't you think?"

"Isn't there any concern about old wounds reopening and the war starting up again?" Geordi asked.

Ilena waved a hand in the air. "Impossible. We have all lost so much that even the Populists, those who started the fight in the first place, have recognized the time has come to put aside our weapons. I truly believe that this world now speaks with one voice."

Geordi was left to ponder such convictions as Ilena concentrated on her driving. Within a few minutes, the sojourner rounded a corner and they came to a small, unimpressive building with red flashing lights on both sides of the door. She smoothly placed the sojourner near three other vehicles, all the same general shape but in different colors. Gesturing for them to follow, she led the way toward the dark red doors. As they approached, Geordi watched as she fished some kind of card from her wide belt and held it before a scanner. The amber lens shut off and a door unclicked. Ilena tugged for a moment and the steel door opened outward, allowing the trio entry.

The counselor hurried her pace to keep up with the larger woman. Geordi rechecked the equipment in his pockets and then also had to hurry to keep up. While he prided himself on keeping in shape, he recognized that he was nowhere near as prepared for away team missions as Troi. She made certain she had a daily workout, while he settled for once or twice a week. His excuse was that his missions usually involved rewiring or repairing something, not running after Picard or Riker, or dodging someone's weapons fire.

Ilena led the officers to the end of a corridor. An elevator was waiting for them and it, too, moved rapidly. Geordi estimated they descended at least sixty-five feet before stopping. The ride was smoother than he'd expected, too; probably powered by magnetic forces rather than cables and pulleys.

"Welcome to Operations Central," Ilena said, stepping from the elevator as the doors opened.

The brightness of the room took him by surprise. The room was large—about the size of the *Enterprise*'s shuttlebay—and had absolutely blank walls, lit from behind with bright yellow light. In the center of the room were seven people, each seated at a workstation and wearing a helmet-like apparatus that had wires leading directly to the terminals in front of them. The workstations were all sharply angled so the operators sat with their backs to the floor and their eyes aimed directly at the ceiling. Above them the ceiling was affixed with screens that flew past quicker than the eye—at least, Geordi's eye—could keep track of.

"This system is the culmination of research advances made from the five continents, and represents the single fastest computer ever."

Geordi stepped beside one of the workstations. The woman seated by him barely noticed his presence as her fingers flew across wide vertical keyboards. He had to crouch to get a good look at the trio of keyboards and the small screens set in the center. The operator seemed to be managing memory storage, which was allocated by continent, if La Forge was reading the data right.

"We operate five shifts, all day and all night," Ilena continued. "The operators are constantly adjusting resource allocations."

"This kind of resource allocation could be done quicker by some of our artificial intelligence systems," Geordi said without looking up. "We could send in engineers and technicians to help modernize some of your systems."

"Our people are dedicated to helping themselves,"

Ilena said, a small frown crossing her dark features. "I don't know if they would like that."

"If Eloh joins the Federation," Troi said, walking close to her host, "it is up to Eloh to decided how or if we may help. The Federation has always believed that each world is unique enough to decide for itself."

Ilena smiled, first at Geordi and then at Troi.

"Now that's what I meant to say," Geordi put in.

"It sounds perfect," Ilena responded. "I hope your captain explains your policy in just the same way to Premier Daithin."

"You can count on it," Troi said.

Geordi leaned closer to the operator, trying to read one screen. The woman finally turned toward him and brusquely asked, "Would you like to try it?"

"Oh no," he replied, moving back a bit. "I may know the computers back on the *Enterprise,* but I wouldn't dare try and touch your systems on-line. Maybe another time."

"Then back off and let me concentrate! I nearly lost a power grid on Dos Dar." The woman turned back to her work and ignored Geordi completely.

Geordi stood up and moved back toward his host, a little taken aback by the vehemence of her response.

"Not your fault," Ilena said quietly, laying a hand on his shoulder. "We ask a lot of these people; most can only perform this for five or ten years, we estimate, before they need to retire to easier tasks."

"Ah—you're here!"

Geordi turned and saw a man in deep crimson and silver emerging from a door set in the far wall of the room. He had two large circuit boards in his hand and a band with a light around his head. At first glance, Geordi took him to be a technician, but then he noticed the translator casually affixed to a broad pocket and how everyone reacted to his presence.

"You must be from the Federation. Ilena, would you introduce me?" the older Elohsian asked. He was the shortest Elohsian Geordi had yet seen, probably Commander Riker's height, and not as broadly built as most other Elohsians.

"This is Lieutenant Commander Geordi La Forge and Counselor Deanna Troi of the *Starship Enterprise*, from the United Federation of Planets. And this is Conductor General Luth, the man currently responsible for keeping our technology on the cutting edge."

Geordi glanced down at the circuit boards in Luth's hands, and his VISOR ran a complete scan, trying to help him figure out just what the boards might be for.

"What's that on your face?" Luth asked gruffly.

"It's an electronic device that enables me to compensate for my blindness," Geordi explained. "I can 'see' on all waves of the electromagnetic spectrum. It comes in real handy for troubleshooting problems aboard the ship. What are those for?"

Luth gestured with both hands and grimaced a bit. "These are burned-out units from a relay station on an island about four hundred squares from here. I've been studying them to see what may have caused the damage. What do you see?"

"Actually, sir," Geordi began, "I don't want to presume to guess about your technology. I do see, though, a great deal of seawater corrosion around your contacts. What do you use for insulation?"

Luth continued to juggle the two boards, weighing them gravely in each hand, studying them as Geordi spoke. After a few moments he said, "A storm knocked off the metal plating and the water did get in and short things out. But it took only a brief contact to disrupt the system. I'm trying to find a way to prevent that. Can you help?"

"Hmm . . ." Geordi looked a little closer at each of the boards. The problem was in the materials the Elohsians were using for insulation. They weren't stable enough, chemically, for the varying environments they had to survive.

"I think I see the problem," he began.

Troi put a hand gently on his arm.

Of course, he realized, recalling Picard's stern warning about rendering technological assistance during the initial mission briefing.

"I'm very sorry—but I can't help, Conductor," he said, shaking his head. "We have codes of conduct that prevent us from altering a planet's natural state of affairs. As the Counselor and I were just explaining to Ilena—"

Luth glared. "Doesn't your being here alter our state of affairs?"

"Of course it does, sir. But you invited us here. And until we settle the issue of alignment, I am bound not to interfere."

"Interfere?" the older man thundered. "All I'm asking is for some simple technical help, not plans to build a bomb."

Geordi noticed that people were looking away from their busy workstations. This was not good. "If Eloh agrees to align with the Federation, then we'll give you all the help you can handle. But right now, I'm really sorry, I can't do a thing."

"It's time for us to move on to our next stop," Ilena said. She nodded to Luth and began backing towards the exit. "Conductor, thank you for—"

Luth made a rude noise, turned away from them, and stormed back to his office. One of the floor operators gave them all a nasty look before turning his attention back to the panels before him.

"Let me guess, I said the wrong thing," Geordi said once they were back in the elevator.

"Still, the conductor was unspeakably rude," Ilena said. "I suppose because his feelings were hurt he feels such behavior was warranted. Not unusual for a Populist."

Whoa—now where did that come from? Geordi exchanged a look with Troi, who simply rolled her eyes. So much for Ilena's protestations of Unity, he decided. Despite her declaration that the Populists and the Dar were all great friends, and allies in Parliament, it was clear that there was still a lot of bad blood—and old prejudices—floating around.

The three of them continued on in silence back to the sojourner.

"Would you like to see my favorite view of the coastline?" Ilena asked suddenly. Geordi and Troi exchanged a glance and nodded; it wasn't on the official tour, but they could use a break from that right now. Ilena led them down a rocky path past the computer complex and to the ocean. Within minutes, all three were stretching their legs while gazing at a breathtaking view. The sea gently washed up against rock and crags, glistening in the sun. Small birds flew overhead, emitting graceful calls. As Geordi watched, a flock of them gathered together, and then suddenly shot over their heads, moving inland.

"They're called *keeners*. It's harvest time for them now," Ilena said, following his gaze. "They're heading east, maybe fifty or so to a flock. They'll stop every few squares to scavenge for food. They have small sacks below their beaks to store it in until they reach their winter homes. They gather here every year—same place, same time." Ilena reached down and took off one shoe, then put her foot in the water.

"When I was growing up and the war was still going on, I could only come out here after the all clear sounded. The butchers from Hyanth would hit and run, and hit and run—we would never know when they'd show up next. We had to go to school in underground shelters. One year I missed the keeners entirely."

"How could you concentrate on studies with a war going on around you?" Troi asked.

"The war had been going on between the Dars and the Populists for thirty years by the time I was born. My father spent his whole life in the navy. He still can't get used to peace."

"Well, for all your sakes, I hope it lasts," Geordi said.

"It will," Ilena said, drawing her knees up to her chest and hugging herself. "It has to."

"My esteemed colleague from Dos Dar seems to be thinking more with his rear than with his brain, Premier," shouted a stout Elohsian.

"I object to such Populist slander, Premier!" the wounded representative cried.

"No slander was intended," the woman began. "If anything, I was noting the improvement."

In the visitors' gallery, directly to the left of the dais, Captain Picard and Data sat quietly watching Eloh's 'Unified' Parliament. For the last forty-five minutes, the proceedings had consisted of representatives from each continent boasting about something for the official record. This record was immediately available to all interested parties on the planetary data network, and was no doubt influential when parliamentary elections were held, Picard surmised.

The current debate revolved around a claim involving grain production on Regor. Matters escalated until the name-calling began, the likes of which the Captain had not seen since his days as a schoolboy in France.

"For the record, Premier," the Regorian bellowed, "it should be noted that our people increased productivity for the forty-second straight period. This event remains unequaled in our history."

"What matters how many of a thing are made, if that thing is ultimately worthless?" countered his opponent. "Let the record reflect that consumer satisfaction remains highest with the proud product from Dos Dar."

Picard turned his neck to take in the entire room and gauge the reactions of the others. Members from the respective continents made gestures, silently cheering on their leaders. People from the other three continents watched the back-and-forth boasting with varying degrees of disdain and amusement.

Data turned towards his Captain and spoke. "Sir, I find it interesting that this political structure, with its petty bickering and politics, can also be currently found on no fewer than fourteen Federation worlds."

"Interesting, Data." Picard shook his head. "It only confirms my belief that human nature is much the same, no matter how far out in the galaxy one travels. For people to get along, some system must be present that allows them to vent steam. This session appears entirely designed for that function and little else."

"A fascinating observation, Captain," the android said.

Picard nodded to himself. "Data, for this planet to function as a part of the Federation, they will need to be schooled in so many new things starting with improved technology and, I suppose, including *Robert's Rules of Order.*"

"Actually, Captain, *Robert's Rules of Order* has

never been an accepted form of governance during the Federation's existence."

Picard stifled a smile and replied, "It was a small joke, Data."

The second officer frowned a moment in concentration, filed away the reference, and returned his attention to the proceedings.

Picard watched the premier as the boasting wound down. Daithin made few notes on his terminal, he saw, but did make frequent side comments to Larkin. Neither seemed to take the boasting seriously, and they allowed matters to proceed at a more leisurely pace than Picard would have preferred.

"If the Dar and Populist hot-air masses are done, Premier, I wish to petition this body to vote in favor of new business," said one member from the extreme back of the room. His voice was barely loud enough to be heard over the debate.

Daithin's eyes smiled with recognition. "The chair recognizes Waln from Hyanth."

"I will second the suggestion," came a woman's voice from Waln's right.

"Thank you, Waln," Daithin said. "We needed to move on a long time back. Who now has new business for the parliament?"

Waln stood up immediately and tugged at his belt. He waited patiently for voices to die down and then spoke. "Premier, the people on Hyanth have completed their survey of the damage done during the recent uprisings. It will require an extra four months, perhaps even as long as a year for us to return to normal production."

Picard frowned. This was the first he'd heard of any such disturbances.

"Furthermore," Waln continued, "the recent earthquake, in addition to causing the deaths of dozens of workers, has severely compromised the integrity of our Lorcan mining facility. It may need to be shut down entirely."

For the first time that day, Picard saw Daithin frown.

"That will mean a planetwide shortage of current-bearing cable," the premier said. "Are you sure the mine is unuseable?"

"I am sure of nothing," Waln said. "Save that I will see no more of my people die just to provide the world with metal for weapons. Instead . . ."

"Now see here, good sir," began a heavyset woman from three tables over. "Are you implying that the soldiers on Delpine Dar place a higher value on weapons for the good of the world over that of life itself?"

Waln turned toward his attacker and pointed a finger directly at her. "I said no such thing, madam. I did say, though, that I need more time for my people. Surely your army is adequately prepared for any civil trouble." The older man's voice dripped with sarcasm. "We no longer have any wars to prepare for—and we are currently being protected by two starships the likes of which we have only dreamt about with weaponry far in advance of ours."

Picard had leaned forward during the exchange, and Data had watched his captain watch the people. Inquisitively, Data asked, "Captain, is this how parliaments worked on Earth?"

"Mr. Data, I have the feeling governments have worked like this since people created such structures."

"We recognize the worth of your troubles, Governor—but you must also recognize the need of our army to maintain its fighting strength." The woman's allies nodded among themselves.

"All I recognize," Waln said, "is that the high-minded and long-winded Dars may not be willing to submit to the changes to come! You speak only of 'your' army—and not the United Forces of Eloh!"

"Because they do not yet exist, Waln!" the woman shot back. "Today it is the Dar army that must protect my people—an army, I might add, that is the envy of the five continents."

"The *two* continents, you mean," called a new voice from behind Waln. "The Dars are still no match for the Populist retirees from Carinth!"

"I've never heard such rubbish in my life," the large woman called.

"You certainly speak a lot of rubbish yourself, *madame,*" taunted another member of the parliament.

The woman's face turned red, and she pushed back her chair. "Maybe, but let's see your army save you from me!"

Picard's mouth dropped open in astonishment, as the woman continued moving forward with scared politicians moving aside.

This was Unity?

The captain quickly glanced back to the dais where Daithin had finally stood up. Larkin was also on his feet, tapping commands on a console. Summoning help, Picard hoped.

"Enough!" Daithin's booming voice echoed over the chamber, silencing the throng that was now less than a foot apart. Frozen in motion, they seemed ill-equipped for any sort of a battle within the tightly laid-out structure of the chamber. Some members were now prying their feet loose from around chair legs while others rearranged their belts or slicked back their hair.

"The only reason the last unpleasantness lasted for half a century was because *both* armies were superior.

Now Populist and Dar stand together as Eloh's defenders." Daithin took a deep breath and collected himself. "Now take your seats—all of you. You act like a bunch of overage school children bickering in the yard." With that, he nodded toward Larkin, who punched in two commands on the computer. Picard surmised the Elohsian equivalent of an all clear had just sounded throughout the building.

Everyone returned to their original positions, and Waln took up where he had left off. "Premier, to return to my original request for more time in our production schedule—"

"I hear your plea, Waln, I hear it," Daithin said. "I am ordering the matter to be placed at the top of tomorrow's committee agenda. Now then—is there any other new business?"

The next petitioner rose and begin to speak, and Picard turned away from the drama below.

"Mr. Data," he said, frowning slightly. "This world is not fully healed."

"Indeed not, Captain. Such fractiousness among the elected representatives leads one to consider what the general populace is like."

"Indeed," Picard replied. "It's a very interesting period for this world, Mr. Data. Did you notice how quickly the conversation turned from mining to weapons and war readiness? The war may be over but battles are still being waged—albeit through words."

Data nodded. "I am puzzled though, sir."

"Go ahead," the captain prompted.

"How can a people profess unity when it is abundantly clear that such is not the case?"

Picard smiled. "Optimism, Mr. Data. Despite their harsh words, I think they all want to rise above the kind of infighting we saw earlier. Daithin's leadership has them looking to the future."

The question rolling around in his mind was how the Federation could help them realize their dream of Unity.

"If there is no more business today, I declare the session ended." With those words, Daithin slammed a hand on the table and rose. Everyone stood immediately after him and began to file out of the chamber. Picard and Data remained for a moment, taking in whispered comments and the local flavor.

An Elohsian interrupted their observations and told them he was prepared to bring them to the next stop on their tour. They followed him out of Parliament and into the center of town. The buildings they saw were set off in a uniform grid of streets and avenues, and all seemed to have been built from a handful of architectural designs. Without the signs, though, it might have been easy to mistake one street for another. The buildings were all low, no more than five stories tall at most, excepting Parliament, which had obviously been designed to be the city's focal point.

The Elohsians they passed all stopped to take a look at the new visitors, but people did not gawk or point or seem terribly bothered by their appearance. Instead, many smiled or offered the Elohsian salute, which Picard returned. The salute, it seemed, was the equivalent of the Federation preferred handshake.

"Here is the premier now," their guide said, interrupting Picard's train of thought. Daithin was heading toward them from the opposite direction. Larkin was with him.

"I thought we'd take some lunch before the committee meetings this afternoon," Daithin said. He turned and indicated a restaurant just behind them. "Would you care to join us?"

"Of course," Picard said. He and Data followed the two Elohsians into the restaurant—a popular one, he judged, since just about every table was full. Pater, an overweight Elohsian with a very broad smile, gave the ritual fist-to-chest greeting to Daithin, then gestured to a waiting table. A waiter immediately appeared and brought menus—only for the Starfleet officers. Picard looked over to Daithin with a puzzled expression.

"We know the menu by heart," he explained. "May I suggest our mixed vegetable salad with the herb dip. It's got a nice little bite to it."

Picard nodded. Data, however, continued to scan the menu.

"Is there something in particular you would like, Commander Data?" Daithin asked.

"I was just studying the available selections," Data replied. "I do not need to eat although I very much enjoy dining conversation."

"Ah, I see," Larkin said. He and Daithin exchanged an amused glance and then gave their lunch order to the waiter.

"Premier," Picard began. "I couldn't help but notice that the Romulans were not present at today's session."

"Correct, Captain. They had attended yesterday's council, before your arrival and are spending today giving a preliminary briefing to my chief advisory staff. Don't worry, we've arranged a schedule that keeps direct contact to a minimum. I understand perfectly how it can be when you're so close to people you consider . . . the enemy."

"And let me tell you it wasn't easy," Larkin interjected, "given the few days we have to work with. If only *Nelvana Del* wasn't next week, but we can't change our calendars any more than you can change yours."

"Indeed," Picard said. Pater and a waiter returned with several large ceramic bowls. Larkin's was full of a steaming soup, while Picard's salad was a vibrant mosaic of colors. The premier himself seemed content with a noodle dish sprinkled liberally with what Picard assumed were local vegetables, having never seen any of their particular shape or color.

"Outstanding—as always, Pater," Daithin said.

Pater beamed in pleasure at having served his world's leader, and then faded away, smile still in place.

"You seem quite preoccupied with the Romulans, Captain," Daithin said.

Picard sat back from the table and studied the premier. "Only on your account, sir." He paused a moment. "If I may speak frankly . . ."

"Please," Daithin said, nodding.

"We only consider the Romulans our adversaries because their entire code of conduct is something distasteful to the Federation. They grab what they want, and their values remain an anathema to us. On the other hand, should they wish to settle the hostilities between our governments, we'd be only too happy."

"They say the same of you, Captain," Larkin added. "Though in much stronger language."

"I'm not surprised," Picard said. Daithin was right —his salad was delicious.

"Peace is a difficult concept for some people," Data put in. "They require certain challenges in order to remain alive and vital."

"How well I understand that concept," Daithin said. "In the past, we Dar fought the Populists for centuries on end."

"Now, Captain," Larkin said. "What of your battles with the Romulans? I hear tell that of all the Federation starships, yours has engaged them the most often."

"Mr. Larkin, while the *Enterprise* may have had . . . dealings . . . with the Romulans they have not been pitched battles. No state of war has existed between our people in nearly two centuries."

"Come, come, Captain," Larkin prodded. "Their man Plactus has told us of many such 'encounters' with your ship. As I understand it, Commander Sela is practically family."

Picard couldn't avoid wincing at those words. Losing Lieutenant Yar under his command was bad enough, but to be constantly reminded of her each time he saw Sela . . . He pursed his lips a moment before replying. "I will not deny that we've crossed swords with the Romulans, but I like to think each encounter has left both sides keenly aware of the high price such a war would exact." And that was pretty much all he wanted to say about that.

"Well said, Captain," Daithin said. "Well said." He stared into Picard's hard eyes with intensity, but Picard met the gaze and matched it. The exchange took a few heartbeats but left the captain aware of the intense scrutiny he was under. Larkin was doing a good job engaging the Federation representatives in conversation, allowing the ruling diplomat the luxury of observation. Picard resolved to remain ever vigilant.

"Mr. Larkin, exactly what function do you serve on the council?"

Data's innocent and forthright question immediately changed the subject and allowed Picard a moment's relaxation. Larkin seemed thoroughly surprised by the question, and was actually caught with his soupspoon to his mouth and without an immediate reply.

"Why, Commander Data, I serve at Daithin's pleasure. I . . . advise and counsel him."

"Then you do not enjoy an elected position?"

"No, I do not," Larkin replied. "I serve at the premier's pleasure. He, of course, is entitled to advisors much the way your captain can count on the advice of your first officer and ship's counselor."

"You know our ship's operation?" Data inquired.

"The Federation was kind enough to send along some preliminary material so we would be better prepared to meet with you." Larkin smiled. "I remain interested in seeing your ship."

"And you will, Mr. Larkin. It's all on the schedule," Picard said. He's smooth, Picard noted, impressed by the swift recovery and mastery of the conversation.

The captain stood. "And now if you'll excuse us, we have a briefing session scheduled, I believe."

"Of course, Captain," Daithin said. He watched them walk away, eyes squinting in the midday sun.

"What do you think of them, Larkin?" Daithin asked.

"Very bright, very intelligent. And it's hard to believe that Data is an android—an artificial being. Impossible to believe."

"A close to indestructible artificial being, the Romulans say." Daithin stroked his chin absently. "If we'd had a hundred like him, it would have changed the war." He sat up straight. "They make a good impression, Larkin. I like Picard's demeanor. A real leader, but I can also see he's a rarity."

"What do you mean?"

"There's a quality about him that you can just tell makes him stand out from other men. It's hard to tell when he's with Data, but you can see it with his other crew."

"What about the Romulans?" Larkin concentrated entirely on his leader's opinion, adding it to his own observations.

"A very different breed, don't you think? All so imperious and impassive. Their leader, Commander Sela, is definitely an interesting one to watch, but you can tell there's no real loyalty, no real connection between her and her people. They follow her orders because there is no other choice. Picard's people show a connection to him and would probably willingly lay their lives down for him. The Romulans, I suspect, would hesitate. Very different styles."

"Well," Larkin said, "we have got more work to do. The ranking Dars demand more time on the schedule with the Romulan engineers. I think they don't need it but it's a bone I can throw them."

"Do that," Daithin said, now walking away from the restaurant and back toward the imposing parliament building. "A greedy bunch, those, but we're all in this together now."

"The unity you mean?"

"No, I mean now that we've invited both alien races to visit, we must remain united in our dealings with them or it will turn into a disaster. Mark my words."

Larkin regarded his friend and leader. "What do you mean?"

"You saw the fight today. We're no closer to burying the past today than we were when the parliament first met. How can I get the governors to see past such foolishness?"

"Maybe they can't."

Daithin shook his head sadly, slowing his gait. "If not, then we had best be prepared for a new civil war. And then the Romulans or Federation can walk right in and pick up the pieces or bury the lot of us. Our technology has gotten so we're very good at death and destruction. Rebuilding takes longer after each war. We're reaching a point of no return."

Larkin looked over at his superior.

"Worrying about your place in the history books?" Larkin asked, clearly trying to lighten the moment. Daithin, though, was having none of it.

"Much more than that," the premier responded gloomily. "I'm worried that there won't be any history books at all unless we can find a way to keep the alliance together."

Ro made certain that James Kelly's parents had gone on duty before she approached their home. Unlike yesterday, when she walked down the corridor seething with frustration, now she was more than a bit nervous. She had to control her temper carefully and make sure the teen understood that she didn't mean any real harm with her words. Taking carefully measured steps, she reviewed her exit from their conversation the day before and wanted to make sure that the apology was comprehensive. Then, she wanted to make certain that if he told his parents about her actions, the apology would also make its way to them.

Finally, she arrived at the door and pressed the buzzer. Just as before, the door opened pretty quickly, and once again there stood the youth, this time in a bright teal jumpsuit and neatly combed hair. His expression of delight was not at all what she expected from him.

"Ensign Ro," he said, his voice high with excitement.

"Hello, James. Do you have time for me?"

"Time? Sure, sure, come in, please. I've just finished my course work and was about to go meet some people, but they can wait. Please, what can I get you?" He seemed as expectant as a puppy, she noted, and she was thrown by his enthusiasm at her visit.

"Nothing, thank you. James, I wanted to—to apologize for my behavior yesterday. It was rather unbecoming of an officer, and I mistreated you." She stood still, waiting to see what would happen next.

James got himself a glass of juice from the replicator and looked up at her in surprise. "Oh, that. That was nothing, Ensign. I get worse from my dad all the time. It seems I never know when to stop asking about things. It's going to be tough becoming a social scientist if I can't control myself."

Feeling off the hook and washed with relief, Ro took a casual stance. She wasn't prepared to continue the conversation after the apology. She had intended to apologize and leave, but now she was stuck with the eager young man. Again.

"I've been considering xenopsychology or maybe even the diplomatic corps, but I'm not sure. My mom says I can decide after I've started my college-level studies. You sure you don't want anything?"

"Thank you, no." She hoped silence was the proper approach at this point and let him grind the conversation to a halt.

"Well, anyway, the stuff I was just working on involved comparative biology between humans and other bipedal races. When we first met the Vulcans in the twenty-first century, we thought the odds against other humanoid races were remote. But . . . I guess you being in Starfleet, I guess you know that."

"I do. The Bajorans' first contact with another race was long ago and I can't remember which one it was. Our world has not benefited quite the same as Earth when it comes to contact with other civilizations."

"Oh bloody heck, of course, the Cardassian occupation. Gee, I'm sorry to make you think about that, Ensign. Pretty insensitive of me, huh? Anyway, you really should stay and see my parents again. They'll be back at sixteen hundred."

Ro shuffled her feet, thinking quickly. The one

thing she had not planned on doing was spending more than half the day alone with the enthusiastic young man. "I wish I could," she lied. "But I have other duties to tend to now. I will be back this evening to meet with them. I must go now. Thank you again for understanding."

James moved toward her, holding his cup. "Sure, if you have to go. Thanks for dropping by. I'll be sure to tell my folks."

Quickly, but not too quickly, Ro moved out of the room.

Something about the encounter with Kelly left her feeling even more nervous than before. He was always staring at her, always smiling at her. . . .

She stopped dead in her tracks in the corridor. Could it be that—

No, she decided firmly. There was nothing unusual about the way James regarded her.

Just the same, she resolved to keep her next visit with the Kelly family as brief as possible.

Chapter Four

Captain's Log, Stardate 46892.6. Our visit today to Eloh
was both enlightening and fortunate. By that, I mean
that we had no negative encounters with the Romulans.
In fact, they have been keeping to themselves and have
caused us no problem. The trouble I sense comes from
an unexpected source—the Elohsians themselves.
Hostilities between the previously warring factions on
the planet are still simmering beneath the surface.
Fundamental prejudices remain and erupt with alarm-
ing frequency during times of tension. I fear the
Romulans will exploit the tensions and claim the planet
for themselves when no one is looking.

Tonight Premier Daithin is hosting a banquet in
honor of both the Federation and the Romulans. If
Commander Sela is up to something, I hope to spot it
there.

IN THE TRANSPORTER ROOM, Captain Picard surveyed
his senior officers, all in dress uniform. Worf tugged at
his collar, constantly readjusting his shining ceremonial Klingon sash. Both Dr. Crusher and Troi looked

resplendent in their attire, with Troi opting for the bright blue off-the-shoulder dress that was an accepted part of her office. Riker, Geordi, and Data all appeared fit and ready for the event. He knew most of them disliked having to wear the current style of ceremonial dress uniform, and in practice Picard ordered their use sparingly. But he could not afford to skip their use this night—nor could he take chances with any other part of the banquet.

"Before we beam down," Picard began. The fussing and straightening stopped and all eyes turned to the captain. "I want to stress a few points. First, we have much more to learn from these people and I want to make sure you all remain observant. This is essential, especially with a contingent of Romulans in the room."

Stepping onto the transporter platform, Picard turned to his security officer. "Warbird status, Mr. Worf?"

The Klingon cleared his throat. "As of five minutes ago—unchanged."

"Good. Then we can enjoy ourselves, eh?"

Worf suppressed a grimace as Picard gave the command to energize.

Minutes after beaming down, the *Enterprise* contingent was brought to a building that seemed boxy, lengthy, and a little narrow, with twists to the general construction. It was a single-level construct that had silver filigree decorating the outside, just under the roof and around the windows. A small symbol of Eloh, made from a large diamond, was above the doorway, which was rather wide. Darkly uniformed women hiding beneath charcoal cloaks stood at either side of the door—protection against unwanted guests, the captain surmised. Just inside the doorway, Daithin, dressed in bright yellow with dark orange trim, greeted the Federation representatives. He also wore a tight, pointed hat with copper decorating the crest. Beside him, in a deeper shade of yellow, was Larkin.

"So good of you to join us, Captain," Daithin began. He gestured to the room behind him and added, "I trust you brought your appetites with you. My cooking staff has spent a week preparing the best our world has to offer."

"We certainly look forward to the experience," Picard replied. "I do not believe you and Mr. Larkin have met our security chief, Lieutenant Worf of the Klingon Empire. And this is our chief medical officer, Dr. Beverly Crusher." Both crewmen nodded in acknowledgment. Daithin smiled. Larkin just stared openly at Worf.

"People, please follow me to the opening hall," Larkin said. He gestured forward and a very wide door swung inward, allowing the crew to walk into a brightly lit room. More darkly clad women milled about, each proffering ceramic goblets and bottles. None had the universal translator on their dress; only the Elohsian dignitaries, including much of the parliament, did. Alongside one wall was a wooden table with dish after dish of rich, aromatic food. The colors were bright and some glistened from glazes, while others were damp from syrups. A stack of plates was carefully positioned at the beginning of the table, while a gleaming lacquered box awaited the plates at the table's end.

"Rather strong stuff," Crusher whispered, sniffing the air.

Picard's observations were interrupted by the sight of four Romulans already on line at the long table. Sela was not among them, and this made the captain curious.

"Premier, could you please tell me where Commander Sela might be?"

Daithin turned and eyed Picard carefully. Without expression he merely replied, "She was detained, her subcommander, Plactus, tells me." He then turned away and surveyed the room.

Troi, eyes wide with interest, stepped alongside Picard and whispered, "I suspect this is just the first course. I don't see any seating and this is a small room. I believe we should just help ourselves. Don't make a meal of this."

"Thank you, Counselor," Picard replied. "Knowing you, you'll politely try everything and save yourself for later. Have you learned if this world has any dessert to rival your chocolate sundae?"

"Not yet," she said with a twinkle in her eye. "But I'm willing to go exploring." With that, she sauntered over to the table and helped herself to a sampling of the first six dishes. Dr. Crusher immediately joined her, and the feast began.

Picard followed behind, scanning the length of the table to get a sense of the foodstuffs. From what he was given to understand, intercontinental commerce was still being refined, and unique plants and spices remained a rarity among continents. The first one to figure out a good distribution system for such items will no doubt be an economic force to reckon with, Picard surmised. Worf stepped before the captain and gave the table a suspicious look. Picard was privately amused by the action and was tempted to allow him merely to sample the fare, just as Troi teased earlier. However, that would be bad form before the head of state. Politely allowing Worf to precede him, Picard took a delicate but substantial plate.

Geordi La Forge stood near a far wall with a small bowl of nuts in his hand as Data walked toward him, his plate brimming with foodstuffs. There was a companionable silence between the two for a while. While studying Geordi's expression, Data tried to deduce his friend's emotional state. He could tell from the furrows on his brow that Geordi was troubled by something. He decided to try and detect the problem through indirect means.

"So, Geordi, what did you think of the Elohsian computer facilities?"

Geordi looked up and grabbed a handful of nuts. He began popping them into his mouth, one at a time, without pause.

Data decided to try again.

"Are their networking capabilities up to Federation standards?"

Finally, La Forge stopped eating peanuts long enough to answer. "Actually, no, they're years away from that. But they do have an effective network which links all five continents."

Data noted the flat tone in Geordi's voice. The *Enterprise*'s second officer studied his friend's facial expressions. They had varied very little since he initially took his seat. Geordi's answers were informative but terse. Data guessed that something had happened during La Forge and Troi's visit to Carinth Dar. "And they work from a central processing unit?"

"Yeah, and it's like a high-pressure setup that does no one any good. I'd love to get in and redesign it with some isolinear chip boards but we can't touch a thing." Geordi popped a whole handful of nuts in his mouth.

"You do seem frustrated," Data said.

"That's the word, my friend," Geordi said. He shook his head. "How about we just change the subject?"

"Of course." Data paused for a moment, summoning up casual conversation subroutines. "Nice weather we are having, is it not?"

Geordi smiled. "Good try, Data."

"Did I say something funny?"

"It was the non sequitur about something totally pointless and out of place. You might not realize it, my friend, but you're developing a sense of humor."

Data paused and considered the statement. He quickly analyzed the last five minutes' worth of conversation, studying how his question about the weather fit in context. The concept of humor, however, although it was something he had studied in depth for quite some time, remained elusive.

"Tell me, Data, what have you been working on—besides the Elohsians, I mean?"

"At the captain's suggestion, I have been rereading the collected works of Edgar Allen Poe. Captain Picard was correct that the first fictional detective was C. Auguste Dupin, whom Poe created in 1841. Poe also introduced the conventions of the detective story in all of three Dupin stories, totaling a mere one hundred pages of handwritten manuscript. It can be argued, and I think the captain would agree, that all detective characters—including his favorite, Dixon Hill—trace their lineage to Dupin."

Data paused to see what response he would receive from Geordi, but instead could tell that once again his friend was not paying full attention to the conversation. He was somewhat puzzled. Data knew that Geordi also liked detective stories and had indulged Data on more than one occasion by dressing up as Dr. Watson, to Data's Sherlock Holmes.

Clearly, something was still bothering his friend. Data wished Geordi would speak openly about the matter, but the engineer simply popped some more nuts into his mouth and remained quiet.

"Geordi, I get the impression that there is some other matter on your mind."

La Forge nodded. "There is." The engineer lowered his voice. "I just wonder if we're doing the right thing, getting involved here. These people don't seem ready for us. Plus, they need so much help rebuilding, I just want to wade in and start teaching them. And I can't."

"The non-interference directive," Data said.

Geordi nodded. "You should have seen what happened today. It was a mess." He popped another nut in his mouth. "I want to get along with everyone, and when I can't—well, I guess I don't always know how to handle it."

"Counselor Troi usually advises crewmembers just to be themselves. I have noted that this approach is quite effective."

Putting the bowl down, Geordi looked at Data and began to smile slowly. He scanned the room and saw a few Elohsians just chatting quietly by themselves, near the end of the banquet table. "I guess it's worth a try. Anything's better than eating nuts all night."

Picard looked up from his plate to find himself face-to-face with Subcommander Plactus. Federation archives on Sela and her crew were almost nonexistent. Plactus's name did not appear in the current information available on officers within their fleet.

The subcommander stood slightly taller than Picard and had steel gray hair and bright blue eyes. His hair was cropped rather short, and showed no sign of receding. His pointed ears were prominent and almost shone in the bright light that emanated from panels positioned every few feet alongside the walls and ceiling. Definitely older and more seasoned than Sela, probably a career officer, Picard estimated.

"Captain, a distinct honor," Plactus said in an even tone.

"Subcommander, I don't believe I've had the pleasure . . ." Picard began.

"The pleasure is mine, sir," Plactus interrupted. "You are rather well known among my people. After all, we can count on one hand the number of humans to visit Romulus and return to Federation space to discuss it. Yes, we know you well."

Picard gripped his plate a little more firmly and gave a smile with no warmth behind it. "It was an interesting visit. The insight into your culture was most . . . enlightening."

"As it should be, Captain. Our culture dates back centuries—before your people had learned how to speak. That depth of culture has allowed us to thrive and grow, and given us a perspective that enables us to plan for the future."

Picard stared at him a moment, then chose an *hors de ouevre* off his plate. A vegetable—quite tart. Not altogether unpleasant, he decided, and took another bite. Plactus stared at him, waiting for a response.

This Romulan had a lot to learn if he hoped to provoke Picard into anything other than a completely dispassionate discussion.

"Humans and other species in the Federation enjoy the freedom to debate the course their future will take. It is one of our fundamental beliefs that such freedom of choice must be protected."

"I believe, Captain," Plactus said, "that it is the differences between our fundamental beliefs that provide the Elohsians a basis of comparison between our two Empires."

"The Federation is not an Empire, Plactus," Picard snapped.

"As you wish," Plactus said. "Nonetheless, both

governments are here, parading their wares and trying to make themselves appealing to a world that can easily be scooped up by even the Federation without the need to ask permission. We waste time and materiel on this folly."

Picard took another bite, letting himself relax. "Again, you state the obvious. We could take this world but choose not to. You also could take this world but choose not to, for fear of a skirmish you can ill afford at this time."

Plactus glared at Picard. "What do you mean by that, human?"

"I merely observe that the Romulan Empire's resources have appeared thin since your return from isolation a mere six years ago."

"Captain, Subcommander, this is surely not the place or the time for such debates," Daithin said, stepping between the two.

"Of course, Premier," Plactus said, moving off. "It was never my intention to provoke the captain."

"My apologies as well, Premier," Picard said, although in fact he felt he had nothing to apologize for. How long had Daithin been observing their exchange? He had the sense the premier had interrupted them not to stop their argument, but simply because he'd seen enough.

Time to lighten the mood, he thought, and tried another item from his plate. This, too, was tart, although crunchier and with a more pleasing texture.

"Tell me, Premier, what is this called?"

Daithin smiled. "This is *greel,* a vegetable from Numih—my home province. My mother used it in everything from salad to stuffing. A very versatile vegetable and a hardy one as well. It can grow in most any climate. I see that it is in no fewer than four other items on our appetizer menu."

Geordi and two Elohsians wandered over to join them.

"Captain, I'd like you to meet Simave and Dona—Ilena's parents. She was the one who gave us the tour of Carinth Dar."

Picard nodded formally at each, receiving broad smiles in return. The woman, handsome by Elohsian standards, he guessed, took his hand and said in a throaty voice, "Captain, it is a pleasure to meet you. My stepdaughter, Ilena, called us yesterday to rave about how much she enjoyed meeting your crew."

"Simave and Dona were career diplomats who helped negotiate the peace treaty between the Populists and the Dars," Geordi offered.

Picard smiled at the news, certain he'd found people sympathetic to the Federation's way of life. He was unsure if they remained influential, but if the couple already had a good impression of the Starfleet officers, so much the better. "A very impressive accomplishment," Picard said. "How did you achieve such a feat where others failed?"

Simave smiled and gestured toward the ceiling. "The stars, Captain. Our technology had finally managed to bring radio signals from space to the common people. We finally were able to show that there were other civilizations in space and that we were all part of a greater community."

Dona nodded and continued. "Simave's telling just part of it, Captain. We reasoned with both sides that sooner or later some spaceship was going to find us and we had better be ready to deal with alien races from a position of strength rather than have people find us divided. Eloh has much to offer the universe, I feel, and I was able to convince key leaders on both sides that I was right."

"We used the stars as a way to show that the

philosophical and petty political differences between Dars and Populists was nothing compared to races that could fly from star to star. We were denying ourselves our rightful place among the starfaring races by impeding planetary development with useless warfare. There were adventures to be had among the stars, worlds to win, and greater struggles to be had for gain than proving one way of thinking was better than another. It took Dona and me a few years to bring everyone together on this point, but we won out."

Picard nodded thoughtfully, but was mentally alarmed at the tenor of the conversation. He knew a world capable of decades-long civil wars would be aggressive, but to stop fighting among themselves to take on other worlds—well, that was something else entirely. The Elohsian way of thinking would bear greater scrutiny. He made a note to discuss the matter with Troi when the banquet was over.

He continued to make small talk with the couple and Geordi until Larkin approached, followed by a serving woman carrying a tray with steaming gray towels. She handed towels to each of the four and then patiently waited to retrieve them. When the tall, silent woman had departed, Larkin waved a hand toward the door at the end of the room. Another darkly clad woman was waiting by the handle, ready to open the way ceremoniously into the next chamber.

"This way, Captain, if you please," Larkin said smartly.

Picard led the roomful of people to the doorway and waited patiently as the thick, heavy door was opened. The woman showed no strain but it obviously was an effort. Inside, the next room was slightly larger, with small tables and high, straight-backed chairs. Again, a long table was set into one wall. This room was somewhat dimmer than the previous one, with fewer lighting panels; these were muted as well. On the table was a selection of six steaming cauldrons. The containers were each distinctively colored with graphics depicting local vegetables, fish, and fowl.

Larkin led Plactus to the head of the line and loudly explained the nature of each dish, for all guests to hear. The Romulan officer picked up a wide, deep bowl with three compartments and selected one fish, one bird, and one vegetable soup. Larkin nodded silently in approval as Plactus completed his way down the table, and then gestured for the remaining Romulans to follow. Larkin then motioned for the *Enterprise* crew to serve themselves, following their counterparts. Picard allowed his officers to precede him and once again took his place behind Worf. While this meant little to Picard, he recognized that the Klingon warrior in Worf liked leading the captain, standing in harm's way.

Even on the soup line.

Peering around the Klingon, Picard watched his officer carefully smell each soup, selecting just two, both fowl. "The idea, Mr. Worf, is try one of each variety," Picard said quietly.

His security chief turned stiffly, and nodded. "I know, sir, but these others smell like *veQ*," came the soft yet forceful reply.

The captain nodded, and then smiled. "Didn't your mother ever tell you that vegetables were good for you?"

Worf grunted and moved back into line.

As the various officers completed the line, some took seats at the tables while others continued to mill about. Picard took the advantage to wander about the warm room, exploring the construction and trying to better understand their architectural philosophy. He guessed that the structure was rather old, perhaps more than a hundred years. There were signs of weathering and hard use, but everything seemed structurally sound and well maintained. The windows were shuttered with brass fixtures that held solid boards, blocking out prying eyes and, unfortunately, the pleasing twilight. There were but two doors noticeable in the room, so Picard wondered about the arrival and removal of the soup tureens. Perhaps a mechanism that moved the long table into the kitchen? He began to look about the room, but his attention was caught by the sight of a Romulan centurion heading straight for Worf's table.

The Romulan had finished her soup and was carrying the empty bowl. Worf was politely sipping from his bowl, using the deep-bowled spoons that were provided. His expression told Picard that neither was to his liking, despite the meat content. The security chief looked up and glared at the centurion standing over him. She, too, was clearly not to his liking.

"So, Klingon, what's it like serving aboard a ship of sheep?"

Picard noted the woman was young for a centurion. She had closely cropped black hair and a very interesting twist to the tips of her ears. The upswept eyebrows allowed for a liberal amount of eye shadow, which was used to give her features an exotic look. It more than made up for the face, which was rather plain.

"I serve with people from thirteen different races, none of which house sentient sheep," Worf responded.

"And yet you do not command them." The Centurion leaned in closer to Worf and smiled. "We Romulans have always wondered why your people allowed themselves to be beaten into submission."

Worf's nostrils flared for a brief moment. "No such event took place, Centurion."

"My name is Telorn, Klingon," she snapped, cutting him off. "I am Centurion Telorn of the *N'ventnar,* a ship you will come to rue."

Worf set down his soup spoon and took a deep breath. He stood, and Telorn took a step backward. Picard saw her tense, the muscles in her legs coiling for action.

Please no, Mr. Worf, he found himself praying silently. *Not a fight. Not here. Not now.*

The Klingon looked at Telorn for a moment and then said stiffly, "I am Lieutenant Worf, Centurion Telorn. And I am pleased to meet you."

Before the Romulan could respond, Worf plunged ahead. "As for our relationship with the Federation, we sued for peace at a time when it best served our interests."

The woman placed her bowl on the nearest table, catching the interest of Data, Dr. Crusher, and Dona. "You serve willingly, then?"

Worf nodded and gritted his teeth, his hands clenching and unclenching, muscles rippling beneath his skin.

"I have always thought Klingons would make good serving people."

Worf grunted. Picard started to put his bowl down in case his officer lost control.

"I believe we have nothing further to say," Worf began, and started to move away. She sidestepped and came directly into his path, their chests brushing.

"Not so fast, Klingon. We are ordered to fit in here, and so I am under obligations to make—what's the human phrase?"

"Small talk," came the sudden reply from Data. He had stood up and rapidly approached the pair, shielding their confrontation from Daithin. "In fact, Centurion, I am most interested in finding out more about the way the Romulans see Eloh fitting in with the rest of the Empire. I have many theories and would like to see if any of them match your own scheme."

During the rush of words, Worf stepped back and around Telorn. Picard was pleased by Data's improved ability to sense emotional distress and act to help a fellow officer. The leaps and bounds his internal programming had made since they first met nearly seven years ago never stopped amazing Picard.

A moment later, Larkin led everyone to the next great door, which opened onto a room with long banquet tables. This time, both sides were adorned with platters of food, ranging from cooked meats to raw fish, and with an astonishing assortment of vegetables, fruits, and condiments. Following the previous pattern, Plactus was led through first, but the Starfleet officers were given first turn at the buffet. The difference here, though, was that as each person finished filling his plate on one side, a serving girl in a darkly shaded gown took the visitor to a specific seat.

By the time Romulans, Starfleet officers, and Elohsians had completed their first visit to the buffet table, Picard noted that people were paired up in an unusual fashion. At the other end of his table, Dr. Crusher was placed next to Plactus, a military man, while at the table to his back Geordi was placed next to Ilena's parents. Amusingly, Data was placed next to the centurion who had unsuccessfully tried to provoke Worf, and he still attempted to engage her in a political debate. Picard noted that he himself was placed opposite Sela's still-empty seat and next to Daithin, who had the head of the table. Larkin was placed at the head of the second table, where Worf had his back to the captain, not at all to his approval judging from his deep scowl.

Before anyone could take a first bite of their entree, Daithin rose.

"My friends from the stars, before we begin our main meal, I want all of us to take a moment and give thanks. I know we each have differing beliefs, but we all recognize the existence of a guiding force that brought life to the universe and gave us all the intelligence we have employed to bring us together. Let us give thanks for our existence and for the fine food before us. May no one go hungry, may no one live in want, may no one cower in fear."

There was a moment's silence, and then all the Elohsians deeply bowed their heads, touching the edge of the tables. Daithin smiled serenely and brought his hands together in a soft clap. With that, everyone looked up and dinner began.

The meat was delicious, with a kind of thick, naturally seasoned gravy served on the side. No doubt containing thousands of calories. No matter, the captain told himself, he'd leave the nutritional assessment of the meal to Dr. Crusher. For his part, all he cared about was the taste.

"When the tour is done tomorrow, Captain Picard, I hope you will save some time for me to introduce you to my favorite pastime," Daithin said. "It's called Start. I'm sure you will find it mentally stimulating."

"Thank you, Premier, I will make sure to arrange the time," Picard politely replied.

"Commander Sela tried it herself the first day they were here, and she has already requested a game set for her personal use," Daithin added.

"Premier," Picard continued, "I couldn't help but notice over the last few days that there still remain tensions among the warring factions. What is being done to maintain harmony?"

Daithin chewed his dinner for a moment, obviously weighing answers in his mind. He stole a moment to glance toward Larkin, who was deep in a conversation of his own with Commander Riker and a Romulan centurion Picard did not recognize. He pushed some food around on his plate and then took a long sip from his goblet. "A simple, straightforward question, Captain, and one certainly deserving of a simple, straightforward response. I wish I had one.

"The Populists and the Dars have been at each other's throats for millennia—or so it seems. In a few short years we've managed a fragile peace, and it's good of you to note that we have not perfected our cherished unity. I see it as something to continue to strive for, something to keep us going as a people. By joining the galactic community, we hope to see examples of how this has been done throughout the stars. The council and parliament have done everything we can by making unity and acceptance of others a core part of our school curriculum and religious activities. Our own holidays and festivals, such as *Nelvana Del,* are also designed to bring people together in large public ways. And yet . . . and yet . . ." Daithin let his words trail off, his eyes searching the pastel ceiling for answers.

"And yet, Captain," he continued, "people won't forget the smallest slight that one clan or family line may have done to another. Port towns resist Dar merchants moving in because of attacks made generations ago. Scientists carefully shield research rather than go further with the aid of work done on other continents. I even heard that once last year a farmer let a field rot rather than use Populist field hands. Without unity, I fear for this world's prosperity. We try and we try, but it gets frustrating."

Picard nodded in sympathy and said, "It was much

the same on my world, Earth, Daithin. Old religious differences or skin color led people to fight, kill, and destroy. It was many centuries before we put that behind us. I have a feeling that if humans, as fierce and stubborn as we are, can do that, then it can happen here, too."

"Let us hope so, Captain," Daithin responded.

Before either man could add anything, there was a stirring among the diners, and everyone looked up. Making a rather theatrical entrance was Commander Sela in perfect Romulan dress uniform, complete with a rarely seen cloak that swirled about her compact form. This was a warrior who commanded attention and, if not respect, certainly fear. Her face was a stone mask of seriousness, and Picard noted that the attractive details of her eyes and mouth were missing, buried beneath a combative attitude.

The door to the main chamber had barely closed by the time she reached Daithin and Picard. Formally, she stood by her empty chair and uttered, "I deeply regret my delay, Premier, but as you well know, the duties of office come before all things, including dinner."

Daithin smiled and gestured to the wall-length table still filled with food. "No need to apologize, Commander, no need at all. After all, we had only just begun and there is so much left to be tried. Fill your plate and join us, please." As Sela nodded and strode off, Picard watched Daithin. As soon as the Romulan had turned, his eyes registered the annoyance her late arrival caused. Picard assumed Sela arrived late to be theatrical, but it may have backfired.

No sooner had Sela taken her seat than Picard spoke up again, moving Daithin on to a different conversation. "I hear from Commander Riker that you intend to tour the *Enterprise* tomorrow. I believe you and your advisors will be impressed. Knowing the commander, he's having the decks polished and the screens shined."

"Surely you're joking, Captain. I'd much rather see the ship in its everyday state."

Picard smiled and let the premier know he was embellishing the state of readiness for effect.

"I would say that Premier Daithin found much to his liking aboard the *N'ventnar,*" Commander Sela commented around a mouthful of meat.

"Oh yes, Captain, their ship, the *Bared Fang,* was quite a sight," Daithin agreed. "Obviously both ships are way beyond anything Eloh has today. I tell you, it inspires me no end to see what the future will hold, no matter which Empire we align ourselves with. Just walking the decks I could sense the power there was to command. Have you been on a Romulan ship, Captain?"

"No, Daithin, he hasn't," Sela injected. "At least, not that I am aware of. Captain Picard has, however, visited our homeworld—unannounced—and for that I salute him." She waved her goblet in Picard's general direction and took a long drink.

"On the other hand, we did offer you the opportunity to visit our ship openly and without escort." He referred to the time Commander Sela voluntarily came aboard the *Enterprise,* the same time she had first proclaimed that she was the daughter of his dead security chief, Tasha Yar. The alluring mystery in that claim had not worn off on Picard and, though nearly two years had passed since he heard those words, he still had no evidence to support or refute the charge. As a result, he remained coldly fascinated by her.

"The openness you so casually display to all will one day prove your undoing, Captain," Sela said.

"On the contrary, Commander, I believe it is just that willingness to accept others that will prove to be our strength."

"You dilute your people with culture after culture, constantly blending and softening. That is why we will be here a century from now while other races are homogenized out of existence. You can see what happened to the Vulcans, Andorians, and Benzites and now you can watch it happen to the Klingons."

An audible growl rose from the next table but Counselor Troi kept Worf in his chair with a glance. All eyes were focused on Sela, and only now did Picard notice the silence in the chamber. "Your accusations are baseless, Commander," Picard said. "All the races you name enjoy the full benefits of Federation membership—technology, resources, defense—while maintaining their own cultural integrity."

"Officers, please," Daithin said. "I'm sure each of you has a story to tell. But not tonight. Please, Captain, Commander, enjoy this meal."

Sela glared at Picard for a moment and then returned her attention to the barely touched plate before her. The captain merely picked up his fork and took a mouthful of vegetables. He paused a moment to glance over toward Troi, who smiled at him. Satisfied, Picard concentrated on his dinner.

While eating, he did manage to overhear snippets of conversation from further down his table and at the one behind him. Geordi was holding forth on computer theory and Dr. Crusher was questioning child care options among the working classes. Worf seemed content to remain silent, watching over the proceedings. No doubt, he was preparing for more baiting.

Down at the other end of his table, Plactus, Picard

noticed, was certainly interested in whatever Crusher had to say. To his surprise, they were discussing families.

"A son in the military," Crusher was saying while Plactus contemplated the food on his plate.

"He will go far, that one," Plactus said with boastful pride. "And you, do you have offspring?"

"Yes, I have a son, Wesley, now completing his work at Starfleet Academy."

Plactus smiled at Crusher, showing worn teeth. "So we both will have sons in the military—excellent."

"Starfleet is not the military and you know that, Plactus," she said.

He took a drink from his mug and gestured for a refill. "Should there be a fight, it will be Starfleet who defends the borders. That's military and you know *that,* my dear doctor."

"I wouldn't want my son to be a soldier, Plactus. He's brilliant and will probably be designing new engines or inventions that will revolutionize the way we all live."

Plactus eyed Crusher carefully at those words, something working behind the gaze, Picard noted. He had rarely heard her boast so openly about her son's being a genius, but then again, she was a mother not about to be one-upped by a Romulan's warrior son.

"How so?" he asked.

"I don't know yet, but when he lived on the *Enterprise* he did some pretty amazing things without formal training. I can only imagine that when he graduates he'll be ready to do something currently indescribable. As a result, I hope, our children will never have to meet in battle."

To Picard's surprise, Plactus laughed at the sentiment and drained his newly refilled mug. Carefully wiping his mouth, he looked again at Crusher and smiled. It was a calculating smile and not at all genuine. "I hope that is true, Doctor, but who can tell what will happen tomorrow? Eloh's sun may go nova. We may be at war. We may become brothers. You may finally recognize our moral superiority."

Crusher made a face at Plactus and shook her head. "I think not, Subcommander." With that, she turned to her other side and began speaking to Conductor General Luth.

The remainder of the dinner was uneventful, but the silence at Picard's end of the table, with Daithin, Sela, and himself, was palpable. He would have to correct that when the meal continued into the next chamber. No doubt dessert, but the captain hoped against after-dinner drinks for fear that any real alcohol might exacerbate a tense situation.

Soon enough, Larkin rose and nodded toward three serving women. At first they circulated the room with more gray towels, and then they carefully covered the now mostly emptied serving dishes and platters, being careful to remain silent in their actions. Finally they turned in unison and another woman took her place by the next door. Picard guessed it would be his turn to go through the door, but he was surprised to see Daithin stroll ahead of the others. Perhaps the premier led the way since this, in theory, would be the final room during the banquet. His stomach hoped so since it was full, despite polite portions allowing him to sample most of the dishes. A workout was definitely needed in the morning.

Daithin stood before the door and waited for Sela and Picard to catch up with him. The Elohsian nodded to the woman, who nodded back and then pushed, rather than pulled, and the door opened. As expected, the decor of the room was at once spacious and full, with small tables in the center and the usual lengthy wall table filled with desserts. Unlike the other rooms, though, the lighting was cheerful and the walls were filled with bright murals. They were all geometric designs definitely pleasing to the eye. Picard particularly liked the one directly above the sweet-smelling desserts.

"Premier, this is a marvelous place with which to end the banquet," Picard exclaimed.

"Yes, we do like to finish with a bit of a splash, yes indeed." Daithin smiled.

"If you don't mind, I will let my counselor lead my people since this is an area in which she excels."

"By all means, Captain, by all means. It's nice to see that you allow others to blaze trails rather than save them all for yourself."

An interesting observation, Picard noted, and filed it away with the others collected already for later contemplation. In the meantime, he gestured for Troi to take the lead, and she passed him with a wide grin. Dr. Crusher sidled up to Picard and whispered, "You know, if there was one more room here, I think I'd burst."

Picard nodded and replied, "I don't know about you, but I think it's just going to be coffee for me tomorrow morning."

Troi gazed at the various delicacies, allowing Larkin the privilege of explaining each dish to her despite the small blue placards next to each setting. With her plate amply loaded, she moved off toward the far table and took a seat. Politely, she awaited company but carefully eyed the foods before her. As she waited, a small, dark-paneled trolley was wheeled into the room and a serving woman with hair in yet another elaborate design went directly toward the counselor.

"May I offer you a beverage?"

Troi smiled in surprise. "I didn't think you were allowed to speak."

The woman nodded solemnly and said, "We speak when we have something to offer. Our role here is to fully support the diners and staff, not become a part of the event itself."

"Do these banquets happen often?"

"No. The parliament has a meal like this at the beginning of each assembly. We had the largest one when the peace was declared. Now, would you like something hot or cold?"

The Betazoid selected a frothy hot drink that had some spices sprinkled on top. The hostess indicated that given Troi's choices for dessert, this would be the most complementary drink. One whiff and Troi beamed in agreement. She strode off, inspecting one of the murals, when Plactus stepped toward her.

"Counselor Troi, I believe," he said, in a smooth tone.

"Yes, Subcommander. What do you think of the painting style?"

He merely glanced at the wall for a moment and admitted, "I know so little about art, it does not pay to ask me. But, may I ask you something?"

"Of course," she nodded, wondering at Plactus' sudden interest in her.

"We have not seen much of you on this world and wonder why the ship's counselor is not attending more of the informational sessions?"

Troi sipped at her drink and considered. "Actually, I have been part of the away teams studying the planet."

"I am surprised that you did not attend the parliamentary session yet. I would imagine a good captain would want a counselor's interpretation of the people."

Troi studied Plactus, who remained unmoving, hands clasped behind him. He had declined all manner of dessert and seemed intent on talking with her. "You seem to know a good deal about how we should do things."

"We study the Federation quite carefully, Counselor. We watch who is near our borders because they might pose a threat to our security. Did you know, for example, that we have had troubles of late with Corvallens?"

The mention of the Corvallens made Troi stiffen. Did Plactus know she was involved with the recent incidents involving the defection of Vice Counsel M'ret? The deception had involved Troi disguising herself as a Romulan. Plactus must be toying with her. Or was he? Troi could read nothing from the Romulan.

"Oh, yes, we had one near us that seemed engaged in piracy," Plactus continued. "We may be many things, but not pirates. Am I right, Counselor?"

"'Pirate' is certainly not a name I would associate with a Romulan," was all she managed to say.

Plactus beamed. "True. In fact, we blew up such a pirate ship recently. If I'm not mistaken, the *Enterprise* was nearby at the time."

He knew! Troi forced a curious expression to her features. "If we had been nearby, I certainly don't recall being there when it occurred. You're not saying we had anything to do with piracy."

"No, no," Plactus said reassuringly. "Pirate is certainly not a name I would associate with the Federation. Instead, I just find it interesting how often we actually manage to blur the lines between our peoples. Comings and goings across the border in both directions. You'd almost think we were friendly neighbors."

Troi recalled the days she spent as an imperious Romulan, summoning those feelings of discipline. She wanted very much to redirect the conversation. Plactus obviously enjoyed baiting members of the *Enterprise* crew for the Elohsians' benefit, but she was not going to submit.

"We are not friendly neighbors, Plactus," she said. "The goings-on you mention involve spying and deceptions that are forced by the hostile state of affairs between us. They will remain hostile, too, until you recognize the galaxy *is* big enough for the both of us."

"Of course, Counselor," he said. "Your bluntness surprises me. If you were Romulan, I'd say you were capable of command . . . of, say, even one of our warbirds. Perhaps the *N'ventnar* or the *Khazara.*"

Oh yes, he knew and he was having fun taunting her with the information. The Romulans might not be pirates but they were sadists. "Both seem to be fine representatives of the Romulan Empire," Troi replied in as hard a voice as possible. "Both ship's captains— Sela and Toreth—far better exemplify the Empire than their underlings."

"Well said, Counselor."

Troi decided to take the offensive. "It's even more interesting to note that the Romulans must use subterfuge to get what they want. It must be difficult to spend every waking moment looking for the next way to take advantage of your opponent."

Plactus rose to the bait, acting annoyed at Troi's turnabout. "Our methods have worked for a millennium and we remain a force to be reckoned with. On the other hand, you sound like your precious Federation is above subterfuge of its own. Using unidentified Betazoids during negotiations, hiding Vulcans on our homeworld, probing our borders with every passing sensor sweep . . ."

"I think the continuation of this conversation serves little purpose, Plactus," Troi snapped, cutting him off. She had heard enough.

"I don't think so, things are getting interesting," he said with a sly smile.

"I believe I said the conversation was over, Subcommander," Troi stated firmly. He continued to step closer.

"You heard the counselor," thundered Worf, striding over and catching their attention. Both looked at the imposing Klingon, who seemed to get larger by the second.

"Thank you for the interesting chat." And as suddenly as he approached her, the subcommander wandered off, immediately engaging Waln in some new conversation.

"Thank you, Worf," Deanna said as the Romulan left hearing range. She let out a deep breath and leaned against the wall, suddenly feeling drained.

"The captain did say we should not cause any incidents," Worf said matter-of-factly. Troi could not tell if he was teasing or being dead serious.

"My hero," she said with a grin and then grew serious as she mentally reviewed the confrontation.

Troi and Worf were quickly joined by Riker.

"Plactus knows I posed as Major Rakal," Troi said. "He knows I was on the *Khazara*. How could he possibly know, and why bring it up here?"

Riker thought a moment before answering. "Plactus was testing us, Deanna. He tried to provoke Beverly just as that centurion tried to provoke Worf. They want us to look bad but we haven't risen to their bait."

"But, Will, how could he know?"

"I don't know Deanna, but it could mean trouble. We'd better tell the captain."

* * *

The room quickly filled as people took small desserts, reflecting the amount of food consumed prior to this final stop. In a break from previous arrangements, Elohsians were clustered together while Romulans stayed near a corner, having taken the smallest portions possible while still remaining polite.

Picard listened to Troi's report, his face growing dark with concern and anger. "Toreth, of course, reported the deception to the senate and now it's one more piece of information for their files. So be it. It won't have any bearing on us this mission. We won't let it."

"Of course, Captain," Troi said.

"I believe that if we convened our group right now, each and every one of us would report a confrontation with a Romulan. This is a deliberate gambit on their part." Picard returned his attention to Troi. "I hope it didn't ruin your dessert. The pastries look delicious."

"They were, Captain, but I've lost my appetite," she answered. "We'd better not stay in a cluster; it's counterproductive to the spirit of the evening and might let Plactus think he won some victory."

"I agree," he said. Mug in one hand, he purposefully walked toward Commander Sela, who was near her countrymen but not part of a grouping.

"Our earlier conversation was certainly not dinner talk," he began. "I was not trying to irritate you."

Sela stared at Picard with no discernible expression on her face. She merely looked down at her nearly finished plate and contemplated it.

"We each have a job to do, and parading our philosophies so nakedly before Daithin is not how I intend to win this world."

"So, you expect to win it, Captain?"

"Of course, Commander. Starfleet has entrusted this mission to me and I would be something less than officer material if I didn't approach each assignment expecting to complete it satisfactorily."

Sela seemed to consider his words, the soft tone, and the force of character Picard radiated, even standing before her, drinking something smelling sickly sweet.

"I, too, expect to come out of this victorious. Only one of us will be satisfied."

Now it was Picard's turn to consider this woman. Her cold confidence continued to fascinate him because he recognized that beneath the icy exterior was a woman of tortured emotions. She was half-human and half-Romulan—very few such hybrids were known to exist in the universe. Just as other interspecies offspring had trouble adjusting to their dual natures, he could only imagine what Sela was going through, committed to one culture while still holding on to vestiges of her past. Surely something of Tasha Yar survived within her.

"Commander, I must compliment you and your officers on the way you have comported yourselves. I know this is difficult given our past . . . differences."

"I act as the situation demands, Captain. In fact, the way I act now is directly because of you."

Picard looked at her in astonishment but said nothing.

"Yes, Captain. After all, coming to convince the Elohsians to willingly join the Romulan Empire is not exactly a choice assignment. In fact, some might see it as a form of punishment." Her glare grew even more intense.

"You've cost me, Picard. Cost me in ways you've never imagined. I fought my way to the top and was given command of key operations. With each success I was given more authority and more power. I was feared and my very word meant life or death. In a short time, I conceived two very unique plans. Had they worked, I would have challenged the powers that be for a seat of power. The praetor himself would have feared my success.

"Instead, both plans failed. *You* spoiled them both, Picard. First, you ruined years of planning and work that would have left the Klingon Empire ripe for the taking. Just payback for the abuses we suffered at their hands decades ago. You and your Klingon servant—Worf—spoiled that.

"And there was, of course, your miraculous mission on my homeworld. We're still hunting down Spock and his paltry underground. Mark my words, Picard, they will be found and their insurrectionist movement will be stopped before much longer."

Picard calmly took the verbal lashing and just watched the officer. Emotions foreign to most Romulans—or their Vulcan cousins—were on display, and he remained captivated.

"You may think what you will, Sela, but from my brief visit to your people, they seem ready for something . . . different. The way of life I saw was not at all the way of life of a strong people. They may be better off if they follow Spock's way."

Sela listened to Picard's words and remained silent for a moment. For just an instant, Picard thought he might have reached something within her, made her reconsider her course of action.

She shook her head.

"You cost me," she continued. "Two defeats that turned out to waste untold man-hours and resources that I'm now told could have been used successfully elsewhere. The Romulans are a very unforgiving people, Captain. I was duly punished for my failures, and this is the result." She gestured toward her colleagues, who by now were at least mingling a bit with members of the Elohsian party. Picard noted his own officers were also fully engaged in mingling.

"I have been reduced to command of an old, failing starship peopled by a crew of officers that no one in the fleet wanted. This diplomatic mission is the best assignment I've had since the demotion. They said this was to see if I had learned my lesson." Her eyes grew wide and she looked directly at Picard. If possible, her face hardened all the more.

"I will win this world, Picard. And I will do it following my orders and by playing within the Elohsian rules. I shall bring this world's flag to the praetor and then see how I fare against the senate. You're very good with words, Captain, but to win a world you need more than that."

With that said, she turned away from him and walked off toward Plactus, who was speaking with Dona. Picard watched her stalk off and pondered her words. He resolved that he would keep a closer eye on her, if such a thing was possible. His thoughts, though, were interrupted when Simave and Larkin wandered by, each finishing a steaming mug of something strongly sweet.

"All in all, I think this turned out wonderfully," Simave offered when they paused by Picard.

The captain nodded and smiled. "Indeed. The food on this world is quite a treat. People may come here just for that, should things work out in the Federation's favor."

Larkin looked down at Picard with a touch of surprise. He placed his mug on the nearest table and asked, "Do you really think Federation tourists would come to this world just to eat?"

"There are those who line up to be first to visit any new Federation member world. Being this far out, there would be trade ships and diplomatic missions and, of course, Starfleet vessels patrolling the new borders."

"And just how much protection would Starfleet offer?" Simave asked.

"This is neither the time nor the place to get into such specifics, sir, but all worlds are offered protection by patrolling vessels, and if this were to be the new border, then it would be monitored and protected by a starship assigned to this sector. We would be able to answer a distress call, more often than not, within hours."

Larkin nodded silently, storing away the information. Like Daithin, he seemed an information sponge, and continued to allow those around him to probe and inquire. Picard had seen his like on many other worlds and noted, with mild interest, that world leaders always seem to need someone just like him.

"And now, Captain, the hour is beginning to draw late. Would you do us the honor of going first?"

"First? I don't understand, Larkin."

"It is our custom, at the end of such an event, to have our guests of honor conclude the evening with a short speech. Something to signify the importance of the event and give the guests words to remember."

"I had not been so informed and have not prepared anything."

Larkin merely nodded and said, "That was a mistake from my office, then. My apologies. Could you say something anyway?"

"Of course. Give me a moment to prepare." With that, Picard stepped away from his hosts and moved slowly toward his crew. Deep down, he suspected that Larkin did not tell him on purpose, and this was another little test to see how the differing worlds handled unprepared scenarios. No doubt, though, his years of experience in diplomacy would enable him to best Sela in a match of words. He hoped.

No more than five minutes later, Daithin stood before the exit door with serving women flanking him on both sides. The Elohsians assembled recognized the formation and quickly grew silent. They had placed their plates and mugs on tables and stood in rapt attention. Federation and Romulan officers quickly matched movements, although a look of confusion was found on more than one face.

"My people, my guests, this has been a truly marvelous evening, truly marvelous. But we grow tired and rest is required for tomorrow's challenges. We have asked Captain Picard from the Federation to honor us with the first closing approbation. Captain?"

For a moment Picard thought he was about to testify before a court—something he also had experience with. But he banished those stray thoughts, plucked his uniform straight, and stepped up by Daithin. The premier sidestepped to the left and created a space for the Starfleet officer.

"Premier Daithin, on behalf of the United Federation of Planets, and most immediately my crew and myself, I thank you and the people of Eloh for your kind and generous hospitality this evening.

"Our very credo is to explore, seek out new civilizations, and study the wonders of the universe. During my years of such exploration, I have helped discover new worlds and explanations for what has become of older civilizations. I have seen new life and far too much death.

"I have also seen, in my lifetime, peace settle in between peoples that never imagined such things happening. Just as Eloh itself has healed divisions that many probably considered irreparable. We share your joy in such unity. As you leave a better world for your children, it is our intention to leave the universe a better place after we have left it. We do that in the form of help. Our ships and personnel can help disaster victims or teach the latest planting techniques to worlds in need. We've kept the corridors of space safe for merchants, visitors, and newly discovered peoples.

"Recently, the Federation has helped discover, and now protects, a marvelous new doorway to the other side of the galaxy. With our help and protection, scientists are now beginning to learn what's out there. Something people have only dreamed about.

"We do not set these goals because we feel they are the only way to ensure our point of view prevails. Instead, we have established the United Federation of Planets to preserve each world's identity and let people grow and evolve as they choose. But each world knows that it can expect help from a neighbor, not exploitation. They can grow safe in the knowledge that they can take a risk and learn from the experience. And should disaster fall, that help is not far off.

"We bring this same set of assurances to Eloh and the Elohsian people. Our experience here has been short, but I would say that this is a young world, having grown up in a terribly short amount of time. Such survival against the odds is impressive. It's that independent spirit I have felt here on Eloh, and bask in it.

"I have no doubt that tonight symbolizes a great step forward in a friendship between peoples, Romulans included, that can even be a turning point in our galaxy. It's an honor to be here and participate in such a moment. I thank you for the invitation and the opportunity to come and know you and your families."

Picard smiled warmly toward Dona and the others. All had stood rapt while Picard spoke. The captain's love for performing Shakespeare certainly stood him in good stead here. Mentally reviewing the just-completed speech compared with comments he had heard during his stay, Picard was satisfied that he said enough to be substantive but kept it short enough so as not to bore. All in all, a good performance. The assessment was confirmed by the big grin from Deanna Troi and the happy look in Will Riker's eyes. Even Dr. Crusher offered him a discreetly placed thumbs-up. Worf remained stoically silent, but when Picard caught his eye the captain received a knowing, albeit short, nod of the head.

Across the room, Sela, Plactus, and the others stood still; no emotion was visible from any of them. The commander's arms were crossed, holding her form tight, not allowing Picard even to guess how his words were received by the Romulans.

Daithin stepped before Picard, all smiles. "Marvelous, Captain, marvelous. We've recorded those words and will broadcast them on tonight's news feed. No doubt they will be much discussed at tomorrow's school sessions. And now, would you join us up here, Commander Sela?"

The Romulan leader purposefully moved through the parting crowd, her arms hidden under the cloak and her expression unchanged. When Daithin once again sidestepped to make way for her, she took her place at military attention, adding a smile for the benefit of her audience.

"The Romulan government also thanks Eloh for its kind invitation to visit and get to know your world and your people. This is something new for us and a sign that the galaxy is changing. Old rules and old ways do not always work in new circumstances. We have learned this and have acted accordingly. Your world, as you know, lies directly between border spots between the Klingon–Federation and Romulan governments. Yesterday it could easily have been a spoil of war, but not today. No, today brings about a new kind of diplomatic war. An opportunity to win a world in ways unfamiliar to many. It's a way I am personally unfamiliar with, but I have chosen to brave this new challenge by going at this with vigor.

"The Romulan people have also explored much of the galaxy. We have exalted in those challenges and tamed worlds for our people to grow and expand. It is the Romulan way not to back down from hardships or challenges. This is the kind of challenge many relish. Being my first such experience with it, I cannot honestly tell you how I feel about it. What I do know is that my people will put forth a way of viewing the universe and not shrink from it. There is a way of life that has proven successful, and it is a way that will endure because of that single vision.

"Eloh has much to offer that vision. You are a planet of warriors who have learned to stop squabbling among yourselves and work together for the good of your world. That shows a courage and sense of character which we find appealing.

"To commemorate this newfound friendship between our people, I wish to leave you with more than words for future contemplation. On behalf of the Romulan people, I wish the parliament to accept a physical token of that friendship." With that, Sela gestured to a legionnaire by the far door. He stepped forward with an ornate box, patterning itself in some ways after the Elohsian mode of decoration. The colors even matched that of Daithin's most favored golden clothes. Good touches, Picard considered.

As the legionnaire placed the large container by

Daithin's feet, Sela proclaimed, "We have brought from our homeworld to yours a selection of our finest incenses. We burn them to help focus our thoughts, allow the aroma to remind us that nature's resources can be used to buoy the spirit and enable us to achieve success. We wish for Eloh to achieve such success and hope that you derive as much satisfaction from this blend as we have over the millennia."

Sela stepped back, a smug look of satisfaction on her face. The Romulans remained a tight group in the back of the room, but knowing looks were exchanged.

Picard, who by now was standing alongside Riker and Troi, was distressed. "Should we have brought something, Counselor?" he whispered.

"There was no way to know this would be required of us," she answered. "I can't even begin to guess how this will influence the parliament. After all, it's just burning spices, not new weapons or ships."

"But," Riker added, "their gesture can be perceived as the first of many such 'gifts.' The parliament may not be above bribery."

"Agreed, Will," Picard whispered.

Daithin looked down at the box, smiling, and then looked out among his people. They were chattering among themselves, and so many voices prevented the universal translators from picking up more than a word or two at a time. No one could tell how this gift was being received.

"Thank you, Commander Sela, thank you. Your gift is a generous one and will be appreciated by our people as much as is possible."

Sela stepped forward and asked, "What do you mean?"

"I mean, thank you," he said more slowly. "You see, well, you see, Commander, unlike the extraordinary senses the Romulans possess, and those of the Federation, the people of Eloh have a rather . . . limited sense of smell. Only certain plants and herbs from our own planet are noticeable to us. Your incenses, sadly, are not. The thought behind the gift, though, means much to me and the parliament. Your gesture will not be forgotten." He waved his hands in a dismissive gesture signaling, rather abruptly, Picard thought, an end to the banquet. An odd note to end on, he considered, and he wasn't sure how this would play in the decision-making process to be concluded in a few days.

Sela had stormed from the festive atmosphere into the now empty main dining room. Plactus and some of the party followed her, not caring that their every motion was keenly noted by the *Enterprise* officers. Grabbing Plactus roughly by an arm, she demanded, "Why did you not inform me of this?"

"But Commander, we did not know!" Plactus stepped back, away from the fury of his commander. She stepped forward, keeping their conversation loud but extremely intimate.

"Imbecile, you were supposed to know everything about these people before tonight. We have been here longer than those Federation fools, and they didn't make the blunder, we did! If we lose this world, Plactus, it will be your head I give to the praetor, not my own. And then your family shall know disgrace and lose their rank, their home, and their place among the people. Not many families can say they helped lose an entire world. Pray this is not the case, Plactus. I will not suffer a defeat at Picard's hands again!"

She swiftly moved away from him and her fellow officers, making a straight line back into the ultimate room and headed for the exit, and actually pushed past a few Elohsians to get out. On her way, she walked by Picard without a glance.

"A rather upset woman," Riker wryly noted.

"Wouldn't you be, Will?" Troi asked.

"Of course, but I didn't make the mistake. Or in public."

"But we could have, Number One," Picard interjected, all business. "We didn't know about their sense of smell, either. What else might we not know about them?"

"Good point, sir."

"Yes. Doctor, I want to see if we can't get one of the Elohsians to submit to a thorough physical. I'd like a better understanding of how they work and what else we may need to know. Perhaps during the tour tomorrow."

Crusher nodded affirmatively and gave her captain a tight smile of sympathy. How easily this could have been the Federation's blunder, she realized.

Once the crew had reassembled outside the large banquet complex, they took their usual positions around Picard. He quietly tapped his comm badge and merely said, "Picard to *Enterprise*. Beam us up."

Chapter Five

RIKER, being the conscientious first officer, knew in advance the banquet would be a long night. He made certain Data would take the evening shift while arranging for himself to take first shift on the bridge, allowing Captain Picard the luxury of sleeping in or time alone to compose his report to Starfleet. Since Riker wasn't due to return to the planet for the duration of the voyage, he knew he could force himself to remain alert earlier and catch some rest when circumstances allowed. Despite the Romulan presence, Riker felt as if this might actually be a quiet mission. He certainly appreciated some action in his life, but he didn't necessarily want the fate of a planet altered just to satisfy his cravings. Instead, he decided that a workout was in order as the shift ended.

The first officer left a quick update on the ship's log and then stood ramrod straight. Squaring his shoulders, he took one last look at the main viewscreen and its placid view of Eloh. Nice-looking planet, he considered. Maybe a shore leave here wouldn't be such a bad idea. Then he strode briskly up the ramp that led to the upper ring of the bridge. Lieutenant Worf remained at the tactical station and barely afforded Riker a glance.

"Shifts have changed smoothly, Lieutenant," Riker said. "I'm going to the holodeck for a workout. You have the conn."

"Aye sir," Worf replied, logging the change in command with a brief movement of his left fingers. As Riker moved off toward the turbolift, Worf turned around and added, "I have uploaded several new Klingon training programs. May I suggest you try Worf Tango Five?"

"A tango might do well, Worf," Riker said, breaking into a big smile.

Worf let out a heavy sigh and returned his gaze to the tactical station, avoiding any deliberations on the concepts regarding human humor.

The ride down to the holodecks was swift, and Riker allowed himself the opportunity to consider training programs and relaxation options. He might try Worf's new workout, although the Klingon programs tended to leave him stretched out a bit much, so he'd have to follow the program with one that involved a whirlpool or sauna. Maybe the soothing vapors of an Argelian spice bath.

With his mind drifting a bit and stifling a yawn, the first officer did not notice that the holodeck doors were opening and a young man was emerging. They collided with a dull thud, bringing Riker's thoughts from the sensual pleasures of Argelius back to the *Enterprise* at light speed. He steadied himself and then the youth, quickly asking if he was all right.

"Yeah, I am," the young man replied. Riker looked at him without recognition, which surprised him, because he thought he had come to know everyone aboard the ship, at least by sight if not by name.

"I don't believe I know you," he began.

"James Kelly, just signed aboard," the jumpsuited teen replied. "You must be Commander Riker. I've heard about you."

Riker smiled and let the holodeck doors close without notice. "Have you, now?"

"Yes, sir," he said, letting a smile cross his face. "My parents say they hear good things about you and . . . well, I've heard from others."

"How long have you been aboard?"

"Just a few days, sir. My parents are pretty happy to be here."

"And you?" Riker asked with genuine interest.

"I guess so," was the reply. "There certainly are some very impressive people on this ship. It must be great being part of the command crew." Kelly did not seem at all nervous around the officer, Riker thought, but was certainly distracted by something on his mind. He then remembered his own advice to Ensign Ro regarding consideration for the civilians aboard the ship. Now was as good a time as any to practice what he preached. "Sorry for banging into you," he began again. "I had my mind on something else entirely and didn't see where I was going."

"You too?"

Riker was intrigued by the tone in the voice, so he gestured toward the just-closed holodeck. "Would you care to discuss it?"

Kelly hesitated for a few moments and then nodded. "I guess it couldn't hurt."

"Computer, access program Worf Tango Five and prepare to execute."

The holodeck computer twittered electronically for

a moment and then replied, "Program loaded and ready to run. Convert to human norms?"

"Negative," Riker said with a smile. "Stand by." He waited a moment for the doors to open and turned toward Kelly. "This should be interesting," he said.

As the doors opened, Riker was surprised to hear birds chirping in the distance. Tendrils of purplish smoke did not surprise him since most of Worf's scenarios involved less than ideal planetary conditions. The Klingon had once explained that this kept him sharpest. Riker had then countered that the security chief wouldn't know what to do if a confrontation involved sunshine and clear skies.

Continuing to gesture, Riker led Kelly into the alien environment. Kelly stared in wide-eyed disbelief and slowed down considerably.

"Our security chief, Lieutenant Worf, programmed this himself. I don't recognize the landscape—don't suppose you do, either. I haven't tried this yet—and won't until we're done talking. Now, then, James Kelly, what's on your mind?"

"It's kind of foolish, sir, and certainly nothing to trouble an officer about."

Riker smiled kindly and said, "I'm also a human being, James. Forget the uniform for a moment and let's hear this man-to-man."

"Oh, but, well, it's just so trivial, sir," Kelly began. "Maybe not. I can't seem to get it off my mind." Kelly stared out at the lush jungle setting. There were trees with thick branches and vines; spotted here and there were burbling holes in the ground from which the purple steam escaped. While life forms could be heard, none could be seen, but Kelly stared out, trying to find them.

"Let me guess," Riker prompted. "Family problem?"

"No, sir."

"Troubles with your studies?"

"No, sir."

Riker thought for a moment and then snapped his fingers. "It's a girl, right?"

"Sort of," Kelly said. "A woman, actually."

Stroking his beard with his right hand, Riker grinned. "Ah, I see, an older woman." He realized he had to be careful here, not sure of how far to push the youth and how far to remain a responsible adult.

"How much older, James?"

"I'm not sure, sir. Several years, I think. Never mind."

"Come stretch with me," Riker coaxed. He extended his left leg and began stretching out the muscles. James fell into step, trying to match the officer move for move. He was, however, considerably shorter than Riker and certainly not as broad or well conditioned, despite being much younger.

"Older women can be tricky to deal with. I was seventeen when a girl of twenty-four made a play for me and I was in way over my head. I do know, though, of several relationships that have worked quite well with vast age differences. So let's see . . . is she aboard the ship?"

James grunted as he switched to stretching his right leg. "Yes, sir. She's really amazing, with the most stunning eyes I've ever seen. There's so much about her I don't know yet, but we've spent hours talking and she's just incredible."

"Well, that a good start," he replied. "What do you know about her?"

"Not much. Yet. We've only spoken twice and we spent most of the time discussing the ship and how it works. She knows so much. . . ."

"So, she's been here longer than you?"

"That's not hard, Commander. I think it's been a year or so for her. I had trouble keeping up with her energy and pace but I think she's worth it."

Riker began moving his body in a rhythmic way, as if following some inner music Kelly could not hear. "All this from two conversations, eh?" Riker said as he continued his exercise. "Must be one impressive young woman." The teen tried to keep up and failed in the attempt. With his peripheral vision, Riker watched and was silently amused. At least the young man made the attempt, which gave him high marks in Riker's mind. "We have several options to work from. Let's see which one sounds right to you."

Kelly nodded, grunted, and then began listening intently.

Ro Laren could think of nothing more desirable than fresh clothes and something warm to drink. The tall, lithe woman nearly stumbled into her cabin after spending the previous five hours repairing a short-circuited workstation on the bridge. Just as Ro was originally anticipating a night's peace, she was summoned to the bridge by Data, who was duty officer immediately after the Elohsian banquet.

The problem on the bridge required her experience, especially since most of the night shift crew were ensigns with little practical troubleshooting experience. The problem was relatively minor but intricate given the microcircuitry behind the wall paneling by the science stations. As the last officer to complete any work on the station, Ro was the ideal person to get back into the systems, find the problem, repair it, and then test the new circuits. Fortunately, no additional irregularities were detected and an engineering crew would report in during first shift and inspect the work.

The burned-out circuit boards and isolinear chips would also be brought to engineering for inspection, to better learn what caused the problem and how to prevent similar trouble in the future.

With the starship in routine orbit, her work was peaceful enough, although she could not shake the unease she felt knowing that a Romulan warbird, albeit in worn condition, was also circling Eloh. She had put those thoughts behind her and replaced them with images of her bed. Tapping the entrance pad to her cabin, Ro stepped in, called for lights, and took a step in before she saw it.

On her desk, which was usually immaculately neat with what few things she kept atop it, sat a canary yellow box with a crimson ribbon around it. With two fast steps, she was at her desk and stabbed at her computer console. "Computer," she snapped. "Detail personnel in and out of this cabin during the last six hours."

"Ensign Ro Laren and Ensign Marguerite Nipar," the computer quickly replied in its characteristic, mechanically female voice.

"Which department does Ensign Nipar report to?"

"Ship's stores."

Ro was momentarily confused since she had not ordered anything, but then she realized the packaging implied a gift. Calming herself, she wondered who might want to send her such a thing. After all, this day did not correspond to any Bajoran or Terran holiday, nor was it her birthday—an occasion not usually celebrated by Bajorans. Then a likely candidate sprung to mind.

"James Kelly," she said aloud in a surprised tone. She had suspected the young man was more than casually interested in her, but for him to send her a gift—this was trouble brewing. Worse yet, unlike a burned-out circuit board, this was a problem with which she had absolutely no experience.

Taking the hard-backed desk chair, Ro studied the package and allowed herself to guess the contents. After considering and dismissing a dozen possibilities, she tore at the ribbon in frustration. Inside was a perfect baker's dozen of glazed fruit candies, each an iridescent color, no two alike. Definitely a romantic gesture, she concluded, but wasn't sure how to respond. She gently lifted a bright violet candy and, as she popped it into her mouth, realized that there was nothing in the *Starfleet Officer's Manual* that could possibly cover this situation.

The worst part was, the candy was good.

Dawn on Dos Dar was a thing of breathtaking beauty. Sunlight filtered through a large bank of clouds, coloring the skies in pastels of yellows and oranges. Mountains seemed to skim along the edges of the clouds and snowcapped peaks reflected the colorful rise of the sun. A perfect day, Geordi considered, as he studied the cloud formations from aboard a small aircraft. Once again he was accompanied by Counselor Troi and Ilena; this time they were visiting the planet's chief water purification plant.

The night before had ended on an odd note, and he reviewed those details as the landing party returned to the planet for more tours and studies of the civilization. Later, they would return the favor and host a party of Elohsians aboard the *Enterprise*. The consensus among the away team was that the Romulans seemed to score a significant point with their physical gift the night before. Troi did what she could to downplay the meaning of the gift as the officers walked toward their cabins, but Picard was resolute that this cost him some maneuvering room.

Geordi had argued that the gesture may have been good but it was flawed, given that the incense was useless to a people of limited natural senses. If anyone understood that, it was La Forge, but the comments did not improve the captain's humor.

Geordi's own humor did not seem much improved from the previous day. Troi had tried to stimulate him beyond moping about the encounter with Luth. She did what she could to focus him on the current agenda and put the past behind him. Instead, he spent last night and now this morning brooding over the *Enterprise*'s role on Eloh. Was it right to tease these people with the knowledge that so many better ways existed to improve their war-torn world? Were they any better than the serpent offering Eve even a look at the apple? Despite his years of Starfleet training, his every fiber wanted to help the people get on with their lives and discover the glory of space exploration for themselves. Instead, La Forge had to remind himself of the specific instructions given the crew by Picard. Under most normal conditions the rule wouldn't be necessary, but this was one way to prevent the *Enterprise* and the Romulans from engaging in some form of one-upsmanship that would only harm the ill-prepared populace of Eloh.

"Isn't it beautiful, Counselor?" Geordi asked, as much to change the subject for himself as to reconnect with Troi and Ilena. By then the craft had begun to clear the mountains and head for the large structure ahead.

"Yes," she replied, a hand resting against a window, toying with a dark curl. She continued to stare out the window, watching the scenery, a look of contentment upon her face. "That's one thing I miss about being aboard a starship—the natural beauty of a sunrise or a sunset. Oh, I could program them into the holodeck, but to wake up in the morning and look out your window to see this . . . makes me want to go on shore leave."

"I'm glad you're enjoying the view," Ilena said from the copilot's seat. Today she wore a bright tan and green outfit with yellow trim, and an ornamental band of copper circled her head, reflecting sunlight. "As a little girl, each morning I would see the sunrise and for a moment forget we were engaged in a terrible war." She had met the landing party at the parliament building and escorted them to a nearby airfield where the small six-person craft was waiting. It was smooth and shone in the twinkling starlight, an elegantly designed vehicle. Some of its allure had been ruined when the pilot, a former soldier named Doral, said the craft was a modified fighter aircraft.

They moved swiftly through the sky and Geordi had chatted with Doral about the aircraft's capabilities. During the hour-long flight, Troi had similarly engaged Ilena about the previous night's party. It was obvious to Geordi that Troi was gently probing to see what the local opinion was of the Romulan act. He recalled Troi telling him that the one thing that was universal on almost every planet the *Enterprise* had visited was gossip. At first he chuckled over the concept, but then he weighed that view against his own experiences and realized, with some surprise, that she was dead right. Gossip was a subject to which the chief engineer did not usually give much importance, especially since he spent his life as the subject of such whispered comments, innuendoes, and speculations. At first it was his blindness followed by the arrival of the VISOR, and then his posting aboard the

Enterprise, and finally, once aboard the mighty starship, his hard luck with women. Far too much time was spent idly wondering about the habits of others, he concluded long ago, and it was not something worth bothering about.

Geordi periodically listened to Troi's conversation and got the impression that Ilena didn't consider the gesture as damaging to the Federation as the *Enterprise* officers did. On the other hand, he thought, she seemed predisposed to like the Federation, so her view may not have been the most prevalent one. Geordi disliked being a pessimist and tried to concentrate on the day ahead.

Once the vehicle landed, Geordi thanked Doral for the conversation and then extended a helping hand to let Troi gingerly step out of the craft. The two followed Ilena as she walked them across the landing strip to another sojourner, this one bright green. She had warned the two that it would be another fifteen-minute drive to the purification plant, but she had hoped the visit would be worth the travel.

They traveled in companionable silence, studying the structure and shapes of the buildings, the clothing worn on this continent, and the way people acted when they saw their first aliens. Like everyone else seen so far, the Elohsians wore simple, solidly colored clothing, with many decorative touches. Unlike Regor, the people on this continent had taken to sporting oversized pockets, almost all them bulging with something or another. They had hip pouches attached by a belt as well, and those pouches had many colorful patterns. Geordi thought the look was comfortable as well as practical. As he understood it, most of the people in this area worked solely on the purification plant, and deep pockets meant a convenient place for tools. Most citizens took the presence of the Federation people in stride, maybe because they had seen Romulans days before, or because after so much warfare they had a high threshold for surprise. Those who stared did so with smiles on their faces, so Geordi thought he could relax.

Ilena drove the sojourner to the purification plant with little problem, and she managed to chat the entire way, explaining some of the background involved in the importance of the plant. During the recently concluded war, many lakes, rivers, and reservoirs were contaminated by shrapnel, chemical by-products of munitions plants, and far too many remains of the dead. As a result, water was needed for the remote areas and desalinization plants were also required. However, it was decided just as the war ended that too many precious resources were being wasted, so the planet as a whole had to do as much recycling of raw materials as possible. The purification plant about to be visited not only recycled and freshened water from a nearby river, but also had facilities to handle major chemical products. It was an engineering marvel, to hear Ilena boast about it. Geordi did note that she made sure to add that the river here was ruined by Populist chemical weapons and that it was a Dar scientist who found the key method to reverse the damage.

As the sojourner rounded one final corner, Geordi got his first full look at the plant. It was an immense, boxy structure, all in a solid gray color with piping and steam valves, using nearly every engineering trick he had studied when at the Academy. The technology possessed by the Elohsians was decades—if not two or three centuries—behind the rest of space, and in moments Geordi knew he could work on ways to improve efficiency. There was a sense that the building had started out with one configuration and had hastily been amended over time. A great deal of pipe connected smokestacks and buildings, as did catwalks and scaffolding. Still, the sheer size of the structure was impressive and the fact that it existed to help people was reassuring.

Geordi let out a low whistle as they stepped from the car, and Ilena beamed. "This is one of Eloh's prides," she announced.

"I can see why," Geordi said. He had automatically opened his tricorder and begun taking sensor readings of the emissions. Mostly, this was to confirm his guesses based on the amazing sensory array he already had via his VISOR. Pleased with the results, he folded the device shut and stuffed it back into a pocket.

"How many people maintain the operation?"

Ilena began walking backward, concentrating on Geordi's answer, but her unhesitating manner indicated she had been here many times before and was familiar with the layout. "There are over a hundred people working during any of four seven-hour shifts. This facility is never closed, but we have built-in redundancies that allow us to take pieces off-line for inspection and maintenance."

"How old is this place?"

"I believe the main portion of the building was constructed about sixty-five, seventy years ago. However, as the war arrived and escalated, the wise Dars living here saw the need for more capacity. They began expanding the original site about twenty-five years ago, and then after the era of unity began, Populists and Dars conceived of the current incarnation before you."

Geordi nodded, taking in the scope of the work done, and imagined that the control centers would be a sight to behold. He picked up his pace, suddenly eager to walk around the entire plant, looking in every nook and cranny and possibly trying out some of the controls. He caught himself and turned to check on Troi, who returned a reassuring smile.

"Sorry, Counselor, but you may be in over your head here." Geordi immediately caught himself, thinking he had insulted the counselor about her height. "Technically, that is," he apologized.

"Don't worry about it, Geordi," she replied, seeming more amused than annoyed at Geordi's embarrassment. "It's important to see how things work around the planet. While you concentrate on the sheer mechanics, I will have a chance to watch the typical workers in action. We'll both get something from the experience, I assure you."

Geordi smiled at Troi's encouragement and quickened the pace. As they drew closer to the plant, La Forge slowed down for a moment and began sniffing the air. Troi noticed his action and imitated him. "What is that, Geordi?"

"This plant may purify its water, but the stink is pretty bad," he commented.

"Ilena, does the odor bother you?"

Ilena stopped leading, noticed the visitors were several feet behind her and Geordi was making a pained face. "What odor, Geordi?"

"Of course," Troi said, smiling. "Their olfactory senses are less developed and they *can't* smell the chemicals. This doesn't bother them at all."

"No, it doesn't," Ilena said. "Do you think you need a mask or something? I'm sure we can find. . . ."

"Don't worry about it," Troi said reassuringly, despite instinctively wrinkling her nose. "The smell just surprised us. If it doesn't bother you, we won't let it bother us."

"Easy for you to say," Geordi whispered in Troi's

ear. "I'm probably going to be climbing around equipment and getting real close to this stuff."

Within another few minutes, the trio were by the main entrance and were greeted by a safeguard officer. La Forge noted that there were none at Carinth Dar's computer headquarters, but here was a live, uniformed soldier, complete with Elohsian rifle and sheathed knife. Ilena flashed him a shiny piece of plastic and the guard nodded in approval.

"We can't be too careful here. A few decades back, during the war, there was a guerrilla attack and we lost several lives and six months' worth of work. Security has been tight here ever since. While you could not possibly pass as Elohsians, they had to be sure I was the proper guide."

"How odd to suspect one's own but not strangers," Troi noted.

"Not at all, Deanna. There's no way anyone could pass themselves off as you, or you pass as one of us. But *I* could be a disguised terrorist or a psychotic and cause unimagined damage."

Troi nodded, but was still bothered by the idea.

Once inside the building, the engineer recognized the same basic interior design as in the great banquet hall. Fairly unremarkable architecture that was more function than decoration. Nothing in the way of local statuary or pictures on the walls. There was a large screen that continued to run a message warning people about color-coded areas to avoid. Pictographs also showed people which areas controlled water, chemical waste, and research and development sections.

"You know, Ilena, I'll want to see all three areas," Geordi commented. "I'd like to be thorough."

Troi walked up beside the still-moving guide and

leaned in to whisper conspiratorially, "I believe you have candies on Eloh."

"Yes, of course. You tried some last night. Are you hungry?"

"No," she laughed. "On Geordi's home planet there's a phrase to describe the way Geordi is acting."

"Oh?"

"It's called being like a kid in a candy shop."

Ilena slowed her pace, stared at La Forge and considered the counselor's words. A smile crept across her face until she laughed out loud. Geordi stopped, looked at both laughing women, and frowned. This only made them laugh a bit more. Troi, getting back to business, took Ilena's arm and started her walking once again.

After an hour of inspecting the chemical waste sight, Geordi had a stiff back, but was impressed with the design and function of the facility. He had taken extensive notes and readings with the tricorder and spoken with each section's main engineers throughout the plant. They proudly showed him graphs and charts that indicated how much raw material was recycled and reused during a given year. Productivity was up for the seventh straight year and there was no letup in sight. Geordi filed that knowledge away and looked up, and his jaw simply dropped.

"Oh, it's you," Luth said.

Geordi looked up at the conductor, resplendent in his crimson outfit, this time without the headband equipment. While Geordi obviously registered surprise, Luth seemed less than thrilled to see the chief engineer again.

"Good morning, Conductor," Troi interjected.

"I knew the Federation was due here today, but I should have given it more thought and realized you would be the one sent. Ready to tease me again with your technical brilliance?"

La Forge was flustered, and it showed. He hated himself for feeling so silly in front of the administrator and he knew he had to control those feelings immediately. "Just as you are Eloh's technology expert, I'm the *Enterprise*'s. I've just spent the last hour looking around, and I must say, this operation truly impresses me."

Luth grunted but smiled a little. "I'll be in the main control room. If you're that fascinated, stop by and see the real workings up close." With that he turned on his heel and strode off. His body language convinced Geordi he made no friend today.

"I don't know about your time on the starship, but around now, most people take a break for a small meal," Ilena finally said. Geordi could tell she was trying once again to soothe the tension in the air. "As I understand matters, it's not like your big breakfasts but more like a snack. Ever since the wars, we've always preferred small meals throughout the day rather than big ones. The banquet or a celebration is the exception, making it all the more memorable. Are you hungry?"

Geordi shook his head and stared further at the unending stream of tricorder readings. Troi, though, thought some food couldn't hurt. She had awoken early on the *Enterprise* and had still felt full from the previous night's meal. Therefore, she skipped her morning meal and was only now finding herself hungry.

Ilena smiled and said, "Fine. I'll take Deanna to the canteen and you can keep working. We have to leave in about two hours so you can be back aboard your ship when Premier Daithin arrives."

"Yeah, I'd like to take more readings, but outside this time. Do you think the guards will mind me wandering around?"

"You've been given complete access by the parliament itself, and they rarely seem to agree on anything. That's a major victory for you, Geordi, so by all means, enjoy your walk. We'll meet up with you in the research labs in about three-quarters of an hour."

Deanna gave Geordi a smile and a wave, saying, "You can enjoy the fresh air. I want something warm and tasty."

Ro popped another piece of the candy in her mouth as she brooded over her situation. This time she was seated in the Ten-Forward lounge because Ro had not uncovered any answers in her own quarters. A change of scenery, she had learned, could sometimes change a point of view. She barely noticed the savory strawberry flavor, and she chewed it thoroughly. Ro had also managed not to notice the approaching figure of her friend, Guinan.

"A little early in the day for you, isn't it?" The gentle, friendly voice always soothed Ro's fiery temper and made her instantly relax. Ro knew little about Guinan's background and less about her friend's current situation. The Bajoran knew Guinan volunteered to serve aboard the *Enterprise,* since she and Captain Picard shared a bond that was a mystery to all. Like Ro, Guinan and her people suffered grave harm—almost wiped out as a race by the soulless Borg. Guinan always seemed unruffled by the various comings and goings of alien races, many new even to the long-lived hostess.

"Just something to drink," Ro replied, then noticed that Guinan had already placed a tall glass of fruit juice before her. "Uh, thank you."

As expected, Guinan took a seat opposite her and just watched the goings-on.

"I suppose you're waiting for me to pour my heart out to you, right?" Ro asked with an annoyed smirk.

Guinan smiled sympathetically. "Is your heart full?"

Ro rolled her eyes and tried to get angry, but Guinan continued to sit and look beatific.

"I received a box of candy this morning."

"That's nice. You probably don't get that often," Guinan observed.

"That's true. And you know why? Because I'm not romantically involved at this time."

"Someone's obviously trying to change that. Do you know who it is?"

"Yes, and that's the problem. He's a teenager."

"I didn't know you liked your men younger," Guinan quipped.

"I don't! I mean, I don't like them at all . . . I mean, he's just a kid and I'm probably the first non-human he's seen close up or something. I don't know. I'm just supposed to be a guide to him and his family, help them adjust to life aboard the ship . . ."

"Nice idea," Guinan interrupted. "Yours?"

"Of course not. Riker thinks it'll teach me something." Ro took another drink from her glass, finishing it.

"And what have you learned?"

"Commander Riker knows how to get me into trouble." She attempted to take another drink, noticed it was empty, and fairly slammed the glass back onto the table. Guinan ignored the action, remaining perfectly composed.

"Are you sure you didn't bring this on yourself?"

Ro gave her friend an annoyed glare. "Quite sure, Guinan. The boy seems to think the universe of me and I've done nothing to lead him on. In fact, I've tried to discourage his interest and keep things professional."

"He may think you're playing hard to get. What does he know about you, anyway?"

"Not much. I've tried to keep me out of the conversations."

"A woman of mystery. Some men like that, you know. I once had a suitor on Risa that tried for weeks to find out even my name. Handsome. For a Tellarite."

Ro grimaced at the image of a pig-snouted Tellarite making nice to Guinan. "He's not a man, barely beyond being a boy. How do I discourage him without failing at my task?"

Guinan folded her hands before her, leaning slightly over the table. "Have you considered being honest with him? Let him down gently with the truth?"

Ro considered the words and then tried to imagine the conversation. She had images of James Kelly not getting the message, Ro getting exasperated, and finally putting the boy out an airlock.

That might not be the best course of action at this point.

Geordi had turned away from the departing women and begun moving toward a clearly color-coded exit door about a hundred yards down a right-hand, bright blue corridor. While he was making his initial notes, he found his mind wandering toward food after all. Too late now, he considered, and concentrated instead on the building itself. The engineer noted coolly that beyond the signage and chromatics, the building's insides were unremarkable, unimpressive, and clearly uniform, right down to the noxious odor. He had already grown accustomed to it, but was thankful he'd be here only a little while longer. Since the structure was built mostly during a war, he was sure that little thought was given to making the place esthetically pleasing, or as efficient as possible. He nodded to various workers as he passed them. Most used a hand gesture or smiled in return, but no one spoke to him. La Forge was used to this reaction when visiting new worlds. Despite having the same basic humanoid appearance—two arms, two legs, one head—there was enough different between the two races to make the Elohsians a bit cautious around him. The VISOR certainly didn't make life any easier for him since it worked like a beacon, making him an unwanted focal point of curiosity.

Geordi carefully noted the tricorder readings as he walked up to and then through the door. Measuring for air purity, he was checking how the filtration systems functioned and if the workers were truly safe. Walking with small, measured steps, La Forge altered the bandwidths for the next set of readings and concentrated almost exclusively on the palm-held device. As a result, on more than one occasion, he nearly walked into low-hung pipes or jutting corners where an old part of the original building had been affixed to a newer one. Geordi did pause at this and take new readings, studying how carefully the two pieces fit and whether anything could escape from the seams. Within seconds he was pleased that the construction seemed airtight.

Finally, Geordi stopped, pocketed his tricorder, and looked up toward the sky. He decided not to totally ignore the nice, pleasant late morning but instead, relish it. Troi had a point, he admitted to himself, it's a nice change of pace to have nature itself greet you with the kiss of a warm breeze and see natural sunlight brighten the sky. He stretched out his back a bit and twisted and turned in every direction, loosening up.

Without warning, though, there was a rumbling sound and then a flash of light from a far corner of the mammoth building. The shaking was violent enough to knock La Forge off his feet and send him smack onto the hard cement ground. Kneeling, Geordi immediately tried to look for some clue as to what was happening. Then he heard a loud explosion, felt the ground beneath his feet churn again, and watched with growing horror as pieces of the building were vomited toward the sky, belching flame and gases in a curling plume.

He could hear the screams and cries of workers from nearby, around the corner. Geordi hurriedly slapped his comm badge and called, "La Forge to Troi!"

Instantly, he heard, "Troi here, Geordi. What's going on?"

"I'm trying to figure that out! Are you and Ilena okay?" He had already whipped open his tricorder and began jogging toward the front of the structure, which continued to vibrate and make groaning noises.

"We're a little shaken but fine. Where are you?"

"Just coming around the side of the building toward the main entrance. Does Ilena know what happened?"

"No, but I can sense from the workers that this is new to them, too. They're on the verge of panic."

"Okay, then we have work to do. I'll see what I can do to help the engineers. You contact the captain. La Forge out."

Geordi began to run full out, rushing to get to an entrance and find Luth, their chief engineer. People were scattering and pouring out of the building, some coughing and others helping a few who seemed to have suffered injury or smoke inhalation. He scanned for Luth's body signature and realized that like a true engineer, he was likely to be inside the building, trying to contain the destruction. Working his way through the people and smoke, Geordi was soon inside the building. The light panels continued to function but the smoke created a hazy look to the corridors. The floor was slick with moisture and at first he didn't want to look down; but he finally did and noted water mixed with Elohsian blood was plentiful. Ignoring that with his VISOR, Geordi threaded his way around people and, stepping over debris of unknown origin, came closer to the main control room. He feared for what he would find inside.

Once at the doorway, he could hear a voice shouting orders, reassuring him that someone was taking charge. As he entered the room, he saw Luth hunched over a control panel while two other women scrambled to fix wiring that fell from a jagged open panel. With his tricorder, Geordi tried to estimate the damage and danger to the people, but it was hard to tell. The room was small and would feel cramped once he went in further, but it could not be helped. At least it would be quieter than the hysteria still ringing through the halls.

"La Forge, we need help!" Luth called out between coughs.

"What's the situation?" No question about it, La Forge was going to help, regulations be damned. Human life will always take precedence and he could face any consequences later—if there was a later. Geordi hurried over to the man and noted the sweat that streamed freely from his hairless brow.

"There was an explosion in the main processing core that has ripped apart the very center of this building. Our internal sensor devices are down and I've got everything off-line. I can't tell where the injured and dead are. More important, I can't tell the extent of our damage. If we can't contain the chemicals, we'll pollute the air and water for this entire continent!"

La Forge nodded, whipping open his tricorder. "Give me a schematic of the plant to work from and I'll try and figure out what's going on. Do you have backup systems at all?"

The older man snorted a little and gestured toward two coughing women working through the smoke to get some bulky computer equipment running. "Yes. That's just what my aides are doing, but it's going to take time to reaccess the power supply and the computer mainframe. I don't have time."

Geordi nodded, enjoying the familiar sensation and adrenaline rush. Finally he was going to do something productive and prove to Luth he knew what he was doing. Locking the tricorder on a display screen, he scanned in the building's schematic and then left the room, following the map that led toward the center of the disaster. Along the way, La Forge continually stopped to help people in need.

First, he helped four people out from behind a jammed, blackened doorway and directed them to safety. Another couple were stuck behind a doorway that had been blocked by falling debris. It took several minutes of prying with a long, heavy tool to free them. His muscles ached, and he was getting exhausted by the heat, stench, and tension. He next found one person with an arm pinned back by a fallen tool container. The effort took more of a toll on him, but at least this was an easier rescue.

That proved to be fortunate because the final effort was a fifteen-minute attempt to help a women get out from under canisters that were filled with cleaning supplies. More than once, Geordi had to slow or stop his efforts and take some cleansing breaths before continuing. While the Elohsian sense of smell was almost nonexistent, Geordi's nostrils burned with the odor of disinfectants and cleansers. Worse, it took the engineer several moments initially to detect the buzzing sound of live wires loose somewhere nearby. While the woman moaned from her injuries, La Forge had to stop his initial rescue attempts first to locate the danger. His VISOR danced with flickering light shifts, indicating the location of the problem like a beacon. But getting there was not going to be easy. First, La Forge had to climb atop some of the spilled canisters surrounding the woman and carefully edge his way toward the sparking wires protruding just inches from a destroyed wall. Once he got closer, the *Enterprise* officer had to find something insulated to reach out and cap the sparking, exposed wires.

By training, La Forge had a healthy respect for fire and naked electricity, but he also had a personal relationship with the element. At age five, he was trapped in a massive fire just before he received his "new eyes," and it scared him silly for years. He always suspected that his decision to get into the technical side of Starfleet had something to do with a desire to learn how to control such destructive energies.

On more than a few missions, he was exposed to phaser blasts, explosions—both natural and man-made—and many fires. And each time he encountered the heat or saw the flames, he always paused for a moment, looking at the scene through the eyes of a terrified youngster. Now an adult, he always took a deep breath and did whatever was required. These days he had come to take a pride in being able to handle himself during a crisis and not be frozen in place, needing to be rescued by his parents.

A sudden flash of inspiration hit La Forge, and he gingerly turned around and examined the two nearest canisters. If they were really cleaning supplies, then there might be rubber gloves to protect the hands. The first one turned out to be all liquids and solvents but the second had two very large rubber gloves attached to a hook on the inside of the lid. Slipping them on, La Forge was now able to shimmy his way toward the wires and, using some rudimentary tricks he first learned at his dad's side, managed to close off the exposed wires, seal them, and even push them back inside the wall.

He took off the gloves and wiped his brow. While his rescue attempts were useful, they delayed him from getting toward the scene of the problem. Already winded, he worried about having the stamina to finish the job, assuming there was anything he could do. Pushing the thoughts aside, Geordi moved on, waving his tricorder before him like a flashlight and constantly sampling the air, seeking clues as to the magnitude of the conflagration.

Finally, he left connecting corridors—and dead bodies—and emerged into a giant-size cavern of a room. There were flames traveling across pipes, which crisscrossed the now-blackened ceiling, where there was any ceiling left standing. White, gray, and black smoke poured from the now twisted machinery, and Geordi grimaced as he noted the limp bodies along ladders, railways, and cross beams.

The engineer was not alone, though. He spotted five people scurrying about with oversize tools, and work was proceeding on damage control. His tricorder continued to whir and click, scanning the scene and trying to gauge the depth of the problems. Geordi's body tensed as he read the numbers on the small screen. Another power surge was building from equipment which lined the curved wall directly opposite him, and he screamed a warning to the repair crews.

As the words left his mouth, the surge peaked and another explosion let loose with devastating effect. La Forge was lifted off his feet and slammed back against a tool cabinet. More smoke obscured even his VISOR's ability to scan the scene properly. His ears, though, registered the screams of more injured Elohsians. As he scrambled to his feet, the engineer winced a little, realizing he had injured his left knee and right ankle. The initial thought was to summon Dr. Crusher and an emergency medical crew, but he didn't want to risk more lives until the situation was contained.

With each step wearing him down, La Forge worked his way over and around fresh debris toward the nearest Elohsian. The man was trying to crawl toward a computer bank, ignoring the bone protruding through his shoulder. "Gotta stop . . . the storage tanks from rupturing . . . gotta reroute . . ."

Without another word the man passed out from his pain and La Forge turned away and studied the man's objective. It was most obviously a master control panel with a computer interface that regulated the treatment chemicals from their storage tanks to the treatment center itself. Without control, the pressure could build and rupture the entire delivery system. Worse, La Forge recalled from Luth, the danger of contamination was high. He figured that at the very least the continent of Dos Dar was threatened.

Reaching a toggle switch, La Forge tried to access the intercom system but saw sparks instead. The internal wiring was shot, which might mean control of the stream was useless. His tricorder confirmed the grim news, and the engineer looked up. The pipes carrying the purifying agents were all overhead, leading from the master tanks into this room. There was no question that the only way to prevent the problem from occurring was to climb up and manually turn off or redirect each flow from the five master pipes. At least two of the normal catwalks were twisted beyond use and an additional ladder was littered with Elohsian bodies.

Before taking another step, La Forge stopped to inventory his condition. He had cuts and scrapes on his hands, which meant he'd need the gloves he carried to prevent infection from any of the chemicals. He felt a few pulled muscles around his shoulder blades, and the constant headache from his VISOR was worse than usual. The injured knee was stiffening but the ankle seemed better than he first thought. Were he on the *Enterprise,* he would direct another qualified engineer to handle the repairs, but there was no one else around, so La Forge got what he wished for: direct involvement with Eloh.

As he began climbing up toward the first main pipe, he tapped his communicator. "La Forge to Troi. What's your status?"

"Ilena and I are helping organize the evacuation, Geordi. Your signal is distorted, where are you?"

"Inside the core, helping Luth figure out what went wrong. I'm going to have to manually shut down the chemical pipelines—all five of them."

"You sound uncertain of the job," Troi commented. La Forge could imagine her concerned expression and it gave him momentary comfort.

"Yeah, well, I'm a bit more banged up than I'd like, but there's no one else around here and Luth is worried about feedback or contamination of Dos Dar's water." Geordi edged further up the core, noting the sounds above.

"I've alerted the captain. He and Data are with

126

Premier Daithin and they have agreed to postpone all additional plans for the day until this is sorted out. Daithin suspects a terrorist."

"So does Luth. I guess the unity may have a few cracks in it after all. I'll check back with you soon. Out."

Five minutes later Geordi was a step away from the pipe. It was about half his size, dull brown, and rather wide. He could hear the chemicals rushing through the metal and wondered about the pressure inside. Rather than dwell on imaginary disasters, he shook his mind clear and began inching toward the manual releases. They seemed to be well-maintained knobs, dials, and wheels, all of which displayed the pictographs he had seen used throughout the building. That gave him a fighting chance of not making a fatal mistake, and he smiled.

The wheels yielded with the high-pitched sound of metal grinding against metal, and Geordi's muscles cried in protest, but he managed to get the first pipe shut down and secured. *Not bad,* he thought. *I may pull this off yet.*

Pipes two and three weren't too difficult to get to and were also fairly easy to access and control. The constant crawling, climbing, and twisting gave Geordi's muscles new things to complain about, and the engineer realized he was going to be in sorry shape when this was over.

Looking over from pipe three, La Forge realized getting to the penultimate pipe was going to be the most difficult. He had no visible way of crossing over and the main controls seemed to be obscured by pieces of the ceiling. Worse, now that he was closer, Geordi noticed the rubble atop the pipe was gleaming with a reddish hue. *Uh-oh,* he thought. There must be a crack in the pipe and a chemical was leaking.

First he had to cross over. He looked around for a rope or something he could use to attach to the pipe he was standing on. With nothing in sight, he turned his attention to the walls around him. Tucked off to one side was a collapsible ladder covered in emergency markers. He realized these people had to be prepared for disasters, considering it was a valuable target during the civil wars. That meant he would have a way to cross over and possibly stop the leak.

Gingerly, La Forge placed the extended ladder between the two pipes, a span of about fifteen feet. He tested to see how secure the hold between the pipes would be and then placed one foot on the first step. It held under his weight, and he let go the breath he had been holding. With grim determination, La Forge began crossing the gap between the pipes, constantly scanning with his VISOR to check for hidden dangers. About two-thirds of the way across, he detected a problem and a fresh wave of sweat broke out over his forehead.

The dripping chemical must have been some form of acid because it had begun to eat away at the clamp holding the ladder in place. La Forge quickly calculated that the rate of erosion might be faster than his ability to cross the final five feet. He didn't want to risk any kind of a leap, given how sore he felt and how high he was from the hard cement flooring. Chancing it, he decided to scramble across faster than before and hope the stress wouldn't cause the ladder to collapse from under him. Five feet became four; then, by the third foot, he was feeling more confident. He could hear the metal twisting but he figured he would make it. After all, this was another typical scrape he had gotten himself into, and somehow he managed to survive them all—so far. Sooner or later he realized his time would come, but deep down inside he knew it wouldn't be today. Looking at the chemical residue, he knew he was right: the erosion wasn't as great as he had feared and he didn't stay to prevent the drip from further damaging the ladder. Instead, he concentrated on finding a way to shut off the flow through this massive pipe before the spillage caused greater problems.

It took a hard five minutes of muscle-straining effort, but he managed to shut the pipe and he heard the flow of chemicals slow to a stop. There was no finer sound, he decided. After that, the final pipe was a breeze, and within twenty minutes La Forge was safely back on the ground, secure in knowing the disaster had been diverted for the moment. There was much more work to be done, but the repair crews could take over.

By the time he was ready to return to the control room, the bone-weary, sweat-drenched engineer found a working intercom and reported his findings so Luth could properly direct repair crews.

Sticky with sweat and smelling of chemical smoke, La Forge walked back into the control room. By then, five more workers had returned to their post and things were humming. A ventilation fan had kicked back on-line and the room was cleaner-smelling and brighter. Luth was hunched over the command board, though, and seemed displeased by what he saw.

"Fine work, La Forge," Luth grunted. "I guess your Federation is as good as you say. You've saved an awful lot of people today."

"What's the next step, Luth?" He chose to ignore the praise and concentrate on the more immediate problems. For a brief moment, though, he did feel really good about making a contribution. Geordi stood behind the large man and watched the shifting screen and charts. Power fluctuations had stopped and the water pressure had been evened off. He was also pleased to see an atmospheric diagnostic show that it was safer to breathe throughout the entire complex.

"We check the records and sensors, La Forge. Ever since the war, we Dars have been very security-minded. We know where the explosion occurred, and in a few minutes a security and engineering detail will go to the blast point and investigate for clues. I'm punching up the various readings from just before the explosion. I hope we find something because if we don't I'll be angry and no one will be there to feel it."

Instinctively, Geordi stepped back, sensing the seething emotions from the conductor. He watched silently, once again the observer, and took interest in the crisis management being displayed. This was a side of Elohsian life he never expected or wished to see on display. Still, he admitted, the people were good and efficient. They moved with authority and knew their tasks, so talk was kept strictly to the facts. Only Luth allowed himself the luxury of speaking off-the-cuff and, at that, only with the Starfleet officer.

"Ah ha. Finally I'm getting some readings. This could be telling," Luth muttered as he slowed the scroll of information and then isolated some specific facts. He leaned even closer to the screen now and practically pressed his nose to the surface. Suddenly, he leaned back, eyed La Forge, and turned his attention to a secondary screen to his left. Geordi couldn't tell what was on the screen but it seemed to confirm Luth's suspicions. The conductor turned toward Geordi, his dark features comprising the ultimate poker face.

"You see, La Forge, our sensors take bioscans every thirty seconds in every room and corridor, plus outside on the compound grounds. Every employee here has his life signs on computer file, which we use to check for infection, disease, or even chemical imbalance. It also helps track down who may be missing during a crisis such as this. We've used these scans already to identify the dead you found.

"We've also just narrowed down the readings of the only person near the blast point within an hour of the explosion." Luth turned slowly in the chair and looked directly at La Forge. "And the readings are not Elohsian. I believe they're human."

Geordi felt his mouth drop before anything else happened. "Could that possibly be right, Luth? I have been the only human—ever—to visit the plant, right?"

"Right. And that makes you, sad to say, our chief suspect. I've already alerted the safeguard chief to join us. Please stay in here a bit longer."

"Of course, Luth, I'll cooperate with any investigation you have. Let me just notify Counselor Troi."

"I'd appreciate it if you didn't touch anything on your person right now. Just in case."

La Forge nodded glumly. He knew he didn't plant a bomb, but how to explain this to the war-weary populace? Standing still, he watched how the others in the room, who all heard Luth's pronouncement, kept their distance. It meant moving around him or avoiding being within three feet of him, and they shrank away.

After a few minutes, the tallest Elohsian Geordi had yet to meet walked into the room. He dwarfed even the more average-size Elohsians and filled the control center. The broad-shouldered mass suddenly made the *Enterprise*'s chief engineer feel very small. He was dressed in a dark green and had a bright silver insignia that seemed to be his badge of office. The man also wore a thick belt with a variety of armaments on display, leaving no doubt that he was responsible for maintaining the order here.

"Mr. La Forge, I am Lan Kris, chief safeguard officer at this facility. It seems we have a problem."

Now that's an understatement, Geordi thought. "I agree, but I will do whatever you feel is necessary to properly investigate this matter. But I would like to contact my captain and inform him of the situation."

"That's rather polite of you, sir. I had expected you to invoke diplomatic immunity, something we were warned of before you arrived. This will make the investigation work more smoothly. I will insist, of course, that you remain here until the situation has been thoroughly investigated. Our chief magistrate has already set aside court time tomorrow, should it come to that. Now you may contact your captain, and then we will escort you to a comfortable room."

All business and no nonsense with this man, Geordi realized. He swallowed, nodded, and touched his comm badge. "La Forge to Captain Picard." In a few seconds he got a response. "Captain, there's been a bit of trouble here."

"Yes, Counselor Troi told me about it. What's the current situation?"

"Sticky, sir. Their security tapes indicate only a human was near the blast site, and guess who's the only human here?"

"Do you require assistance, Mr. La Forge?" asked the captain, his filtered voice growing deep with concern.

"Not at the moment. I have agreed to stay behind and wait for the outcome of their investigation. I'm sure I'll be all right. I just won't be able to help out on the tour this afternoon."

"Forget that, Geordi, we've put plans on hold while this mess is being sorted out. Make sure you can call us if you need any help. I would appreciate it if the authorities there can provide Premier Daithin and myself with a copy of the complete security records."

Geordi looked over at Lan Kris, who stared back at him. Finally, after a few lingering moments, he said, "We will do that if Premier Daithin asks."

There was a pause and then a new voice sounded over Geordi's badge. "This is Premier Daithin. I think it will be in everyone's interests if we can see the information gleaned to date. Yes, I believe that will be helpful indeed."

"It shall be done," intoned the officer. Geordi gave him a thankful smile that was greeted with a stony face.

Lan Kris stepped toward La Forge and held out a hand. "I would appreciate holding on to your communications device and recording machine." Geordi looked down at the tricorder and slowly pulled it from his pocket. He handed it and the comm badge up to the Elohsian officer. Kris studied the items in his hand and then looked inquisitively at the VISOR.

"He needs that to see, Lan Kris," Luth said in a most sympathetic tone. Geordi smiled at the conductor and remained standing still, hands clasped before him, unsure of how to act. Probably with as little movement as possible, he concluded.

"I will advise Ilena and your companion that you will not be rejoining them. I will have an officer take you to the waiting area. I'm sure this investigation will not take long." With that, Lan Kris walked out of the room, pausing to lean forward so as not to bump his head on the doorway.

"I am not pleased with this at all, at all," Daithin said. Standing by him were Picard and Data, both of whom remained still and silent. They had offered to help and to follow all Elohsian protocols, which made Daithin feel a little more in control. Things had been proceeding quite well up until this moment. A day earlier, Commander Sela and Subcommander Plactus were in this very office, discussing all manner of military support and protection the Romulan Empire could afford Eloh. Tapes they brought of their military might were most impressive to Daithin, who watched alone with Larkin. He kept imagining how these weapons would have turned the tide of the war had the Dars, or more happily, the Populists, had access to such firepower.

Today, Captain Picard and Lieutenant Commander Data made a similar presentation. Daithin was interested to note that while the Romulan counterparts emphasized weaponry and ship size, the Federation representatives discussed peacekeeping measures. During their time together, Daithin grew more comfortable talking with Data, realizing he was more than a walking computer system. He displayed in his own way a personality, and one that Daithin couldn't help but like.

"Has the Federation ever experienced a civil war, Captain?" Larkin asked from his quiet place in the back of the room.

Picard seemed startled by the idea behind the question and emphatically replied, "No, sir. I won't lie to you and say things have been harmonious since the Federation was founded over a century ago. Planets have bickered and some have even left the Federation over policy matters, but no, we've never gone to war with one another."

"Then you have no idea what it is like to fight your friends?"

"No, sir. But my home planet, Earth, certainly had its share of nation—state civil wars until worldwide unity was achieved. Some were the fiercest fought and bloodiest battles in our history, so I understand it intellectually."

Daithin pondered the answers and realized that his frame of reference and Picard's were rather different. The human was certainly an eloquent speaker, as he noted the night before, but Picard seemed not to have a warrior's soul. Such a spirit motivated the Elohsian people and had formed their being for countless centuries. The Federation offered him a chance to evolve that soul from one of war to one of construction and prosperity. While he could not change his own nature, he could create an environment so that a generation or three down the line would find a new breed of Elohsian. He liked the idea of being such an architect and appreciated much of what the Federation had to offer.

The meeting, however, was marred when word arrived of the explosion on Dos Dar. It brought back bitter memories of similar attacks and how narrowly he himself had avoided being killed during such skirmishes. He especially disliked the fact that it would alter or perhaps ruin his plans for the future of his world. Would the representatives of the two governments want to leave? Was one responsible? Could one have made it seem like the other was behind it? While the Federation's words were pretty, Daithin's very nature left him unsettled. How could any such civilization be so high-minded? Questions and more questions rattled through his mind, taking his attention away from the guests patiently standing before him.

"I'm very sorry, very sorry indeed, Captain," Daithin said in a quiet voice. "We'll have to reschedule everything once this works itself out, even if it means some shorter sessions than planned. I do appreciate the willingness of your officer to remain behind until this is resolved. I'm sure we'll contact you when we have some answers."

Picard obviously wanted to stay and help, but he took a deep breath and said, "Very well, Premier. We'll be returning to our ship then." With that, he and Data left the building to transport back to their ship. Daithin imagined beaming to and fro, hurtling around his world in the blink of an eye, and wondered how that might alter his recently unified society. So much to think about, so much to ponder.

Larkin watched the men leave and then took a seat by Daithin's elbow. "What do you make of them, Daithin?" he asked.

"I like them, Larkin, I truly do. They are so unlike us, though, I wonder how we could coexist."

"Are the Romulans that much more like us?" Larkin always probed, never letting a single answer be enough. Mostly this stood him in good stead with Daithin, and over the years the premier had come to trust him completely and care for him more as a brother than an assistant. Their talks were mutually satisfying although at times, Larkin would probe deeper or not let a subject drop to Daithin's liking.

"Maybe. Their weaponry is certainly impressive, but it makes me wonder why this Empire of theirs would willingly negotiate to have us join them rather than simply conquer us. They could, you know."

"I like their fighting spirit," Larkin offered.

"Yes, they are certainly like us in that regard. But enough of that. Will this throw the schedule beyond repair?"

Larkin shook his head, to Daithin's pleasure. After all, with the celebration coming, they could ill afford losing time with either government. Moving ahead, he asked, "What do you make of the explosion?"

"Until the data arrive, I cannot even hazard a guess. Certainly not something the humans would have done."

Daithin looked deep into Larkin's eyes. "Until the bomb went off, I never would have considered that, either. Now I don't know."

Geordi was swiftly escorted to a small, well-lit room. It must have been a conference room, since it had a pentagonal table and five matching purple chairs around it. On the pale gray walls were monitor screens that could have been used to assist the meetings. A small table was set by a far corner, and on it was a pitcher and five small glasses, also pentagonal. The security officer allowed La Forge to indulge in some water for now. Everything else would progress as time allowed.

Seating himself at the conference table, Geordi was left with his thoughts, not to mention stiffening muscles. He was reminded of the old saying about being careful what you wished for. La Forge had moped all along about wanting to help, and he was given a chance to help but was now suspected of being a terrorist. It brought a bitter chuckle to his lips and he shook his head slowly to try and clear his thoughts and sharpen his mind. After all, until Picard could figure something out, the engineer was on his own.

As he replayed the last hour in his mind, he considered Lan Kris's comment that he had been warned diplomatic immunity might be invoked. Obviously this was some new concept on Eloh, and that meant he was warned. By whom? The parliament? Larkin?

Who stood to gain the most from these events, Geordi asked himself. The Romulans. Who would know about the concept of protecting diplomatic members? The Romulans. Who most likely sabotaged the plant? The Romulans. But when and which member of their team? Geordi felt his hands grip themselves tighter and tighter as he realized how hopeless his situation might be and began to wonder idly about forms of punishment on this faraway world.

Chapter Six

PICARD SAT ALONE in his ready room, reviewing the purification plant reports on his desktop screen. Slowly he reviewed the sensor scans that distinctly showed a human being near where the bomb went off. His cup of tea had grown cold and ignored as the captain concentrated on this new turn of affairs. He considered that this would be a major obstacle in convincing the Elohsians that the Federation was a good partner, a better one than the Romulans. To date the Romulans had offered presents and behaved themselves. No doubt this would influence members of the parliament, who seemed easily swayed. Picard had earlier convinced himself that these politicians were all relatively new to their tasks, most of them having been soldiers of some sort just a few short years previously. Politics was a different kind of war to wage and not everyone seemed equally equipped to handle the new responsibilities.

Picard turned away from those meandering thoughts and returned his attention to the report on the explosive itself. It was a concussive bomb, placed well enough to cause the maximum amount of damage without totally destroying the plant. He was pondering the implications of the location and the importance of the plant when his door chimed.

He beckoned the caller to come in and was greeted by Riker, Data, Troi, and Worf. All looked solemn, concerned over the fate of their colleague and the blow this dealt to their diplomatic mission. With a gesture, Picard invited his colleagues to take their seats. Worf and Data chose to stand, and Picard snapped off the viewer and turned his attention to his officers.

"Have you found anything that can help Geordi?" Picard asked.

"Unfortunately, their sensors monitor the complex rather thoroughly," Data noted. "Seventeen minutes before the explosion, Geordi was by the key juncture."

"Captain, have they determined the size of the bomb required to cause that much destruction?"

"Not yet, Mr. Worf."

"Commander La Forge was carrying only his tricorder; surely they will see that he could not have carried anything resembling a bomb."

Picard gave his security chief a tight-lipped smile. "A good point, Lieutenant. But we must await their report and see if we need to make such an argument."

"How is Daithin taking all this?" Troi asked, crossing her legs.

"He's very concerned, Counselor. Both he and Larkin seemed genuinely shocked by the news. It seems that since the unity, there has not been a single recorded act of terrorism. Therefore, he has asked that both Romulan and Federation personnel remain aboard their ships until this is sorted out."

"A wise move," Riker noted. "Do you think this will cost us Eloh?"

"It's too early to tell, Number One. We're awaiting a revised itinerary from Larkin, and we'll see if that weakens our ability to present a clear case. When we can prove Mr. La Forge is innocent, then it falls to someone to find the true culprit. When we learn who that is, then I can better gauge how this will end."

"What if your culprit is not found?" Troi voiced their worst fears.

"I can't say for certain, Counselor."

"Terrorists usually claim credit for their wanton acts," Riker commented. "Someone will surely want to announce their identity and explain why this was done. Of course, they may strike again."

"My fear exactly," Picard said. "Should it happen while we and the Romulans remain here, then we may be victims ourselves."

"And where were the Romulans during all this?" Riker asked.

"A small party was on Hyanth, studying wreckage caused by the last civil war," Picard replied. He touched his cup lightly, remembered the tea had cooled, and ignored it.

"The Romulans visited the purification plant before we did, right?"

"Yes, Number One."

"Could they have planted the bomb before we even got there?"

Picard leaned forward, considering his friend's words. The Romulans were certainly not above such duplicity, and they were on the planet before the *Enterprise* even arrived in the solar system. Motive and opportunity were certainly present. Should matters come to a trial, he would have to request a set of the bioscans from the day the Romulans paid a visit.

"I think you may have a point, Number One. Eloh's sensors, near as we can tell, are not as fine-tuned as our own. Sela, being a human-Romulan hybrid, or so she claims, would be an anomalous reading to the Elohsians. After all, Commander Sela could show up as a human and may well be a suspect, as could almost any non-Elohsian. I wonder where she was today?"

"She may have triggered the device from orbit, choosing a time when our personnel were on the planet," Worf stated.

"Sela certainly has a grudge against this ship and her crew. She admitted as much to me last night," Picard mused aloud. "We'll have to increase our investigation to be prepared. Mr. Worf, please find out exactly where Sela was both today and the day the Romulans visited the purification plant."

"Actually, Captain, I have another line of reasoning."

"Well, Mr. Data, go ahead," Picard said, unsure of what his second officer was thinking.

Slowly, Data began to pace the room, hands behind his back. Picard instantly recognized the mannerisms from previous encounters and inwardly smiled at the realization that Data was in full detective mode. "Since you have had me thinking about crime fiction lately, I would like to venture an opinion. We realize that Geordi could not possibly have planted the bomb. Also, the Romulans make too obvious a suspect. Instead, I would contend there is a third possibility as yet unidentified."

Picard nodded. "If you can find something, Mr. Data, then by all means, look into it." The captain got to his feet. "You have your assignments, so let's get to it. Dismissed."

* * *

Riker took his place in the center seat, allowing his captain time to prepare his report to Starfleet, or rest. While he remained aboard the ship, his captain was constantly going between the *Enterprise* and Eloh, which consumed a lot of time; plus, there was the tension generated by the events. The tall first officer regarded the small world on the main viewer. Eloh may have looked like a nice planet, but once again, looks have been deceiving. While he enjoyed the banquet and the people he met the other night, Riker had come to realize that the people were fractious and quick-tempered. They have bent over so far in favor of a tightly structured world government that it meant they lived and died by their rules. It barely masked the tensions still evident according to the reports Data had already filed. Whereas Picard may have been the patient conciliator, Riker recognized that he usually could not stomach such problems and would just as soon notify Starfleet that the Elohsian people were not at all mature enough to make this momentous decision today.

Unfortunately, waiting was not his strong suit, and he got up and began to walk the bridge. He made himself seem busy by checking the progress at each station, chatting up the secondary officers who had arrived to start the day's second shift. It was clear that word of La Forge's situation had already spread among the crew.

As he strolled by the conn and Ops, he leaned over to watch Ensign Ro complete an orbital survey. She looked up at him with an expression that read all business. He tried to smile at her, felt awkward, and just watched the telltales on her board.

"Orbit is probably the most boring time for you, isn't it?"

Ro looked up at him and replied, "I guess so. But I must remain in case we're needed to do something other than go in circles."

"Maddening, isn't it?" His grin grew wider and his eyes twinkled.

Straight-faced, she replied, "I would have to agree."

"Then this will make dealing with the Kelly family all the more palatable, right?"

Ro stiffened slightly at mention of the name, and Riker noticed it. He asked, "Something going wrong, Ensign?"

Quickly, she replied, "No, sir. The family seems quite . . . nice. The parents are certainly adapting quickly, and their son, James . . . seems unusually interested in the ship's functions."

Riker paused a moment, mentally placing a comment just made by Ro. James Kelly, he realized, was the young man with whom he had spoken the other day. Earlier he hadn't made the connection between the love-struck teen and the family he had assigned Ro as a lesson. Well, he realized, with only a thousand people aboard such coincidences were bound to occur.

"I met the boy the other day. We worked out together and he seemed interested in more than the ship."

Ro studied Riker's expression, opened her mouth to make a comment, thought better of it, and returned her attention to the operations panel before her.

"As you were, Ensign," Riker said idly, and moved away toward the aft stations.

The next several hours moved slowly for the bridge crew. Riker finally busied himself at one of the aft terminals, working his way through secondary scanner readings. Data conducted his work at the Ops station, where a slightly amused Ensign Ro watched his work from the conn. Throughout the time, Data continued to work and would occasionally pass theories by Ro, who was not a student of Earth detective fiction and was unfamiliar with the android's forays as Sherlock Holmes. Worf was poring through Elohsian records as well as *Enterprise* sensor scans of Romulan transporter activity.

"Commander," Worf rumbled after a long, silent stretch of work. "Everything I have seen indicates that Commander Sela was part of the landing party that visited the purification plant. The visit was exactly two days before our crew was taken to see it. Sela was also said to be aboard the *N'ventnar* when the bomb went off. Our sensors indicate that there was extensive communications and transporter traffic at the precise moment the bomb went off, so we cannot isolate a signal that may have triggered the device."

Riker had walked over to the tactical station during the report and glanced down at Worf's panels. He began stroking his beard thoughtfully and considered the information. With a practiced hand, he quickly reran the logs of Romulan activity, trying to find a damning clue the security chief may have missed. Frustrated after two minutes of work, he commented, "If they *are* behind this, then they masked their work really well. Thank you, Worf." The Klingon grunted in frustration and returned to his own work, reviewing all the information a third time in the vain hope of uncovering something useful.

Riker strode down the sloping walkway and returned to the center seat, where he used the small controls in the chair arm to switch from dry Elohsian plains to the ship's sensor array. He carefully scanned those screens, looking for something—anything—that might give him a direction in which to look. The minutes ticked by slowly and he prepared to return to his other studies when Data caught his attention.

"Commander, I may have something of use," Data said.

Riker sprang from his seat, walked over to the forward station, and peered over his friend's shoulder. At first he couldn't tell what Data had accessed, but things began to make sense as the explanation began.

"I have been doing a systematic sensor study of the entire planet, matching it against our initial scans. I was following a theory that if something changed, we might be able to use that as a clue. Since our orbit has not varied, the theory goes that the scans should match exactly, taking into account weather patterns, tides, and the like."

Riker wanted to grab Data by the shoulders and demand he get to the point, but he recognized that lengthy explanation was something Data seemed to prefer, making sure he was not misunderstood. Just as Captain Picard allowed Data such leeway, Riker felt he must follow that example, no matter how frustrating that might be.

"Some ten kilometers from the purification plant on Dos Dar is an anomalous reading. In fact, sir, it is shielded from our sensors, and that does not match standard Elohsian technology as far as we have studied it."

Riker leaned forward, almost brushing his beard against Data's ear, and watched the parallel scans. The readings, taken just two days ago, did not show any such small structure. And now here was a strange artifact, something definitely bearing investigation. He patted Data reassuringly on the shoulder and then quickly moved to the aft science station. With practiced ease, he called up more detailed sensor comparisons and determined the shielded space was large enough to house at least two living beings and their equipment. He called out, "Data, you've found something really interesting. Something I think we're going to have to pay a visit. Mr. Worf, please contact Larkin at the parliamentary office."

Within minutes, Larkin had been found and was in contact with the *Enterprise*. His expression was hard for the first officer to read, but Riker suspected the aide was annoyed by the intrusion in his daily affairs. This exchange would call for top-notch diplomacy. "Mr. Larkin, my apologies for interrupting you, but we think we have found something and request permission to beam down and study it."

Larkin seemed only vaguely interested by the news. "What is it, Commander Riker?"

"We're not sure. It wasn't on our sensor scans just two days ago, and it is now shielded. It's also fairly close to the purification plant and we'd like to take a look and see what we can find."

"I will contact Lan Kris at the plant, and his men can investigate this for you," Larkin said dryly.

"I would appreciate it, sir, if we may see this for ourselves. No offense, but our equipment may be able to help."

"And I would rather we keep this an internal matter," Larkin said diffidently.

Riker took a deep breath and tried to be as authoritative, yet as cordial, as possible. "Mr. Larkin, the fate of a member of this crew is involved. I believe that gives us the right to be a party to the investigation. We will, of course, abide by your local laws, but you must admit we do have the ability to scan for things you cannot."

Larkin sat silently, contemplating the request, obviously trying to find a way around the situation, a way that would leave Riker aboard the starship. Time passed slowly and Riker tried to contain his sharpening feelings of frustration.

The Elohsian folded his hands and took a deep breath, measuring his words. "Very well, Commander Riker, you may come and see this. Lan Kris will be waiting for you at the plant. I should point out to you, sir, that if this proves useless, and your man is found guilty, the current law calls for death by slow torture. Larkin out." The view screen once again showed Eloh.

"Just lovely," Riker muttered. "In that case, we're going to have to be convincing." The commander began on his way to the turbolift, his voice snapping commands. "Mr. Data, Mr. Worf, you're with me. Ensign Ro, you have the conn." With that, the three officers disappeared.

Geordi had just finished a small meal provided by the tight-lipped Lan Kris. The food was nowhere near as impressive as the banquet, but it did wonders for his growling stomach. To the engineer, the hours seemed to crawl by and his thoughts had not coalesced into anything remotely resembling a conclusion. He had totally abandoned the political upheaval on Eloh and was mentally trying to recalibrate the warp core —something to keep his mind off his own troubles.

His thoughts were shattered—and an imagined breach was now imminent—when the door opened and Luth strolled in, looking down at La Forge. The expression was the displeased look Geordi had come to expect from the conductor. Obviously Luth had remained busy with the repairs, since his crimson robes were streaked and stained. The foul odor from the fumes had clung to him, and it made Geordi's nose wrinkle.

"Are you being treated fairly?"

"Huh? Sure, Luth. I have no complaints."

The larger Elohsian took a seat and looked at La Forge with a grave expression. "Although the evidence points directly at you, let me assure you that I know you are not the culprit. No one would have set off such a device and then gone through as much exertion to save the lives of others. You knew what you were doing, and for that I thank you."

La Forge didn't know how to respond. Luth certainly had changed from the experience, and a wave of relief washed over him. Still, he was intimidated by the man and felt he had not given his all at any time they met. "How are the repairs coming?"

"Slow. We have the breaches sealed and have finished pumping out the last of the sewage. Now we are working on rewiring so we can be back on-line within a day or two."

"Looks to me like you have some real good people to rely on, Luth," La Forge offered.

"I agree. Still, your expertise would be nice to have," Luth said. He patted the air with a hand and added, "I know about your rules, and while I don't like that they can't help me in the short-term, I do understand the larger implications. But tell me, honestly, what do you think of our technology?"

Geordi let out a deep breath and then launched into some lengthy opinions, none of which violated the Federation's rules. He was finally making a constructive contribution and found himself enjoying a talk with another engineer. Suddenly, time's crawl quickened.

Riker looked up, and up, at Lan Kris. The Elohsian did not seem to care one way or another that Riker, Worf, and Data had come to join him on the search. He did look at each officer slowly, taking in the vast

Robert Greenberger

differences between human, Klingon, and android. Riker's practiced eye took Lan Kris's measure and he began to imagine confronting him or one just like him in a conflict. Another reason, he decided, that Eloh should be part of the Federation.

The first officer appreciated the perfunctory introduction although Kris did not even bother to introduce the more heavily armed guards that flanked him at the landing site. Instead, he gestured the three officers toward a larger version of the sojourner Geordi and Troi had enjoyed earlier that day.

The ten-kilometer trip was totally silent. Riker had tried to engage Kris in conversation at the beginning but it was obvious the content wouldn't help the investigation, so Kris remained silent. While Worf usually preferred such silence, Riker liked chatting people up, getting a better sense of who they were and how they would react to a given situation. Riker may not have been as patient a man as Picard, but he was also a skilled card player and knew how to wait someone out. Eventually he would learn about Kris and be better able to adapt to the unfolding circumstances.

Riker noted the sun beginning to drop behind the mountains, recognizing that night would fall shortly and their hopes of finding anything significant were unlikely. He feared they would have to return in the morning and Geordi would spend a night in prison for a crime he did not commit. Within fifteen minutes, the twisting route had led them to a fork in the road. Data's tricorder indicated they should head right, but on foot, since the structure was just a hundred meters away and silence might be called for. Kris nodded in agreement, and with hand gestures signaled to his people to take prearranged positions. Riker noticed with amused satisfaction that Worf continued to

150

watch Kris's every move, his Klingon and Starfleet training meshing rather well for a change.

The road was paved with some natural material, and dirt, gravel, and weedy-looking bushes lined both sides. They were near the main mountain range of the continent and the terrain would get rockier and steeper nearby—and more dangerous now that shadows were lengthening by the minute. Kris took the point and had a hand-weapon in his left hand. Data took a position directly behind him, carrying his tricorder but leaving his own phaser pocketed. Kris's men had received silent instructions to take the right flank and position themselves about twenty feet behind Kris and between their leader and the ultimate goal. Riker decided he and Worf should take positions on the left flank, finishing the formation. The group began walking, and as they did, Riker silently withdrew his phaser, opting to be prepared. Out of the corner of his eye, he noticed Worf had already done the same. While Worf scanned the darkening terrain, Riker moved alongside, almost in lockstep, toward their goal.

The meters narrowed and they topped a small rise. Kris crouched as he took the top and looked down. Data had silently shown him the tricorder reading, indicating exactly where the structure was: below them by about forty meters. Again, Kris waved his hands and the security people moved out, flanking the rise. Riker and Worf hung back a bit more, just in case defensive screens were involved. No one could hear a sound, so Kris began moving over the rise and down toward their objective. In a few moments, the duo were directly behind the security officer and they got their first glimpse of their goal: a flat, wide, rust-colored building that seemed prefabricated and held together with just a few efficient joints. Definitely for quick assembly or an even quicker getaway. No defensive screens or weapons were visible, nor were there any markings on the walls. What they did notice, though, was that the side door was open—not an expected opportunity.

Worf looked around the vicinity and then noticed a small figure getting smaller, almost hidden by the rapidly approaching nightfall. He called out, "A man, running away from here." With that, Kris and Worf simultaneously broke into a dead run, trying to catch up with the suspect. Without hesitation, Riker began striding to catch up and keep their quarry in sight. As he moved along, Riker would occasionally lift and aim his phaser, trying to get a bead on the figure, but the fugitive was a good runner, zigging and zagging to avoid such fire. Riker cursed himself for even trying, noting that neither security man made the effort since it cost them speed. Forcing himself to go even faster, Riker could feel muscles and tendons stretch. It had been a while since an away mission forced him to such exertions.

Being taller, Lan Kris moved ahead of the Klingon early in the chase, but Worf made sure that his counterpart wasn't leading by that much. Still behind, Riker calculated that they had gained on the man, human from what he could make out in the dimming light, and they would be upon him soon enough. The figure wore a light beige jumpsuit and seemed not to be armed.

All of their time observing the terrain proved to help Riker when he noticed the man break to the left, toward the mountains, jumping over rock outcroppings and avoiding the worn terrain. Riker had earlier noticed that there was a dip in the land in that direction that would give him some added momentum. Shouting Worf's name, Riker broke left and felt himself gaining speed as he tried to gain ground without stumbling on the graded terrain.

The man did indeed seem to get larger, and Riker was satisfied that he was one step ahead of Lan Kris—for a change. He heard rocks being moved by booted feet and surmised Worf was right behind him. Feeling confident from the knowledge, Riker pushed himself even harder, trying to get to the man first. The distance was rapidly diminishing from a hundred meters at the beginning of the chase. Now it was a mere forty meters. Then twenty.

The objective did not seem to notice the approaching men but continued to run in a uniform zigzag pattern, only varying how often he shifted direction. Sooner or later, though, he would tire and be caught. Riker was certain of this, and as if to prove him right the man seemed suddenly to slow down. He reached down toward a calf; must be a cramp or pulled muscle, Riker speculated. Whatever, now was his chance and somehow he found the energy to go even faster. Ten yards became five, and the man was slowing with each footstep.

With a final effort, Riker launched himself into the air and tackled the large fugitive with a resounding grunt. The two tangled on the ground, kicking up dust, pebbles, and brush. Riker could sense Worf's arrival but also knew the Klingon would hang back, allowing Riker the glory of the battle.

Such observations were banished from Riker's mind when a loud crack sounded from their left and then the man shuddered, fell, and lay still. Worf, Lan Kris, and the others all fell to the ground, searching for cover where there was none. Riker crouched behind the still form, looked over his shoulder, and saw nothing but the mountain range. No movement at all except for the fleeing birds that were frightened away from their homes by the loud sound. After a minute of silence, the people got to their feet and moved toward the body.

"Dead," Kris said, the first word he had spoken since they left the sojourner. Riker, sore from the exertion, knew that already. Protruding from the man's body were four arrowlike projectiles that had pierced his torso, instantly killing him. Blood slowly seeped from the wounds into the brush and dirt. Kris knelt down, carefully examining the projectiles while Worf pocketed his phaser and removed his own tricorder. He used its recording function to get a complete visual record of the man, the surroundings, and the distance to the mountains. Riker puffed, catching his breath and his wits, and was perfectly content to allow Worf to carry on the investigation. He watched as Worf switched the tricorder to biological scanning and took a medical report in case the authorities refused Dr. Crusher the chance to study the deceased. Worf was nothing if not complete and methodical in his work as security chief, which pleased Riker.

"He's a human, isn't he, Worf?" Lan Kris asked, moving closer to his counterpart.

"Yes. Not one of our crew."

Worf opened a small, transparent container from his pocket and unscrewed the top. "Lan Kris, I would like to take a blood sample for study on our ship."

The tall Elohsian nodded and then roughly pulled out one of the protruding devices. "Take this, too. We call it an *erewhan;* it's used by hunters today, but was the weapon of choice by guerrilla warriors during the war."

"How were they fired?"

"Four *erewhan* are loaded onto a platform that is

steadied by the forearm, and the target is found with an electronic scope that is designed to detect biological functions. Quite effective at night, as you can tell. A most efficient weapon."

"Noisy, too," Riker said as he finally stood and moved around the still body, careful not to get blood on his boots. The surrounding dirt was already turning a muddy brown from the growing pool.

"The *erewhan* are fired from compressed gases loaded in the chamber," Lan Kris added.

"Very effective," Worf commented absently, and continued his studies with the tricorder.

Lan Kris remained silent for a moment, considering the night sky and then the mountains. "Can your recording device find people in the mountains?"

Riker, having finally started to breath slower, tapped his comm badge. "Riker to *Enterprise*. Lieutenant D'Sora, please concentrate sensor sweeps on the mountain range within a ten-kilometer distance from my position."

"One moment, Commander," came the electronic reply. Everyone waited quietly as the *Enterprise* complied with the order. Finally, she signaled back to say, "We have detected three life-forms, Elohsian we believe, moving quickly away from your position."

"Can we follow them in the sojourner?" Riker asked Kris.

"There are no roads in the mountains, just dirt trails worn down over the years. If they're moving quickly then they are using some smaller ground vehicle and using night for their cover. Rilen, once we return, requisition compatible vehicles equipped with night scopes, and go investigate the mountains."

"Yes, sir," the guard said. Riker noted it was the first time he had heard one of the guards speak. He wondered for a moment if this was normal for Elohsian security or the people were intimidated by Lan Kris's demeanor.

Once Worf completed his scans, Kris directed his people to drag the body back to the building where Data was continuing to study the contents. He stood in the doorway as the group returned, his tricorder closed and put away.

"Well, Mr. Data," Riker asked as they got close enough to speak without yelling across distance.

"This man was, I believe, a mercenary, Commander. All the equipment here employs stealth technology that would enable him to enter most non-Starfleet constructs and bypass security channels. The equipment is illegal in the Federation but easily obtained through black market channels or pirate races such as the Orions or Cardassians."

"Any evidence of the bomb?" Worf asked.

"No," he replied. "The man left behind very few incriminating items. He had Elohsian clothing in a small satchel and enough food to stay here, hidden, for two more days. Another bag contained what I believe to be precious metals native to Eloh. He appeared to be under surveillance; otherwise he would not have been killed so quickly after we arrived. This was a premeditated operation."

"Lan Kris, I think this will convince you and the premier that we are dealing with something far larger than sabotage on the part of Commander La Forge," Riker said authoritatively.

"Commander Riker, I will relay this information back to the parliament. Under the circumstances, I would imagine your Commander La Forge will be free to leave."

"Then we accomplished what we came for," Riker

said. "I hope this restores our good reputation before the Elohsian government."

"That's not for me to say," Lan Kris commented.

Riker watched Kris and the guards secure the building, ignoring Data's offer to provide copies of his recordings. The group moved back to the sojourner, still dragging the man's body behind them. While it was good that Geordi La Forge was to be freed and declared innocent of the bombing, it rankled the *Enterprise* officers to learn that this incident had uncovered a new layer of concern regarding this world. New questions were raised, and this posed new threats to the crew. Riker wondered, as they rode back to the purification plant, whether Eloh's strategic location was worth the trouble.

Chapter Seven

RIKER DID NOT LIKE RED TAPE.

While it was common for most worlds to have their own version of bureaucracy, it nonetheless consistently annoyed the first officer. He suffered the small-minded administrators not at all well and usually found himself deferring to Deanna Troi or Captain Picard in getting past the latest roadblock. This time, though, he was determined to see this particular one through without getting angry. Riker decided it was not inappropriate to expect Lan Kris to release La Forge as soon as the group returned to the purification plant. Instead, the tall security officer launched into (what was for Kris) a long explanation of the legalities involved so the engineer would not be released any-time soon.

Returning to the *Enterprise,* Riker immediately contacted Larkin to ask for an expedited release. Instead of cooperating, Larkin agreed that Lan Kris had quoted the proper administrative chapter and verse. He would, though, try and have the man released as soon as possible, possibly late tonight—tomorrow night at the latest. Riker thanked the man through gritted teeth, and cut off the communication. Exhaling to release the tension he felt, Riker then left the bridge for the captain's ready room to make a full report.

As expected, Picard was already poring over both Worf's and Data's tricorder readings. The captain remained calm behind his desk and worked through the documents for another minute before Riker captured his attention.

"I see they have done a thorough job of finding everyone employment," Riker quipped.

Picard merely looked up at his first officer. "You don't like the Elohsians, do you, Will?"

"I have spent far too little time with them to determine my exact feelings, sir, but you can keep the bureaucrats."

"Indeed."

"Sir, you've been down repeatedly: what do you think of them?"

"Number One, they are a people who have suffered a great deal and are determined to do everything possible as quickly as possible to grow. They may be trying too hard."

"I agree, and from the reports, they're still liable to lapse back into war. I don't think they're Federation material," Riker concluded.

"Perhaps," Picard agreed. "However, it appears that we have a new problem."

"Absolutely," Riker agreed.

"How did a human get here before us? I am baffled by his presence."

"I'm more concerned about the mission he performed and the secret he was killed to protect. Could the Romulans have set this up?"

"No, I don't think so, Will," Picard replied with a shake of his head. "This may involve them, but they would sooner use a Romulan agent than a human. They are convinced of their moral superiority and would proudly execute this entirely on their own."

Riker once again began stroking his beard, forcing himself to put his own thoughts and feelings in order. "Have you been in touch with Daithin since we learned this?"

"No, Larkin continues to tell me Daithin is meeting tonight with the parliament to discuss the latest events. That is one session I would like to witness."

"What do we do next?"

Picard was silent for a few moments, evidently gathering his own thoughts, separating them from his personal feelings, ever the commander. "Someone is out to sabotage the negotiations. The agendas are already disrupted and Daithin has yet to resume normal plans. We will not have time to go past the fourth day, and the pressure on all of us appears to be mounting. Neither we nor the Romulans are expected back on the planet through today. I suppose we'll know more when the parliament has its recess. I have Worf and Data working on new theories and contingency plans. Dr. Crusher has also begun to review the sensor information and is examining the blood sample. Until we know what they reveal, we will sit and wait. Geordi will be freed soon enough, I imagine. At least he is no longer in danger of local law."

"A good thing, too," Riker added. "The penalty for sabotage is slow torture, a leftover law from their civil war. The war may have ended some years ago, but I don't think their legal system reflects that in the slightest."

Picard leaned forward. "Now that is interesting, Will. They have made a big show of their unity and how they are now cooperating freely with one another. Yet, there remains prejudicial tension in parliament and you now report their laws are harsher than necessary during peacetime. The Federation has yet to accept a world that does not have a stable, unified world government. I get the feeling the Dars and the Populists are still at war, but now with words, not bombs. This world may not yet be ready for any intergalactic alliance."

"Would you rather they join the Romulan Empire?"

The captain's face scowled. "Of course not. However, I do not know if this world is mature enough to make the decision for themselves. The wars of division may be too recent, and I believe they need more time to heal and learn to truly function together. I would hazard to say they might need at least another generation of peace before they clearly know their own destiny."

Riker considered the captain's words, measuring them against his own observations despite having logged less time among the Elohians. "And yet you've told me some of the people have felt unity on Eloh was a stepping stone for bigger battles. This time on a galactic scope."

"Correct. It may be bluster or ambition. I can't put my finger on it, and that concerns me. I remain increasingly convinced this world's problems are not yet over. I've already begun drafting a report to Starfleet, and these concerns figure prominently. First, I have to notify them of the latest turn of events."

"Sir," Riker began, "I can only imagine what you're putting in your report, but I must stress that from what I can tell, this world is a powder keg. If they choose us it may only delay igniting the fuse. If they choose the Romulans the fuse gets lit for them. Either way, this world needs a lot of help and Daithin alone may not be up to it."

Picard looked up at his first officer and gave him a tight smile. "I agree, but this world asked us here and we must do what we can to convince them not to allow their prejudices to bring the world to ruin. We can offer them the help they need, but I can't say it so baldly. Be that as it may, you need some rest, Number One. Go get yourself a few hours' worth and I'll call if something new is revealed."

Riker stood, smiling for the first time in hours. "Those are the kind of orders I really like, sir."

The first officer stopped quickly into his cabin to clean up and put on a fresh uniform, and went straight to Ten-Forward hoping to catch a friendly face and maybe get his mind off the problems a few thousand kilometers below him. Once inside, he felt himself instantly relaxing. The cool color tones and plush decor always gave people the sensation that they were far from the starship. No Starfleet or Federation symbols were exhibited. This could be a gathering place on any of dozens of worlds, and that was exactly how Guinan treated the place. This was her world, not Picard's or Starfleet's, and she was determined to make people feel wanted.

Riker strode over to the bar where Ben, the gregarious bartender, greeted him with a smile. Ordering himself a hot Tellurian fizz, Riker surveyed the room, searching for companionship. At first he was disappointed; while he knew just about everyone in the room by sight, no one was particularly close to him.

Then Riker spied someone off in the corner, as far from the door as he could get. Now, here was something to get his mind off Eloh.

"Hello, James, may I join you?"

James Kelly looked up in astonishment as Riker grabbed the seat opposite him and settled in. Riker's drink, in a very wide, tall glass, allowed a fair amount of steam to escape. The aroma from the glass was sour and Kelly's nose immediately wrinkled when he first noticed it.

"Hello, Commander." Kelly seemed to get over his shock quickly, and gradually accepted that the second most important officer of the *Enterprise* had chosen to sit with him. "How are things below?"

Riker made a face at being reminded about Eloh. He took a long sip from the drink, savoring the taste before replying. "Not so good, not so bad. A lot of new information to process from today's visit, so we'll see what happens. So, how did it go?"

"Go?"

"The 'situation' we discussed the other day," Riker prompted, his eyes suddenly merry with amusement.

"Oh, that." Kelly shrugged, noncommittal. Riker watched, waiting for the teen to continue. "I don't know if it worked. I received a note on the net, thanking me for the gift and leaving it at that. I don't think she liked it. And it didn't open the door as you expected."

Riker frowned at having his own plan rejected by this woman. He began considering alternatives, ready to help this teen get the girl. It was the romantic in him, he told himself. It was also one way not to think about Eloh.

"There are many ways to develop a relationship, James. You've had girlfriends before, right?"

"Sure. Four before we came to the *Enterprise*. In

fact, I had to end the last one once we found out we got this posting. Boy, did that make Mom happy. She thinks I'm too young for anything serious, but I'm almost seventeen."

"She should be happy about being here," Riker said, getting Kelly off the dear subject of the last girlfriend. "We're a very choice assignment in the fleet." Kelly did at least nod in acknowledgment.

"If the gift approach hasn't softened her up," Riker continued, "have you tried getting to spend more time with her? Maybe a walk in the arboretum. It's idyllic and can lead to some very private, very heartfelt conversations. Or you can program some activity on the holodeck. We have amusements from plenty of worlds, including several two-person games that could show you off. You have to spend time with her, let her see that you're fun to be around. And, James, you have to be yourself. You said you don't know what she wants from a man, so don't be anything other than you already are."

"I see," James said slowly, absorbing all the new information. He seemed to remain amazed that Riker was even talking with him. "It's never been this hard before. Maybe I *am* too young for her. Maybe this is just one big mistake."

"Maybe it is and maybe it isn't," Riker countered. Kelly looked hard at the senior officer.

After another sip, Riker's face turned serious and he added, "And you have to consider the possibility this won't work out. For you. She may be interested in other people or just past a relationship and not looking for one right now. Or she's not ready to get past the age difference, which you still don't know the extent of. Can you handle rejection?"

"I think so . . . sir," the teen answered, now staring out the window, watching the stars lazily move by.

Riker could tell the youth hadn't considered outright rejection as a real possibility before now. Better he learn young, Riker considered.

The first officer took his time finishing his drink and waited for the teen's mind to return to Ten-Forward. Finally, James returned his attention to Riker. With enough having been said about romance, Riker decided to mix in a little business. "Has Ensign Ro been providing you with enough information to make shipboard life easier?"

The boy's eyes widened and he got rather enthusiastic. "Oh yeah, I mean, yes. She's been great. She had dinner with my parents last night and gave them the ship tour they missed the first day. She has been by at least twice a day to talk and answer questions. My dad thinks this is a great program. It's also made some of the other new families jealous."

Jealous? Riker hadn't fully considered the effect such singular personalized attention would have on the other new families. While it sounded like Ro was actually doing her job well, now Riker had to consider ways to fix this latest wrinkle. Ah well, he thought, it's always something. Perhaps he and Troi could devise a more formal system for the others and she could then take charge of it. But first, he had to deal with Eloh. He sighed, realizing he couldn't fully get his mind off the problems below.

"Picard to Riker," came a call over the comm system.

Quickly, Riker tapped the badge. "Here, sir."

"We just received a signal from Larkin. Things moved faster than anticipated and they are now ready to release Geordi. Would you beam down and receive him from the authorities?"

"Of course. I'll do it alone to minimize any further entanglements."

"Agreed. When you both return, get some sleep. I'd like a staff meeting at oh-seven-hundred tomorrow to review all findings and determine how best to be prepared."

Riker looked over at James, who grinned at being part of the ship's business. He appreciated that the youth did not pepper him with questions about how Geordi got detained below. Maybe he was more mature than Riker originally assessed and could handle whatever happened. "Duty calls, James. Good luck."

"Thanks, Commander. Really. Your advice is flawless."

"Flawless, huh? We'll see later." Riker left the lounge and wondered how James's plans would ultimately turn out. He hoped better than this mission.

"I want to thank everyone for attending this session despite the early hour," Picard began, trying to signal that they had business to discuss, but it would be done in as casual a manner as possible. Everyone was assembled around the table and, for a change, they all had cups or mugs before them. Most had coffee or tea, although Worf had a Klingon cocktail that made Beverly Crusher lean away from the fumes. La Forge sat at the table, nursing a mug of black coffee and looked tired but fine after his prolonged stay on the planet. A plate of pastries and fruit decorated the table's center, furthering the relaxed atmosphere. Picard buttered a croissant and then called the meeting to order.

"Doctor, your report please."

Crusher moved herself back to the table, keeping distance from Worf's drink; he remained oblivious to her obvious distaste. "The man died from the *erewhan* bolts, that's undeniable. He's a human being, from one of the Earth colonies, if not Earth itself, from what my diagnostic readings say."

"Data, have you uncovered anything about his identity?"

"Yes, Captain. Based on his DNA sample taken from the blood Worf recovered, Starfleet records have identified him as one John Stormcloud, a convicted felon. He was a mercenary, and Starfleet intelligence reports had last recorded him working in the Onias sector."

Worf downed his drink and slammed his glass down with a dull thud on the tabletop. "Onias is near the Romulan border!"

"I recall, Mister Worf," Picard said. "After all, we were there ourselves not that long ago. Anything else, Mr. Data?"

"No sir. Stormcloud was a low-level mercenary according to reports and was not particularly noteworthy."

Picard took a sip of his coffee before continuing. He wanted everyone to digest the new information and consider how this might influence the next few days. "Daithin has contacted me and said that the incident does indicate a problem, but he is convinced that the security measures now in effect will not spoil the remainder of the visit. He has authorized a resumption of the schedule, although we have shortened a few events and revised the number of officers either we or the Romulans will be allowed on the planet at any given time. The revisions will include the tour of this vessel at fourteen-hundred hours."

"Captain, I must insist that all weapons be left in the transporter room under guard," Worf announced.

"A wise precaution, Mr. Worf. Make it so," Picard replied. He didn't think the issue of weapons was an important one aboard the *Enterprise,* but it was a small victory for the security officer, and sometimes those must suffice. Picard imagined his Klingon friend would prefer the Elohsians stayed on the planet. He might even prefer if the starship left orbit and went home tonight. However, a mission remained to be completed, and everyone had to do his part to see to it the assignment concluded peaceably.

"Who's coming to visit?" Crusher asked.

"Daithin, Larkin, of course, and a small number of parliamentary members. As a favor to Geordi, we're also bringing aboard Conductor Luth, their chief computer man."

Geordi was of mixed feelings at the prospect of discussing issues with Luth. During a crisis he was able to help, but Luth probably still wanted more technical knowledge than La Forge could offer. It would be a cautious tour.

"We have canceled, though, the reception I was planning for them. Now I have Guinan mad at me," Picard said with the trace of a smile. "She said she spent two days blowing up balloons and I was an ogre for spoiling her party."

Everyone around the time laughed at the concept, and Troi beamed approval at Picard. Once again he was leavening the serious business at hand with a dose of humor to remind everyone that they were in this together. Such composure was important to Picard because he needed his crew aware of the severity of the situation but not too uptight, which might mar performance.

"What are the Romulans doing today?" Riker asked between mouthfuls of apple.

"The schedule of events indicates that Commander Sela and her team will be doing a full briefing on Romulan affairs to the parliament," Picard recalled from memory. After taking another sip from his mug,

Picard seemed to make a mental decision and he turned toward his second officer.

"Mr. Data, I believe we can spare you from the tour preparations. I would very much like to have you in the visitors' gallery, observing the Romulan presentation."

Data nodded affirmatively but then said, "We could easily access the transcript from their computer network. We can then see how the world perceives the Romulans."

"Possible," Picard admitted thoughtfully. "Still, I think it is better if we observe the Romulans themselves. Daithin says that they appear unruffled by these events. They're a suspicious group and I think they expected something to mar the week's events."

"Probably were wondering why it didn't happen sooner," Geordi quipped.

"I want all departments prepared for the tour. Counselor, I would appreciate it if you prepare the itinerary and then alert each section as to the plan. Let's conclude the tour with Ten-Forward so Guinan can at least serve them a drink."

"A prudent move, Captain," Troi noted with a grin. With that, the meeting began to break up and the crew exited the lounge, taking their places on the bridge. Troi had stifled a few yawns throughout the meeting, but finally let out one large sigh just as she took her seat.

"A problem, Counselor?"

She smiled sheepishly and then gave the captain her full attention. "I guess I didn't sleep too well last night. You had me up late reading."

Picard looked genuinely surprised.

"Me? How?"

"Your talk the other day about Poe got me curious. I never read him as a child so I selected a few short

169

stories from the library. I just finished 'Ligea,' and I guess it gave me the creeps."

Picard smiled at the concept. "Certainly not under my orders."

"No, but you certainly have a way of inspiring the crew," Riker said with his characteristic smile as he took his own seat. "I started reading some Poe myself, although none of it scared me. I am now reading through 'The Unparalleled Adventure of One Hans Pfaall'—thought it might be my kind of tale."

"I don't know that one," Picard admitted.

"Kind of short but interesting stuff," his colleague said. Then he looked ahead at the viewscreen still depicting Eloh. "Just the kind of adventure I wish this mission was—short."

"Our reach extends well throughout the charted galaxy, and we offer member worlds the opportunity to fully achieve their destiny by joining us in an adventure unparalleled by your imagination." Commander Sela's words floated throughout the quiet parliament chamber. The room was packed with not only elected members, but aides, officials from other areas, and a few "friends" lucky enough to be squeezed into the small space. As people riveted their attention on the coldly attractive Romulan, Daithin surreptitiously mopped his brow. Data, seated as inconspicuously as possible in a rear row, quickly made a scan of the room's air temperature and quality. It did seem above previous norms for the room, and he determined the additional bodies plus an inadequate climate control system were at fault.

For the last hour, Commander Sela had spoken without prepared notes of any kind, describing the strength and far reach of the Romulan Empire. She briefly sketched their history, acknowledging their forebears, the Vulcan race, which now helped rule the Federation. Sela's descriptions offhandedly mentioned the United Federation of Planets, and Data carefully noted she left the usual venom out of her tone when discussing her rival government. Without pause, she continued discussing her people's technological breakthroughs and their many achievements throughout the years, and the Romulans' willingness to share these marvels with the Elohsian people. If the planet truly prized unity, she argued, then an alliance with the Romulan people would be in their best interest.

Data had prepared himself to access Starfleet's files on the Romulans instantly so he could check the veracity of each claim and statement. Not once had Sela made a boast that could not be backed up with creditable information. The android did file away certain "stretches" that might not stand up under additional scrutiny, but they were minor issues. Her case, he concluded, was strong and quite impressive. A subroutine also ran that had Data comparing her oratory skills with some of the most noteworthy speakers in the Federation, including Surak of Vulcan, Adolf Hitler of Earth, Kodos the Executioner from Tarsus Four, and the recently retired Stephaleh from Andor. Later he would prepare an analysis which might prove beneficial to Captain Picard when his turn arrived.

Watching from the lower rows of the gallery were a small handful of Romulans, only one of whom Data recognized: Plactus. The older officer grimly nodded in agreement as Sela punctuated her points, approving her performance, more like a mentor than a subordinate. Daithin admitted earlier, when Data arrived, that he was comforted by the concept of Romulan guards, led by the rather boisterous Centurion Telorn, surrounding the building to add an extra level of security given the preceding day's troubles.

"Should we ally ourselves with you," Waln said from his desk, "that would put us in proximity to the Federation. Should you two come to a new war, what protections would we receive?"

Sela smiled at Waln and waved her arm toward the ceiling. "You've seen pictures of our vessel and learned the specifications. Our warbirds protect the border and would protect that new border between our governments. Should there be another Federation incursion into our space, we would repel that act with our full might. Trust me when I say that our desire for victory in such matters has carried the day for centuries. Your world would be safe."

Data was interested in watching the way Sela became more animated and confident now that she was answering direct issues. Her bearing had changed, and he added these observations to his subroutines.

"Why have we seen no other race but Romulan among your crew, while we have seen a variety from the *Enterprise?*" Waln pressed.

Sela smiled. "Our strength comes from our very core, our center, so to speak. We have brought you the very cream of Romulus with its long, rich history. Warbirds and other vessels contain people from our other worlds, but we wanted to introduce you to the Empire's finest."

"How quickly could we gain your technology, travel the stars?" This from Dona.

"I would imagine once we establish facilities here and begin work on protecting the planet and the new border, we could have Elohsians serving aboard our ships within a year. Two at the most."

This response brought a positive ripple of reaction from the room, Data noted. After all, he reasoned, they desperately want to be part of that galactic community. And fast. No question that the people heard what they wanted. But Sela was not forthcoming with details, and those were what Data suspected Picard most wanted to hear.

"Would many Romulans come and live here?"

"At first there would be just advisors, teachers," Sela said smoothly. "We'd of course like to have officials from our government come and see their new member world. I don't doubt that there would be quite a bit of activity over the first year. This is a pleasing world and I'm sure that some of our people would like to relocate here. Does that pose a problem?"

The speaker was taken aback by the question, unsure how to answer. "I guess not," was all she managed to get out.

To Data, though, he recognized the pattern from many historic Romulan campaigns. Many of the worlds now under their subjugation first welcomed advisors and teachers. The Romulans would then explain they needed more support staff and facilities, and a handful grew to an army, and the army would then deem the planet unstable and additional resources were called in. Before a decade could pass, the planet was tucked tightly in the Empire's fist.

Within twenty minutes, the morning session ended. Sela and Plactus walked through the aisles, sharing a word or two with the members, all smiles. They were now privately giving reassurances, Data knew, perhaps making some discreet deals or at the least making plans for further confidential discussions. Such was the way of politics, he had learned after much interstellar study.

The Romulans were being escorted to the door by Larkin while Daithin was surrounded by fellow Populists from the parliament, all eager for his opinion of the morning's session. Many asked hurried questions, while others hung back just to listen, clearly waiting for a judgment. People continued to mill about the chamber, slowly starting to leave for lunch. Data had left the gallery and edged closer to the Elohsians, boosting his audio receptors to determine the mood of the people. Instead of concentrating on the voices, he heard something unidentifiable but clearly not natural. Data increased the receptors again and tried to isolate the noise.

Daithin gave some perfunctory answers to his colleagues and then swiftly left to follow the Romulans. As he, too, left the building, Data noticed the small phalanx of Romulans escorting Sela and Plactus toward the center of town. Larkin was behind them, waiting impatiently for his leader's arrival, so the premier quickened his pace.

Data took note of the people watching the procession, leaning out of windows and silently taking note of the Romulans with their premier. No cheers or calls; no signs of acceptance or protest. It was a numbness that he had not previously absorbed and he found it fascinating to watch. The streets were unusually quiet for such a gathering, but maybe that was just their way, he considered. He scanned ahead and saw that the procession was heading toward Pater's restaurant, possibly for refreshments and further conversation. The town was like so many others he had observed on dozens of other planets, although their streets seemed a little more rigidly organized, with exactly five buildings on each side comprising a block. The grid style was practical, but he considered that it lacked any real flair or grandeur, something most capitals enjoyed. Data hurried his pace to catch up with the party now crossing the street, nearing the smiling Pater. Just as he reached Larkin, hell arrived on Regor.

At the four corners, just a block before Daithin's favorite luncheon restaurant, fire simultaneously burst out with concussive force. Buildings were instantly consumed with orange and red flames, sending lunchtime strollers scurrying in panic. Many fell to the ground and covered their heads with their arms; others were on fire and rolled on the street to save themselves. An alarm sounded in the distance, and Data watched as the Romulan guards closed ranks around the uninjured Sela and Plactus; he could spy the two twinkle out of existence.

Data was instantly moving, returning his hearing to normal, using his own eyes to record information, and whipping out his tricorder to ascertain additional information about the explosions. The readings confirmed his initial thoughts: the temperature of the fire was currently over one hundred twenty degrees Celsius, too hot to be natural. Fire was spreading rapidly, and Data made a complete circle, studying the patterns which appeared to be nearly identical at all four points of origin. Leaving the tricorder running with instructions, Data sprang into action.

"Data to *Enterprise*. There's been an incident in the capital city."

Almost instantly, Picard responded. "What happened, Data?"

In what for Data were clipped sentences, the android described the scene. While doing so, he noted that the Romulan guards remained, weapons out, merely watching panic envelop the populace. Larkin, covered in bruises, pushed Daithin back toward the parliament chamber with all his might, nattering on about the end of the world.

"Render assistance as is prudent and then report

back. Picard out." Data was already running toward the nearest building, watching people pour out of buildings with large cannisters, vainly attempting to stem the blaze with some chemical. The efforts appeared to slow the inferno not one whit, and the flames moved with a life of their own, engulfing other shops and buildings. Soon, four full blocks were burning out of control and panic ruled.

All evidence pointed to a chemical blaze, but that would not give Data immediate information as to how to stop the inferno. Instead, he deemed it more important to move the people away from the burning structures. With his above-human strength, Data managed to carry people too weak to walk, away from the fire. His ears were attuned to cries of help from within the buildings, and he gave them rescue priority. All of his programming was in full rescue mode, preferring to let the tricorder continue to take readings of the fire itself.

Again and again, Data would rush into a building, returning to the outside with one or more people in his arms. Smoke and debris turned his golden skin dark and smeared with black. His uniform was now torn in spots and burned through in others. Despite the Elohsians' being taller and heavier than humans, he adjusted his musculature to handle their bulk. One time, he emerged from the building with a corpse in his arms and an Elohsian child crying and hanging from Data's neck. It had taken him nearly a minute to free the child's arms from the dead parent and convince him it would be safer outside.

From within the chamber, Daithin watched four one-man aircraft swoop over the streets, spraying a flame-retarding chemical over buildings as yet untouched by the fire. Soon, uniformed safeguard officers filled the streets, carrying backpacks filled with retardants or medical equipment. People were being quickly, but carefully, removed from the site of the raging fires; ropes were hastily put up to block public access. Large sojourners arrived with more people and equipment. With a sigh of relief, Daithin was pleased to see the prepared teams knew their jobs and were moving as quickly as possible. Maintaining a condition of readiness, after surviving by that instinct during the war, had helped the people once again during a disaster. There was no question this was another terrorist attack, aimed at the Romulans and showing little mercy. The Romulan warriors, he noted, had backed away, watching from a distance and offering no help. One seemed to receive a signal, and the group took familiar positions and obviously beamed back to the warbird.

Instead, he was clearly fascinated by the efforts made by the android, Mr. Data. With no hesitation, he continually walked into the flames and emerged with Elohsians. There was nothing stopping him, and Daithin began to lose count of the number of trips the tireless android made. Now this was an example of heroism, totally unlike the self-interested Romulans. But even the android had moved out of sight, and the premier wondered if he, too, returned to the safe haven of orbit.

Daithin was left with no clue as to what might happen next. He feared even contemplating the future.

Data could not help but recall what happened when the Crystalline Entity destroyed the colony that was his first home. People panicked and buildings burned, and the parallels were eerie. He made a mental note to compare data entries at a later time. He then ordered up a quick scan of other personal memories that might be similar. Perhaps there was a paper in this, a part of his mind wondered, while another quickly analyzed that his work was done for the moment.

His thoughts were interrupted when his receptors picked up the creaking sound of a building collapsing. The fire had reached Pater's restaurant and the entire top floor was beginning to buckle from the stress. Data could not tell if anyone was in the building, but he immediately concluded that if the building fell, it would go in such a way as to cause other structures to collapse. Further, he postulated that if the fire remained unchecked, more buildings would be reduced to piles of rocks, starting with the ones nearest to what he gathered was a power conduit. He recalled that the town drew its power from underground lines that were supplied by a station outside of town. However, these juncture boxes were where the power was redistributed and controlled. If Pater's restaurant caused the next building to fall, the power box would be destroyed, causing untold havoc and destruction.

Data's positronic brain ran through every shred of information it had recorded on Eloh, trying to create a plan of action. In the meantime, Data began cautiously approaching the restaurant, trying to determine if there was a point of entry available to him. He almost did not notice the bulk of Pater's corpse, half concealed by tables and chairs, smoke curling up from several spots.

Data made a note to collect the corpse later and to see to it that Pater was properly taken care of. He had meant much to Daithin, and the premier would want it that way. Meantime, he saw a way through a shattered picture window on the right side of the building. The fire had mostly burned itself out on the inside; so intense was its heat that most everything was consumed quickly. He made his way past the dining area and toward the food preparation bay, which separated the diners from the kitchen. Using his keen perception, Data detected that support struts on this side of the building were mostly burned through, weakening the building's overall support. Pieces of wall and ceiling fell apart and to the ground, cracking in pieces as they impacted.

Looking about quickly, Data spied a pair of metal racks that used to hold some decorations. Useless now, they were grabbed by the Federation officer and he quickly twisted them around and around until they were joined together. Strengthened by Data's actions, the metal pike was now used to add support to the wall where he stood. The job was still not over, as he had to check the other building and make sure it was no longer in danger. Finally, he would have to check the power supply and ascertain its integrity.

While walking between buildings, Data heard something crumble and burn, and he looked up in time to see a piece of masonry fall from the restaurant. Holding his hands up, Data tried to shatter the pieces further before they caused him serious harm. His efforts were partially successful as the large piece shattered, but the force of impact still knocked him to his knees, ripping more holes through the trousers. In time, Data was covered with stones, some still smoking from the fire above.

It took him just a matter of moments to right himself, but in that time he also realized his tricorder was crushed beneath the rubble, losing valuable readings. He then noted that the buildings were past any further help he could render. They were going to collapse, and now his priority had to become saving the power supply from exploding.

Gathering himself up, Data pushed through the

detritus and moved beyond the wreckage to get at the power supply station, a small, unassuming, boxlike structure that was dark and totally unobtrusive. At most, he figured that he had four minutes with which to secure the structure or shut off the power feed. Around him, Data heard the same yelling and screaming as before, but the sounds of panic had become calls to organize help. Large sojourners had pulled close to the scene of the conflagration and were applying high-powered sprays on the surrounding buildings. Small aircraft were also dropping powdered chemicals atop the buildings, which seemed to work and retard the inferno's progress.

Reaching the structure, Data looked it over, using his own sensory equipment to probe it since he had no operating instructions. Much of his work would have to be estimated, and he disliked that but had no choice. He immediately felt the warming box, indicating that there already were problems. A small fire of some sort was already inside the structure, and that meant that the power feedback he was concerned about was becoming a reality. There was little choice left to him as he tore a door off its hinges and proceeded to enter the dark, dimly lit station. As elsewhere on the planet, pictograms were used to illustrate instructions or warnings. Data used those as a basis of analysis and went straight to work, using the fire-suppression equipment first, smothering the small flames.

With measured movements, Data rewired control panels and rerouted controls, working as quickly as he dared let himself before further power fluctuations caused greater catastrophes. The time moved slowly and the android did not allow his mind to work on anything more than his surroundings. His concentration was total and he realized that such an occasion had not presented itself in several years.

Just as he completed rewiring one panel, he replaced it and activated a switch that should reroute the last of the area's power back out of the city to another relay station. The telltale flashed from purple to amber and the job seemed complete. Data turned away to leave the building, when there was a soft *whoosh* and a wall of flame erupted from behind the panel. Data was moved back by the force, and the fire seemed to separate him from the suppression equipment. There was no choice but to abandon the building and let it burn down. At least, he concluded as he left the structure, the power remaining was minimal and the damage was contained.

Minutes later, Data found his way back toward the parliament and he looked about. The people were out in force, working on containing the fire and lending aid to those in need. He determined that he had done what was required and it was time to return to the *Enterprise*.

Chapter Eight

OCCASIONALLY, when a starship maintained planetary orbit for several days, the conn and Ops rotations were shortened to relieve the tedium and more personnel were assigned to these positions. On the one hand, it allowed junior officers the opportunity to gain some real experience behind the control stations, and on the other, it allowed the regular complement of officers some time off. The balance was an elegant one, as far as Ro Laren was concerned. She enjoyed the extra free time and had used it wisely this day. First, she had a short but uneventful lunch with the entire Kelly family. Ro took the opportunity to announce that her time with the family was ending since the adjustment was going well and she could do no more for them. The parents took the news well and thanked her profusely for her involvement. James Kelly looked surprised and then unhappy at the news. She had desperately hoped this would also be the end to his infatuation.

After the meal, she did some extra work in the gymnasium, practicing a new set of exercises recommended by Dr. Crusher after her last physical. They worked the muscles in a variety of combinations, making her even more limber and better able to adapt to changing needs on away missions. These were taught to her, Crusher admitted, by Worf, and Ro was amused by the idea that Crusher and her usual exercise partner, Counselor Troi, found these relaxing. Ro had sweated and grunted her way through four repetitions of the exercise, two more than recommended. After the incident on Eloh yesterday, she wanted to be in top condition should she be asked to accompany a party to the planet. The odds were remote, but she could never anticipate when Captain Picard would send her planetside as part of her continuing "education," as he called it.

Clean and dry after her shower, Ro decided to grab a drink in Ten-Forward before returning to her quarters to do some reading. Data's discussions of detective fiction had peaked her curiosity, and she had already known of Picard's interest in the subject. She had used the ship's library to call up one of the more popular Dixon Hill novels, *Under the Sun,* and only this morning had begun reading it. She was determined not to have formed an opinion of it after just one chapter and tried to keep an open mind on the new subject.

Seated at the bar, she chatted amiably with Guinan for a few minutes, enjoying the cool citrus drink and relaxed atmosphere in the room. So much so that she didn't notice the young man's approach until he was right next to her.

"Oh, James, hello," Ro managed to say without emotion. She had truly hoped not to see him again for at least a few weeks, but such was not her luck.

"Hi, Ensign," he said reluctantly.

"Would you like a drink?" Guinan asked pleasantly.

She then ignored the cold stare Ro gave her. She returned the expression with one of her own, which said, "It's my bar so it's my rules."

"Sure, how about a milk shake?" he replied, suddenly all smiles.

"Chocolate or vanilla?" Guinan inquired.

"Strawberry."

"Good choice. I'll be right back." And with that, she left the two alone, which was not something Ro wanted at all.

"Say, Ensign, I really didn't get a chance to thank you like my folks did," James began. "I really liked the way you put up with us all, even with my questions during the tour. I'm also sorry you didn't like my . . . present."

Ro was not sure how to approach the conversation, uncertain of where it was leading. She decided to be polite but noncommittal, perhaps putting him off and making him leave her alone for good. "I did like it, James. The candy was delicious and a type I had not yet tried. It was just . . . unnecessary. I'm just doing the job I was assigned."

"Yeah, I know." He looked away for a moment, obviously wrestling with something on his mind. "But since you *were* so nice to us, I wanted to find some way to thank you. Guess I goofed, huh?"

"Not at all. It was . . . sweet of you."

Looking encouraged by the comment, Kelly appeared to gain confidence and speed to his speech. "Sweet, huh? I guess I was trying to be sweet in return for your, ah . . . sweetness toward me and the family. I mean, you seem all business and all, but you also have a kind side and that's helped Dad a bit. He can be shy and all, but you kept him in the conversations and made sure he got out and met some people.

You're pretty terrific." He then took a deep breath, looking directly at her. "You know, Counselor Troi announced today that there would be a newcomers' get-acquainted dance on one of the holodecks in about two days, right after we leave Eloh."

Uh-oh, she thought. Ro chose to remain silent.

"I'm not sure if I've met anyone as interesting you, and since you were kind enough to spend so much time with us, I did want to return the favor. So, would the prettiest girl on the ship care to accompany me to the dance?"

Guinan returned with the strawberry shake before the stunned Ro could utter a reply. She didn't know what to do. Kelly seemed sure of himself, happy with the prospect, and pleased he got the offer out into the open. As she mentally stumbled through a variety of responses, James silently sat sipping his shake with Guinan nodding at him approvingly.

"You certainly have a way of flattering people," Ro managed to get out. She had no idea what to do in this situation. Telling the boy to go away was probably not what Riker had in mind. But was going to the dance? Ro would most certainly have to have a word with the first officer when this matter on Eloh was settled. New frontiers indeed, she thought ruefully.

"So, you want to come along?"

"James, I'm sorry but I don't think that would be appropriate. I do thank you for the thought." She prayed it would be dropped right here and now. Forever.

Kelly's shoulders sagged and he let out his breath in a long, loud sigh. She almost felt sorry for him but wasn't going to let him drag her to a dance like some prize. He looked over at his half-finished shake and moved it across the bar, back toward Guinan, who wisely kept quiet. James then slid from his seat and walked across the room and through the doors without another word.

"Prettiest girl on the ship, huh?"

Ro glared over toward Guinan, who just grinned that enigmatic smile of hers.

It was no surprise for Worf to see Plactus waiting in Larkin's office, but he was certainly surprised to see Commander Sela standing beside the subcommander, looking not at all pleased to be there. Both ships were requested to beam down investigators to use their more sophisticated equipment to help determine what had happened and who was responsible. Worf was relieved to be part of the away team, once again allowed to make a contribution to the mission. He had suspected the Romulans of treachery, and now he might finally get a chance to prove it. On a table against the wall, next to the various pieces of communications equipment from both starships, were charred remains of some metallic object as well as small plates topped with a gelatinous residue.

The tall, broad Klingon could hear the continuing noise right outside the building, with loudspeakers commanding people to return to their homes and await announcements over the computer networks. A heavy odor of smoke and fire hung in the hazy air of the small office, and it reminded the security officer of many other atrocities he had witnessed over the years.

"Seventy-two people dead," Larkin began in a voice filled with anger. "I can't even count how many are homeless or lost their businesses. We've got scared people, my visiting friends, and I want them calm. Use your tools, find out what you can, and then tell me who did it." The order was most unlike the usually soft-spoken Elohsian, but the circumstances demanded it, Worf decided.

He immediately began scanning the pieces with his tricorder while Plactus used an analogous device. Time passed slowly as both tools did their jobs. Sela and Larkin stood by, impatient for some result to be announced.

Sela strolled over to Worf, looking him over with cold determination, and let out a haughty laugh. "Of course, send the underlings to investigate while the captain remains safe and sound. No leadership, no glory." To that, Worf growled low, determined to remain civil. Romulan taunts carry no honor, he recalled, and were not worthy of a response.

"Well?" Larkin was definitely impatient and seemed to expect the equipment to be waved over the debris and have a culprit materialized before his eyes.

"This is a familiar compound substance," Worf began, cutting off Plactus by less than a second. Worf grunted in satisfaction at being first. "While we know of it, Starfleet does not currently use it in any form. On the other hand, I believe Plactus will agree that it is a more commonly used Romulan substance."

Larkin looked sharply over at Plactus, who seemed unperturbed by the accusation. Instead, he consulted his device and spoke slowly. "I must agree with the Starfleet officer. This is most *possibly* a Romulan device. It is, as he stated, a well-known compound to both governments, so no blame need be placed at our feet."

"Plactus is right," the Klingon rumbled. "However, I can call up computer records indicating this exact method of attack has been used by Romulans in several similar incidents over the past two centuries."

"Can you now," Sela said mockingly. "What makes you so certain that your Federation spy did not plant these devices using the Romulan pattern to frame my people?"

"The so-called spy is dead, and these incendiary devices are volatile," Worf cut in. "They cannot remain in place for more than thirty minutes before detonation. It's a risky piece of business and the sort of a trap that Romulans have been known to use. Also, Larkin can attest that excepting Commander Data, no Federation personnel have been on this planet in nearly twenty-four hours."

"Lieutenant Worf is correct," Larkin agreed, continuing to eye Sela. "Can you account for the fifteen Romulans that were on the planet this morning?"

Sela glanced over to Plactus, who was tapping instructions into his handheld device. He looked up and showed her the results. All eyes were on her, and they saw her surprised reaction turn to bitter anger. "How could this be, Subcommander?"

"We must investigate this further, Commander," was all Plactus would say.

"It seems, Larkin, that Telorn, the centurion responsible for the guards around the parliament, has gone missing." Worf was a bit surprised by the news that the taunting Romulan from the other night might turn out to be a spy. Once again, no single Romulan ever appeared capable of anything but deceit.

"And you suspect her of such sabotage?" Data calmly inquired, as he entered the room. His uniform was still smoky and stained. Ashes and soot smeared his face but he remained unruffled.

"As much as we suspect the Federation of bringing their own mercenary to cause trouble," Sela snapped.

"I must ask that both sides return to their respective ships. Immediately," Larkin announced in an angry voice. "Until we can find out what has happened, all further discussions are off. You will both wait until

Premier Daithin can fully address the matter." With that, he stood and stepped out of the office, fully expecting the room to be empty the next time he walked back in.

Ro was just completing her short tour of duty on the bridge as the latest briefing was breaking up. While she longed to be a part of the Elohsian mission, it was apparent this was not to be the case. At least she had her bridge duty, so she could stay on the periphery and see how the command crew wrestled with each new dilemma. From what she could gather, Starfleet was pressing Picard for action and the *Enterprise* officers were uncertain as how best to proceed next. In addition to the problems below her, she still had her personal problems to contend with. All shift long she had contemplated her situation with James Kelly and was increasingly angry with herself for not knowing how to get out of her predicament gracefully. As a Bajoran, she had endured much prior to joining Starfleet, and then concentrated with all her might to get through Starfleet Academy and serve well before the away team mission that resulted in her court-martial. Dealing with a love-struck teenager should present no problem, yet she seemed immobilized by the situation. Her rational mind analyzed the situation and came up with the theory that this was far more emotionally based and therefore more than a little bit removed from her realm of experience. War, torture, and study were relatively nonemotional issues, so this posed a new conundrum for her.

Crossing the bridge, she stepped into the turbolift with Dr. Crusher, and the two merely smiled a greeting. The two had few dealings with one another, Ro considered, but the doctor seemed a good, decent sort. She was also a mother, and maybe she could provide some help with the problem at hand. All she had to do was ask.

"Doctor, do you have a moment?" Ro began.

A look of concern crossed Crusher's sharply chiseled features. "Are you all right, Ensign?"

"I feel fine, thank you. I need the advice of a mother."

Now Crusher's expression shifted from concern to curiosity and she smiled. "A mother? How can I help?"

"I've been assigned to help the Kelly family get acclimated to the ship, and their teenage son, James, finds me . . . desirable."

Crusher did what she could to hide the smile from her face and maintain a serious demeanor. "A crush, you mean?"

Ro sighed. "I sincerely hope that's all it is. He has pursued me this week with gifts and flattery and has now cornered me into accompanying him to the newcomers' dance. How do I get out of this without hurting his feelings or ruining my assignment? Your Wesley is a teen and I thought . . ."

"He just turned twenty," Beverly said absently.

". . . you might have some insight I can use." Ro stopped speaking as the turbolift came to a halt and the doors quietly swished open. The two women strolled slowly out onto the deck and Ro followed Crusher toward sickbay.

"I can't recall an incident similar to this, Ro, but let me think a moment," Crusher said as the two continued to wend their way around the ship. She remained thoughtful for a few more moments, and Ro was beginning to wonder if asking Crusher had been a mistake. "You know, we're doing the same sort of thing as James Kelly. Here we are orbiting Eloh, doing what we can to win a planet with our sophistication and maturity. The Romulans may have offered them a practical gift, but we're the ones who are offering the biggest gift: security within our borders. James is trying to woo you with gifts and sweet talk. Not too dissimilar at all.

"You know, one of the reasons we're proceeding so slowly below is that we know so little about their culture and beliefs. We know a lot more now than we did three days ago, but who knows what else we have to learn? How do they celebrate holidays? What are their most important values? Do they eat their dead? Who can say—once we learn all that, we may not want Eloh as a partner despite its strategic location." She stuffed her hands in her pockets and stood by the sickbay doors in quiet.

Ro considered the parallels just offered up and noted the similarities. She would have preferred switching places with Picard and matching wits with the Romulans, but these were her own troubles and she couldn't avoid them. Turning the words over in her mind, a thought began to flicker. It quickly flared into a idea, then a plan, and she smiled, the first genuine smile of the day.

"Doctor, you have just given me a way out," Ro said. "Thank you."

"If I did help, thanks, but, uh, what did I say?"

"Should this work, I'll tell you all about it. I must be on my way. I need a favor from a friend." With that, Ro spun on her heel and returned toward the turbolift. Crusher shrugged, smiled, and entered her own domain.

"Surely you see, Captain, that we don't know how best to proceed, either," Daithin said from Larkin's office. Cleaners had come through and restored the room to order since this was the public face of the planet to the visiting starships. He had sent the parliament home and would call them back to session when Daithin felt the situation was safe enough. Similarly, he also sent Larkin away so he could be alone with his thoughts. While he valued his friend's useful advice, this was becoming a matter Daithin felt fell to him, and him alone, to resolve. "I do want to finish the talks but finding a safe haven is becoming problematic. I also have to worry—yes, worry— about the safety of those around us."

Picard's expression was neutral on the small viewscreen seven feet away from the desk. The conversation had gone on for several minutes, and Daithin appreciated Picard's patience and good humor. He never expected himself to be faced with such problems when the starships first arrived. Who could anticipate attacks with links to both the Federation and the Romulans? He was charting new territory here and was being extra careful not to take a misstep. After today's incident, such a mistake could prove deadly.

"Our security officers are willing to come down and use our technology to make any place you desire secure. We can confine our remaining meetings to that room," Picard offered.

"Thank you, Captain," Daithin muttered. The Romulans had made a similar offer minutes before, and he could ask the two sides to cooperate and agree to a location. There remained too many questions to be answered first, he decided, and Daithin knew he had to act like a leader, even if he remained privately unsure of his actions.

"For the moment, I will consider your offer and let you know what I will do in the morning. The hour is getting late and this day has taken a lot out of me, a lot indeed."

"Before we conclude this, Premier," Picard said in that steady voice that Daithin had come to admire, "I would like permission to have Commander Data return to Eloh and investigate the fire's remains. We will, of course, make all such findings available to both you and the Romulans. Additional information may be our best hope of finding out what happened."

Daithin wanted to leap to accept the offer, but he was expected to remain the wise, thoughtful statesman. Interestingly, the Romulans had not made a similar request, but then again, one of their own was implicated. Maybe they were hoping the less sophisticated Elohsians would miss something. Additional information would only help, and he had come to trust Picard's word.

He tried to hedge the moment. "The Romulans have not made a similar offer just yet and I want to make sure they are not bothered by your presence."

"I do not feel we should be prevented from conducting our own investigation just because the Romulans are disinclined to do so." Nothing harsh, just a counterpoint—and a good one, Daithin felt. He was then reminded that it was Data, after all, who risked everything to save lives and much more. The Romulans had merely returned to their ship, saying later they felt it best if Eloh handled the disaster without alien interference.

"Very well, Captain. Data may come down tonight, but please, just him so we don't call attention to your investigations. For now, then, fair night." With a weary sigh, Daithin tapped a control that shut down the communications device. He marveled at the equipment, hoping one or both people would leave the communications gear behind so his people could use it for global broadcasting. It provided a stronger signal and sharper image than anything they had developed.

He paused to wonder if it was something they could replicate on Eloh or whether they would need materials that could not be manufactured on his world. Again his thoughts turned to the fateful decision that needed to be made.

He had heard the questions being asked during the meetings with both visitors. Daithin was shrewd enough to listen as soldiers-turned-politicians weighed each new piece of information as something that might shift the tenuous balance of power. Dars and Populists could easily be at each others' throats with phasers and disruptors rather than mortar fire and *erewhan*. Such a renewed conflict might spell the end of the Elohsian people, and Daithin could not allow that to happen.

Creeping in between Daithin's deliberations was the new thought that perhaps Eloh could bargain for neutrality and declare the entire solar system off-limits to both governments. Would either honor that desire, and was it the wisest course of action for the planet and his people? Moving slowly from the office toward his home several blocks away, Daithin began to dread another sleepless night.

Ashes and soot had been carried by a gentle breeze for many blocks away from the blast sight, coating many buildings with grime. Street lights shone brightly, casting new shadows over the city and giving it an eerie quality the citizens had never known before. Most remained in their homes, following the curfew set by the chief safeguard's office. Those that chose to violate the curfew did so only to go from one building to another, perhaps to seek companionship and a feeling of safety from friends or family. The local restaurants and drinking spots had been shuttered for the night, continuing to lend gravity to the day's events. Night had fallen, the streets were quiet, and fear spread out, making itself at home in Regor.

With so few people out and about, no one noticed Data shimmer into existence directly in the epicenter where four fires shattered a peaceful day. The android held his tricorder away from him and slowly made a circle, initially surveying the origin points of the fire. Knowledge meant everything to Data and he most definitely wanted to spend the next few hours surveying the damage and coming up with answers not only for his commanding officer but for Premier Daithin as well. In his exchanges with the world leader, Data had come to the conclusion that Daithin genuinely wanted what was best for his people, and such feelings, Data had concluded long ago, historically helped make leaders great ones.

Since their arrival on Eloh, Data had absorbed as much information as possible about the world and its people. His internal mechanisms recorded everything and then, at night back aboard the *Enterprise,* he allowed himself the luxury of reviewing the accumulated knowledge and processing it, sifting it through a variety of theories and conclusions, attempting to best comprehend the society. As second officer to Captain Picard, Data knew that forming opinions and conclusions was an important facet of the job. In return, Data appreciated the opportunity to watch two very different human beings act with the information and react to situations as they arose. Picard was definitely the more private one, relishing the chance to ponder the great mysteries of life when not actually exploring those perplexities. Riker preferred grabbing those unknowns with his own hands, feeling them for what they were and dealing with them appropriately. Intriguingly, even their choice of musical instruments illustrated their personalities. Picard had only recently come to play a Ressikan flute, a soft-spoken, eloquent instrument that worked best when played alone. Riker's love for jazz and his own efforts with the trombone were loud, bright, and full of zest.

The tricorder's sounds seemed louder than normal in the quiet night air. Data made no effort to silence them since they should have disturbed no one for several blocks. Everyone who had lived or worked in the area had long since been evacuated and relocated toward the outskirts of the city. Repair crews, he was told, would begin work within days, and the officials had anticipated having things back to normal within two months' time. An efficient management approach, Data had noted earlier in the day. Tonight, though, he concentrated more on the destruction that had been wrought.

An hour, then two, slipped by as Data methodically sifted debris in all four locations. There were no noises save Data's. No passersby, not even local vermin or insect life dared come near the scene of the destruction. The temperature had dropped four degrees since he had materialized on the surface and, had he been breathing, frost would soon have appeared. He analyzed the decomposed remains of different materials, organic and inorganic. Carefully, Data moved within some of the burned-out buildings, adjusting his own eyes to compensate for the lack of light. The work did not bore or tire him, one of the things that made Data perfect for the role he was performing. The ship's command crew was no doubt asleep by now, with the gamma shift command crew well in place. Data had worked the rotation to allow himself to take command during that shift at least once a week, feeling it important that he remain a presence on the bridge for the less experienced officers. Troi had agreed that psychologically, it was good for the younger officers to get the experience Data offered, even though the crew merely steered the ship from star to star or maintained planetary orbit. Rarely, it seemed, the last shift of the day got called upon to act during a crisis. Such matters were good for contemplation another day, he concluded, and returned his main thoughts to climbing a flight of stairs. With each step he internally analyzed the one before him, adjusting his angle of approach and weight applied so as not to fall through charred floorboards.

Before he could reach the second floor, Data's audio receivers picked up a sound not of his own making. He stopped in his tracks and applied all his internal analytic equipment. Creaking meant weight, and his thermal analysis indicated a living being was moving around above him. Someone was definitely on the floor, walking around unhurriedly. Furniture was being moved, and Data concluded his presence had not yet been noticed by the other entity. With the curfew in effect, Data was certain the person was not authorized to be present, and he immediately began to prepare for a possible hostile confrontation. While one hand continued steadily to hold the tricorder, Data's other hand carefully reached down to his pocket and withdrew the phaser, already locked on a moderate stun setting. Dr. Crusher's cursory examinations of the Elohsian physique recommended that a setting higher than human norm be employed.

Slowly raising his head to the second floor, Data watched the figure move around the room, flashing a tight beam of light. Breath was frosting upon exposure to the night air and left a marked trail. Much of the exterior wall was gone; the window was replaced by a garish rip in the structure that exposed the entire room to the night sky. A pale light from a nearby street lamp allowed for additional illumination, and within seconds Data's assumption of identity was proven accurate.

Settling himself on the second floor, Data said, "Commander Sela."

The Romulan whipped about, her sleek disruptor out and aimed directly at his head. When she realized who it was, she smirked and holstered the weapon. "Data."

"I did not know Premier Daithin had authorized you to come down and also investigate," Data said as he remained where he was, making sure the Romulan would not prove a threat.

"He doesn't know," she said and began looking around the ruins. The upstairs room was obviously an office of some kind, with desks and deep shelves lining one wall, the books and papers now a blackened mess. Wall hangings that had bright colors peeking through the charred, grayish color hung askew.

"Then what are you doing here?"

Frost continued to punctuate the conversation. "The same thing as you, I suppose. Trying to find out who did this."

"You truly do not know if your own centurion was responsible?" Data was puzzled by this and waited for Sela's response.

"Telorn was an adequate officer and I cannot possibly imagine why she would want to do this. We gain nothing from this."

"Nor would the Federation gain anything from the first explosion," Data added.

Sela looked over his way, considered his comment, and made a noncommittal sound. She continued to sift through black junk on the floor in no apparent pattern.

"You would then presume to find evidence that

either proved her guilty or pointed toward the true culprit," Data offered.

"You could say that, android. We still can't locate her, which is concern enough. Our sensors should have picked her up hours ago. When I find her, she may just die for being away from her post, or she may die for treachery against the Empire."

"A curious form of justice," Data said.

"Your Federation will one day fall from such soft responses," Sela said, a harsh tone creeping into her voice.

"That is not for me to say," Data replied. "I would suggest, however, that we pool our efforts to find the cause of the explosions and what truly happened today."

Sela stopped working and eyed the Starfleet officer. "Why would you make this offer?"

"Because we both want the same thing: the truth. Together we may find it."

"And do you trust me after our last encounter?" Sela's blue eyes bored into Data, recalling the humiliation and ruination of five years' work thanks to the android, Captain Picard, and Ambassador Spock.

"Deception would gain you nothing, so trust would be implicit," Data responded.

The Romulan considered his offer, shrugged, and went back to work, using her own sensor device and light source. It was larger and made considerably more noise than Data's tricorder, leading him to observe once again that though the Romulans may have had superior technology in some areas, they certainly did not have a total edge over the Federation.

"The chemical material is as we suspected," Data began. "This world is unfamiliar with chemical weaponry, as far as I can tell, and was not as equipped to stop the spread of the fire. It did far more damage than we expected. The actual device that held the chemical is what I would like to find. A piece of it, anyway."

Sela was crouched by a corner, a hand sifting through the material, the other holding her light. A gleam of recognition was visible to Data, and he calmly stood nearby, watching. Her dirty fingers rose, holding a small, greenish bit of material. Placing the light in her belt, she held up her device, scanning it.

Cautiously, Data walked closer and asked if he could scan the piece as well. She nodded, not wanting to speak at the moment. Data ignored the possible slight and concentrated on the readings. "I show this to be a ceramic construct," Data began.

"Yes," she agreed. "Too small to be consequential, but if we can find more of it here, and perhaps at the other buildings . . ."

"You believe this held the chemical?"

"If it is what I believe it to be, yes. Come with me, Data," she commanded, and quickly moved across the room toward the stairs. Data obediently followed, unperturbed by her attitude. Since he regrettably had no emotions to hurt, it did not bother him to let the Romulan lead the way, take charge, or seem as if she was in totally command of the situation. He was, after all, allowed to be here while she was present surreptitiously. Data began to suspect that Sela's own shipmates were unaware of her location and that this was a personal investigation.

Within minutes, they were standing knee-deep in the rubble that was once a storage space above a bakery. Sacks of Elohsian sugar, flour, and some unidentified substances had split open and mixed with the chemical retardant to make a goo that lathered the fallen shelves, ladders, and half the ceiling. While Sela held her light high, Data dug through the mire and concentrated his search for the same bit of ceramic material. Had Geordi been present, his VISOR might have simplified the search, but his own visual receptors would suffice in this case.

After nearly a quarter-hour of silent digging, Data held up three more bits of the green stuff. Sela scanned them and then looked worried. Data could tell without his tricorder that the material matched what they found across the street. "This is of Romulan make, is it not?"

Sela, shaken by the readings, said without really paying attention to Data, "Yes. Some of the ceramic components are clays from Romulus. The chemical compound is poured into these handsize containers within a vacuum. Its acidic content eats through the ceramic and upon exposure to air, ignites and burns quickly. There's no doubt a Romulan was behind this. Damn the praetor, who?"

"Do you continue to suspect Telorn of being the person who placed these devices?"

"I don't know what to suspect, android!" Sela was seething and Data noted, from his observations of Romulans, that her reaction was more human than Romulan. "We did not come here to hand the world to the Federation."

"I agree," he said.

She paused for a moment and looked over toward Data, who was dusting himself off. His words seemed to stop her cold, and Data watched her expression change from fury to puzzlement. He chose to continue his theory. "Neither the Federation nor the Romulan Empire came here to sabotage their own efforts and 'hand the world' to the other side. I can only conclude that there are third-party agents with an agenda we do not as yet know."

"A reasonable assumption, Data," she agreed. "And how do we prove this new theory of yours?"

"I do not know, as of this moment. But clearly, to do this, I believe we will have to work together despite our differing philosophies."

Sela stood still, pondering those thoughts, and Data simply watched her, not certain of how the suggestion would be received. The moments ticked by slowly and all that convinced Data that Sela had not turned into a statue was the continual stream of frosty breath. Finally she made her decision, stepped toward Data, and gave him a rare, genuine smile. He noted that it enhanced her cold beauty as he understood the descriptions.

"All right, Data. If you have a plan, I will listen."

Chapter Nine

Data returned to his pacing, back in detective mode. His thoughts were, for humans, an orderly collection of patterns, deductions, and hypotheses. To Data, though, they were a scramble of incomplete ideas all running on parallel processors and fighting for attention. Even with his amazing positronic brain, it took him some time to sort through the facts, comparisons to similar incidents in his memory banks, random comments that had been filed away and may now prove useful, hundreds of theories, and two separate tracks that involved surveillance on Commander Sela, and one on on comparing Elohsian musical etudes to that found on the Denebian colonies.

Sela merely watched him pace back and forth, but even the cool Romulan had her limits, he noted.

"Why do you move about so?" she finally asked.

"Ah, you are unaware of Terran detective fiction," Data said, a thoughtful expression crossing his face. "I have done a great deal of reading on the subject," he continued, "and find the methods of most fictional detectives quite fascinating. I have emulated their approaches on more than one occasion to satisfactory results. Since we are posed with a mystery, I have returned to that mode of operation for the moment. Does it bother you?"

"No, but get on with it if you have something," she demanded.

"Of course. Do you agree that we are dealing with a third party that wishes both the Federation and the Romulan Empire ill will?"

Sela seemed to consider the question a moment. He presumed that she was weighing the evidence along with her intimate knowledge of the *Enterprise* and its crew. There could be only one answer, but he waited patiently.

"Yes," she concurred.

"Very good. With us both believing in this new theory, then we can better operate together. I have reason to suspect that there is a connection between the dead human mercenary and your centurion, Telorn."

"Unlikely," Sela replied. "Telorn has never left the Empire before this mission. She would have had no contact with humans. The *N'ventnar,* before this mission, was performing duties well within the Empire and away from you."

Data continued to pace, hands behind his back. "I see. Could she have been bought by someone?"

"Bought? I had not considered this, but I suppose after today, anything is possible."

Sela began to move away from the worst of the mire and brushed her clammy, dirty hands on her pants, ignoring the rest of the mess. "If you're right, Data, then the clues we're seeking could be here, right under our noses, and we'd never know. Damn, this is infuriating."

Data had just given her a new avenue to consider, and he knew Sela would need some time to process the concept and see if it was worth accepting. Either way, the very notion would no doubt be distasteful to the proud Romulan and might alter her mood. He merely watched, trying to see if he correctly predicted her action and frame of mind.

"If we're done here," she said sourly, "could we please leave this place? The stink is starting to get to me."

Data stopped pacing at her last words and whirled about. He snapped his fingers and actually said, "Ah ha!" On the one hand, he was pleased that he had correctly presumed she would alter her mood, but then his mind seized on her sentence, and clues fell into place and a new theorem was being developed. All this happened with lightning speed so Sela could not possibly comprehend what her words triggered; she merely stared at him.

He walked over to the table where the three bits of ceramic sat and then bent over them. She watched, curious, as he bent lower and actually began sniffing the pieces. Then he went over to the wall where the pieces were found and began sniffing there, periodically consulting his tricorder, which whirred and beeped on occasion.

Finally, Data stood and entered some information into his ever-present tricorder. He waited briefly for some result to come up on the tiny screen, and then Data walked over to Sela. Holding the tricorder up for her to see, he said, "We have something."

"What?" she asked.

"You mentioned clues right under our noses and then, moments later, the stink, something I had not considered previously. It led me to think of a story I only recently acquainted myself with. One of the great detective stories of Edgar Allen Poe was 'The Purloined Letter.' Written in the nineteenth century and featuring the first of the great literary detectives . . ."

"Get on with it," she ordered.

Data was nonplussed by the command and interrupted his lecture. "The point of the story is that a rare postage stamp was missing, and while local police searched high and low for the item, it remained in the house all the time, affixed to an envelope like an ordinary stamp of its day."

"What does this . . . this stamp have to do with us?" she asked curtly.

"We have a clue under our own noses that the Elohsian authorities would never think to investigate."

"Do I have to drag this out of you, Data?" Sela said, sounding frustrated with her newfound partner.

"I think not. What I have been doing these last few minutes is to acquire a catalogue of the smells associated with the bombs. If we go to the other three sights, I suspect we will discover the same odors, odors which would not usually be associated with this area or even this continent."

Sela began to smile at Data's ingenuity. "Your tricorder readings seem to indicate you have smelled . . . seaweed?"

"I believe so. Let us go to the other buildings before you are missed back on your own ship."

Before another hour elapsed, Data's keen sensory equipment allowed him to find not only more, similar smells, but five more pieces of the ceramic used to house the flammable compound. On the surface, the rough-textured Romulan-made material was damning evidence, but with Data's help, the true story behind the bombs would come out. Sela seemed to understand this without lengthy discussion, and Data approved of her keen, adaptable mind. He normally did not allow himself to dwell on Sela's purported parent, Tasha Yar, but in such prolonged, close proximity he found himself returning to comparisons between the two. Rather than let himself get totally carried away, he ordered up a subroutine that would keep a running file of comparisons for future analysis. He hoped he might find a clue that would help Captain Picard establish her true identity once and for all. What Data did not add was that it would settle the issue for him, too, and that was one matter he felt the need to resolve.

When they had finished with the fourth building, the duo stepped out into the street, remaining away from the pools of light cast by the street lamps every few feet. Both were pleased that no one had interrupted their work, and Data had theorized that when Daithin gave permission for him to beam down, he had asked the local safeguards to steer clear of the area.

"I will return to the *Enterprise* and continue my research. Later, I will notify you of my results. From that, we can consider a course of action. How shall I contact you?"

"I will be in touch," she said simply. Opening her own recording device, she depressed a stud and within seconds, she dematerialized, returning to her own ship no doubt through some prearranged program.

Data, his work done, signaled for his own return home.

Captain Picard started his day rested; he had slept well for a change and immensely enjoyed his breakfast conversation with Dr. Crusher, discussing matters having nothing to do with Eloh. Over the meal, though, doubts and dark thoughts returned to his conscious mind and his mood returned to a guarded, sober condition. No doubt the problems in orbit below him were far from over, and his every action seemed to take on greater importance.

As the turbolift doors opened and he strode onto the bridge, Picard surveyed the area and was content that things continued to run smoothly. Lieutenant Keefer stood from the center seat and relinquished command, officially concluding the gamma shift. Most everyone else was already in place for the day watch, although Riker was nowhere to be seen. No doubt involved in some minutiae of the ship's business, he mused.

Picard then noticed Data quietly working with the bridge's aft science stations. His uniform was dirty and seemed to carry a medley of odors, including smoke, fire, and other things unidentified. It was a thick, unpleasant smell, oddly reminiscent of Eloh. Before taking his command seat, he strolled over to the station and watched Data at work. For a moment, things remained silent, until Picard allowed himself a chance to continue his scan of the bridge. As his eyes rested on the viewscreen, the accustomed view of Eloh was different, altered somehow.

"Mr. Data, did we change orbit overnight?"

Data paused his work and looked up at the captain. "Yes, sir. I needed to change the orbit in order to complete a revised sensor sweep of the planet. I can have us return to standard orbit now that I am done."

"What the devil were you doing all night? What did you find on the planet?"

"It was a most interesting night, Captain," Data began, sounding enthusiastic over his work. "I have pursued a line of inquiry which may produce satisfactory results."

Picard nodded, tight-lipped, waiting for the usual complete report, replete with details.

"I smelled something unusual, sir. First, we detected . . ."

"We?" Picard seemed suddenly concerned.

Data paused to consider his answer, realized his omission, and continued. "Yes. Commander Sela was apparently also conducting a search for clues, although hers was a secretive mission, unknown to local authorities."

Picard uncharacteristically appeared quite surprised. Immediately his features smoothed over and he simply said, "I see. Go on, please."

"We did find conclusive evidence that Mr. Worf's analysis of the explosion was correct. The firebombs did come from a purely Romulan source. Commander Sela seemed unable to explain how this happened without her knowledge. I then detected an odor that seemed out of place. Pursuing that, I found the same trace smell in all four bomb sights, and that research took up a considerable amount of time. When I returned to the ship, I continued my studies which forced me to alter the ship's orbit."

"And you found . . . ?" Picard prompted, growing slightly impatient with the drawn-out response.

"Seaweed."

"Seaweed?" Picard seemed genuinely perplexed. First Sela, and now seaweed. This day had suddenly grown odd, and a sour feeling began to form in the pit of his stomach.

"Yes, sir. The saltwater of Eloh's oceans produce a rather pungent form of seaweed that, when dried, is used to season foods on the Dar continents. This was a similar but not exact odor, and I continued my research until I found a hydroponics plant on the continent of Delpine Dar. Most of the planet's oxygen-producing vegetable life is there, and the plant is in place to increase such production to help restock the continents that were most ecologically damaged during the wars. The smell, I believe, is hydroponically grown seaweed."

"And you believe the people behind the bombs are located on Delpine Dar, at this research center?"

"That is my current belief, sir."

Picard pondered the revelations and considered the next course of action. Of course, it would fall to Data to find this obscure line of reasoning and make it work. Surely, had they known to look for it, the human officers might have scented the seaweed but not given it much significance. But Data was right, the seaweed odor had little business being found in the center of town, near the parliament. Picard the scholar considered that such trace clues had often helped authorities find criminals who usually prided themselves on how smart they were. A little too obscure a clue, perhaps, for Dixon Hill, but certainly not at all beyond the ken of Sherlock Holmes.

"Very good work, Mr. Data. I will give this some thought and plan a course of action. In the meantime, why don't you return to your quarters and change into a slightly less noticeable uniform."

Data cocked his head at Picard's suggestion. He looked down at his regulation clothes and then took a whiff. "Ah," was all he said, and promptly left the bridge. Picard smiled and went to his command seat and thought.

Shortly, he was joined by Commander Riker and, briefly, the captain filled in his number one officer on Data's latest line of reasoning. At the mention of seaweed, Will's dark eyebrows shot up and a grin crossed his face. By the time Picard had finished, Will shook his head in wonderment at Data's skill, and just then, the detective himself returned to the bridge. They beckoned him over to the command center.

"I think, given the circumstances and method of discovery, that we will allow Mr. Data to continue to lead our investigation," Picard announced.

"Agreed," Riker said.

"I believe we will need permission to have Mr. Data return to Eloh and visit this hydroponics research center. I'd like you to take Mr. Worf with you, Data."

"Understood, sir."

"I'll contact Premier Daithin immediately and see if we can't get this investigation moving." With that, Picard rose and moved into his ready room for the conversation, certain the day was not as he originally envisioned it, but was pleased to see things heading toward a conclusion—this might turn out to be a satisfactory mission after all.

Daithin was wondering if this was what it meant to age. He had slept badly for another night and was irritable with his staff when he arrived at Parliament. His shoulders and multitude of scars ached all over, and the leader frowned at the sight of the firebombs' work as he gazed from his window, ignoring his daily paperwork. No doubt about it, he was not in a tolerant mood today. Grudgingly taking his seat behind an ornate desk in his private office, Daithin called up the day's information on his personal computer and hastily scrolled through news announcements and private messages from worried politicians, and ignored his schedule. As he tapped a spoon against his hot mug, he recognized there was no such thing as keeping to the agenda anymore. Every time something happened around the globe, the schedule was the first thing to go. Larkin normally did a fabulous job juggling the dates and appointments, but even he was tested to the limit as the presentations, tours, and meetings with the two races were constantly being altered. While he had gotten to visit the warbird, he seemed destined not to make it to the *Enterprise*.

Daithin stopped tapping the spoon when he realized the rhythmic sound was getting annoying. He blew on the mug and took a drink—never as good as his wife's, but it would get him through the day. The very act of sipping the drink made him long to be at home spending more time with his bride, and to stop feeling the crushing weight of the world on his shoulders.

His first order of business, though, was to restore order to the meetings and swiftly conclude the business with both governments so the parliament could make a decision. For the moment he ignored the possibility that the parliament could not possibly come to a reasonable resolution with these acts of terrorism coloring everyone's perceptions. Daithin had to place his confidence in two alien races, neither of which he felt he truly understood. This left him feeling unusually vulnerable and maybe even a little scared. After all, this was a bigger undertaking than he ever imagined, and sometimes he wished the dreamers, Dona and Simave, never whispered about the stars to the war-weary populace. The battles would have come to a close soon enough, he mused, but then again, maybe not.

He did not like having to revise the appointments again but felt he had no choice, and since he was feeling surly, would do it himself with an eye toward an expeditious conclusion to this once and for all. With rapid keystrokes, Daithin arranged and rearranged the mosaic before him. It took time, which he probably didn't have, given the increasing sounds of the day's business on the other side of his locked door, but he had no choice. The calendar was most important since it set the tone for the day and perhaps the next millennium.

Finally, there came a loud knock. Unfinished, Daithin was unhappy with the interruption, but the knock had a familiar tone. The double rap was used only by his friend, Larkin. Reaching beneath his desk, he pressed a small button that unsealed the door and allowed the shorter Elohsian to enter.

"Fair day, Daithin," Larkin said, seeming in far better spirits than the world's leader. He even wore one of his brighter garments, with flashing yellow and silver filigree trim on both arms and legs. Daithin was grumpy enough that he threw on the first garment he reached in his closet and hadn't considered a choice. He paused to glance at it and realized it was one of the more somber outfits, with rose and deep purple piping along the shoulders and arms with a thick, brown belt and a planetary symbol as its buckle, matching his mood.

"No it's not, so don't lie," Daithin said roughly. He swiveled the computer screen around and gestured at it with a finger. "Here, look at what I've done and see if you can finish it up. I want to notify both commanders of the plans and get this affair back on track."

Larkin busied himself with the screen for a few moments, immediately moving pieces around like a puzzle, then looked up and said, "Oh, Captain Picard is trying to reach you. Are you prepared for him?"

Daithin was not at all ready, but took a deep breath, glanced at the screen to see how the schedule was coming, and decided it was time to get started doing something constructive with his day. Anything. He walked into Larkin's smaller office just down the short hallway, and entered. With practiced ease, he placed himself behind the desk, let the breath out, and activated the screen.

"Fair morning, Captain," Daithin said, completely lying. "Was your officer able to find anything last night?" He desperately hoped for a positive response.

Picard smiled, showing confidence. "A fair morning to you, Premier. Actually, we have a very strong lead that I would like Data and Mr. Worf to pursue. May I have your permission to beam these men down to the hydroponics research center on Delpine Dar?"

Now this was totally unexpected, and it showed on the premier's dark-skinned face. Daithin wasn't sure what to make of this new turn of events. Delpine Dar was one of the more stable continents, and he couldn't imagine how the bombings on Regor and Dos Dar linked with the other continent. "Is it in danger?"

"Not that we know of, Premier," Picard replied. That look of confidence supported Daithin despite the bleak thoughts rummaging around in his mind.

"Very well, then. Let me have Larkin make the necessary security arrangements there. I don't want anything to happen to your men."

"Thank you, Premier. Have you made any decisions regarding today's agenda?"

Daithin was planning on stalling or making something up from what he remembered of the jumbled schedule, but a console on the desk winked purple and caught his eye. Within seconds, the day's schedule flashed on the screen and Daithin addressed the camera, imitating Picard's confidence.

"Actually, yes, Captain. We'd very much like to conduct the tour of the *Enterprise* this afternoon, at fourteen-hundred hours your time, of course. That would put us . . . just a day behind schedule, I believe. This morning I'll finish my interrupted meeting with the Romulan party, so I'll be free by then." His eyes flicked over to the small screen again and noted that Larkin had Picard making his formal address tomorrow morning. He made the invitation and was pleased to see that Picard was more than happy to accommodate the (again) revised Elohsian schedule. But then, what choice did Picard, or Sela for that matter, have? At least he was able to exercise that much control over the proceedings.

When the screen went blank, Daithin breathed easier, feeling a bit more in control. This business about Delpine Dar worried him since it was unexpected, but he was feeling more trusting of the Federation officers and was willing to let the investigation proceed. He summoned Larkin and briefed him on the latest, dispatching him to make sure things would be ready and secure at the center.

The captain assembled Worf, Data, Troi, and Riker in the observation lounge for a quick recap so that everyone knew the basic information. Worf grunted in approval of Data's work and Picard suppressed a smile at the Klingon's reaction to Data the detective. "I'm only sending you two down so we don't attract too much attention to the investigation. I want you both prepared with tricorders and phasers, just in case. We'll have someone monitoring your position to be on the safe side."

"Captain," a voice sounded over the communicator. "We're getting a signal from the warbird—sir, it's marked for Commander Data and is private."

Picard glanced over toward his second officer, and Data, unruffled as usual, merely said, "I have been expecting this call."

"By all means, take it here. We're done for now." With that, everyone slowly filed out of the room, most glancing over at Data to see if he would mention more about the message. Data, though, was damned good at keeping secrets.

Returning to the command center, Picard stopped by Worf and the tactical station, waiting not only for Data's conversation to finish, but for Larkin to contact them with details for the beam down. Standing behind the Klingon, he nodded in silent pleasure that everything was calm and quiet. Picard had earlier ordered the ship back to its original orbit, and the view of Eloh was now a familiar sight. By his estimates, there were two days, three at most before this situation would be resolved one way or the other. On most diplomatic missions, Picard could gauge early on how the mission was going. This one was harder to estimate because of the constant topsy-turvy turn of events. He had absolutely no clue which way things would go when the final vote was taken. The captain was glad he would be able to make his formal presentation to Parliament, preferably after everything had been revealed. Being able to present his case with the full story known would strengthen his cause and possibly even sway the vote in the Federation's favor.

"Can I help you, Captain?" Worf asked in his usual low rumble.

"Just checking the view from above, Mr. Worf. It's not something I take enough time to do."

"I see," the security chief replied stiffly, indicating he truly didn't understand. "If I may ask, Captain . . ."

"Go ahead, Mr. Worf," Picard invited, curious.

"This Edgar Allen Poe—he was definitely a nineteenth-century human?"

Picard cocked his head. "Of course."

"His imagination can rival that of our best Klingon authors, even today," the Klingon admitted.

"I see," Picard acknowledged. "Have you been reading him, too?"

It took the proud warrior a moment to reply. "With everyone else discussing his worth, I grew . . . curious. His stories can inspire the blood, and I see why the counselor was so easily chilled. They will make fine bedtime stories for Alexander."

A few minutes later, Data came out of the observation lounge and reported directly to Picard. "That was Commander Sela. She has sent Plactus to conclude their business with Premier Daithin. When Worf and I beam down, she will meet us on Delpine Dar." A low growl rumbled from behind them.

"I understand," Picard said, ignoring Worf for the moment. "If you have preparations, feel free to make them. But tell me one thing. We didn't discuss this earlier, but what led you to find the odor as a clue?"

" 'The Purloined Letter,' sir," Data replied.

It took Picard a moment, but then he followed Data's line of reasoning. At a glance, he could tell both Riker and Troi obviously did not. "Very good, Mr. Data. Dismissed."

"What was all that about?" Troi asked.

"I recommend you both, like Data, brush up on your Poe detective fiction," Picard replied, letting a smile stay on his face. "After all, those stories won't give you nightmares." His attention turned to other matters, and he rose from his chair and returned to the tactical station where Worf silently maintained his post. From his very body language, Picard could tell that Worf was having a problem. Walking very close to the Klingon, Picard spoke softly.

"Mr. Worf, I know this presents a new difficulty for you," he began.

"Yes, sir," was the only reply, and that through gritted teeth.

"I can think of no better officer to accompany Data to the planet in order to get the job done. You have my confidence and appreciation for the uncomfortable position I am putting you in."

"Understood," Worf replied. He remained stiff, but Picard could see in his eyes that Worf would do the job despite his personal distaste for the new ally.

As the *Enterprise* officers rematerialized on Delpine Dar, their first sight was that of another figure also materializing. Worf made an unhappy face as Sela completed her transport and immediately waved her weapon in their direction. She holstered the weapon and walked toward them, a smirk growing on her face.

They were all standing in a clearing near a lush green tropical forest. In the distance they heard the mechanized hum of machinery, indicating which way the research center was located. Before beaming down, Worf and Data made a quick study of the continent. It was Eloh's second largest land mass, and more than sixty percent of the planet's oxygen came from the tropical rain forests. Worf had commented to the second officer that the Elohsians may have waged a bitter civil war, but were not insane enough to jeopardize their very lifeblood, and so the jungles remained unofficially off-limits. As a result, it was one of the first areas to get back up to peak performance when the unity was achieved. The research center they were visiting was one of the newer symbols of the continent's peace and prosperity. There were water, vegetation, and other natural elements all mixed together. He imagined the Elohsians couldn't sense much of it, which was a pity since the air was filled with life and buoyed his spirit.

No one had asked the Klingon's opinion, but there was little Picard could do but assign his most qualified officer to work with a Romulan. As it was, Worf's racial hatred of Romulans was bred in him at a young age. All Klingons were taught early on who was your friend and who was your enemy. Right after they learned which houses were to be counted as allies, they were taught about neighboring races.

The Klingons had a long memory and never forgave the Romulans for repeated treachery over the years. Nearly a century ago the two powers had been united, although it was a loose alliance that seemed to benefit neither party. Then, just as abruptly as they came together, the two sides ended up being bitter enemies with bloody results. Both felt it was their due to inherit the known galaxy, with the Federation seen only as a temporary inconvenience, despite setback after setback to both sides. While the Romulans stayed away from Federation contact for sixty years, there were constant skirmishes with the Klingon Empire during those bleak years.

Oddly, just as the Klingons were getting used to their independence, circumstances forced them to reconsider their relationship with the Federation and, beginning with the peace conference on Khitomer, a new age dawned for both races. The new alliance was put to the test at Narenda III twenty-five years ago, when the *Enterprise,* NCC-1701-C, came to the Klingon outpost's defense against a Romulan incursion. It was this very attack that initially destroyed the starship but also created the time warp that gave Sela life, and further cemented the friendship between the Klingons and the Federation. Or so Sela had claimed to Picard over a year earlier. Picard later told his senior crew about the boast and Guinan's peculiar endorsement of the probability that the claim was true.

In the years since Data and Worf joined the *Enter-*

prise, each had many opportunities to witness first-hand the Romulans' ability for treachery and deceit, acting in ways that would have brought dishonor to any Klingon house. Still, the Romulans' deceit more deeply affected Worf at every turn. The House of Duras, for example, suffered greatly for their clandestine work with the Romulans over the years. First, it was Duras's father, Ja'rod, who betrayed his people and allowed four thousand to die during the surprise Romulan attack at Khitomer, which left Worf and Kurn orphans. Years later, while aboard the *Enterprise,* Worf was able to defend his father's name and prove the House of Duras was ultimately at fault. Undaunted, Duras's sisters, B'Etor and Lursa, worked closely with Commander Sela to divide the Klingon Empire through civil war, making it ripe for conquest by the Romulans. Again, Worf, with his brother Kurn, helped defend the Empire and saw to it Gowron was left to rule a united, if not entirely happy Klingon Empire.

There remained no question, Worf concluded, that he had cultural as well as personal reasons for hating the Romulans, notably Sela. But the Klingon was also a man of principle, and his orders were to cooperate and he would do so. Grudgingly.

"Commander, I see you have brought a pet," Sela said contemptuously, hands on her hips. Worf loudly growled, but before he could respond, Data smoothly moved between them.

"Commander Sela, I appreciate the need that has brought us to cooperate together. However, Lieutenant Worf is here to work with us. He will be treated as a fellow officer and colleague. If you cannot give him that due, then our partnership will end here." Data stood his ground, making no move toward or away from the Romulan.

"I understand, Data. My people have worked along-side Klingons before, and I can do so for the good of my mission," she said formally but coolly, not at all meaning the words.

Before the conversation went any further, the trio heard the sound of footsteps approaching. Since they were expecting to be met, no one raised a weapon, but Worf allowed himself to loosen up, remaining in combat readiness. Within seconds, people came from behind a cluster of low-sloping trees with leaves that were long and curled. The five Elohsians were led by a woman in the dark green garb Data recognized as that of a safeguard. Her silver badge of office was visible on the belt buckle, while the people behind had the usual dark clothing with ornate trim, these in browns and golds.

"Greetings. I am Lan Mathli, chief safeguard at the research center. These are your hosts for your stay." She then introduced each person, all of whom appeared to be regular researchers given a great opportunity to meet people from another world. Sela, taking the lead, made the necessary introductions and the group moved toward the research center itself. The building was a one-story construct, similar to the rambling architecture of the banquet hall back on Regor. It was newer-looking and had chrome trim in spots near doors and windows. Behind the main building was a gigantic glass structure that was their greenhouse for the various experiments. Grounds-keepers tended the open-air gardens set around the structures, and there was a feeling of peace about the setup.

Once inside, Lan Mathli asked, "How can we help?"

Data stepped forward, beginning to take charge of the discussion. Worf took a step back and observed everyone's body language and placement of obvious weapons. He was taking nothing by chance. "Our own research from the *Enterprise* indicates that your work includes artificially breeding new forms of kelp and seaweed as a foodstuff. Am I correct?"

The shortest Elohsian, nearly Worf's height, nodded. "That's right, Data. It's something really new and we're excited about its ability to help those areas that haven't repaired their farmland yet."

"Where is the new growth located?"

"Why, in the auxiliary greenhouse, not far from here."

Sela nodded and asked, "Do you guard all your buildings? Or are they under surveillance?" Good questions, Worf had to admit.

Lan Mathli shook her head and replied, "We haven't had the need, Commander Sela. There has been no need even during the war. Why, there's just me and two others, and we usually help out with the research since our safeguard duties aren't usually called for."

"They might be soon," Worf rumbled.

"I think it would be best if you showed us this building," Data suggested. Lan Mathli agreed and led the group back out into the filtered sunlight.

During their brief walk, Lan Mathli and Worf were side by side. "It must be very quiet here," Worf said by way of conversation.

"Yes. We Populists knew better than to engage the Dar here. Oh, there were some skirmishes on the coastlines but that had more to do with piracy than politics."

"Did you serve in the war?"

"Of course. I was proud to hold the Populist banner on Hyanth. In fact, I was wounded four times and managed to return to fight each time."

"Admirable."

"It was my duty," she commented. "Now that we have unity, my duty is to protect this place."

"It seems unfitting for a warrior of your caliber," Worf said.

She laughed and replied, "Thank you for saying that, Worf, but I was posted here and this is fine. I think I grew weary of war by the time it ended, and this is an acceptable change for now. I won't shirk from the chance for combat in the future, but here and now I am content."

Data moved toward the pair, obviously intrigued by the conversation. "Does it bother you, a Populist, to be placed among the Dar?"

"Not at all, Data. I defended my homeland from invaders. I hold no grudge against these Dar since they weren't the invaders."

"Interesting. My studies to date have shown a strong instance of prejudice remaining between the sides. You are the exception."

"That's nice to hear," she said, and moved further into the jungle.

This isn't going as bad as it might, Geordi thought to himself as the tour of the *Enterprise* finally was under way. Captain Picard himself was leading the group of Elohsian dignitaries, which was a rare sight for the crew. Normally such tours fell to Riker or Troi but given the importance of the mission, it didn't surprise the chief engineer at all that the captain took the lead. He took tremendous pride in his ship and it wasn't often he got to show it off to world leaders, much as they showed off their own worlds. Dr. Crusher and Geordi were the only ones accompanying the captain since it was decided Riker had best remain on the bridge in case Data and Worf needed help.

Counselor Troi was also dealing with some shipboard matters that had been put off during the Elohsian problems, and she was getting backed up with appointments.

"A bright, clean ship, very bright," Daithin muttered mostly to himself as they entered the crew decks. Larkin and the other parliamentary members nodded in silent agreement. Their pace was definitely leisurely, Geordi noted, and he felt the tour would take quite a bit of time. To top it off, he was also expected to devote some private time to Conductor Luth, who hung at the back of the group, examining everything possible with his magnifying loupe. He curiously avoided asking any technical questions, and Geordi could only imagine that they were all being saved up for later.

"All officers have private quarters," Picard explained. "Junior crew are paired up according to Commander Troi's recommendations." He went on to describe the psychological importance of off-duty time and the recreational options available to the crew. "The recreation areas include a variety of games that test the mind or even the spirit."

"We, too, like games of chance," Larkin said. "Military simulations were an important part of the Populist naval training, which is why we succeeded so often on the oceans, and now our children seem to enjoy pretending."

"Succeeded on the oceans, indeed," sniffed a member of the party, obviously a Dar who objected to the boast.

Picard quickly reasserted himself, bringing the conversation back to games. "Some of my senior officers enjoy a playing card game called poker, while others seem to enjoy the high-spirited competition in more physical matches such as handball or parises squares."

After watching the Elohsians for a few days and reading up a bit on their past battles, Geordi was convinced these people would make fine Dabo players, bringing their high passions to the game. Ferengi merchants would clean up opening an establishment here—another reason the world was better off being protected by the Federation or even the Romulans, who hated the Ferengi almost as much as they hated humans.

The tour wended its way through the ship and at one point, while the group was awaiting a turbolift, a new line of questioning came up.

"Captain, what's the photon torpedo complement of a Galaxy-class starship?" Larkin asked casually.

"Our armaments are housed separately," Picard replied, avoiding the actual answer. "And I hope you can understand that they will not be a part of our tour. Also, please understand that the nature of our weapons is totally defense related."

"What about your shuttles? Do they come armed?"

"Actually, no. They are merely transport vehicles and are not usually expected to encounter hostilities."

"How has this ship fared in combat with Romulan warbirds?" another visitor asked.

"We've sustained minor damage in the rare instances when we have had to defend ourselves," Picard responded. Geordi could see Picard's jaw tighten and was probably the only one to understand how rare that was. He knew these questions were designed to see which ship was actually superior, a natural inclination of the Elohsians, but La Forge also knew that Picard disliked discussing the ship's weaponry since the captain always considered it a necessary evil.

"Will we have a chance to survey your battle bridge?"

Picard snapped about, surprised at the thoroughness of the diplomatic office's efforts. He'd have to have a word with them when this mission was completed. "I'm afraid our reduced schedule will not allow us the luxury."

"Are you able to fire both photon torpedoes and phasers simultaneously and while using warp speed?" Larkin probed deeper than any previous visitor Geordi had witnessed.

"Sir," Picard began, barely containing his exasperation. "I am attempting to show you the full range of this vessel and its crew. We're an exploratory ship, not a warship. Some of the races we encounter prove to be hostile and we must be prepared to defend this ship. After all we have not only Starfleet personnel aboard, but families as well."

Daithin wisely chose then to change the subject as the turbolift doors opened. "These families, Captain, do you find yourself commanding this vessel any differently because of their presence?"

Better ground, Geordi noted, and he listened to Picard's discourse on command styles. It wasn't often he got the opportunity to watch Picard the diplomat, and he admired the way the captain handled these myriad questions without breaking stride.

By the time the group had completed the tour, it was evident everyone needed a break, so the last stop being Ten-Forward turned out to be inspired. Guinan was at her charming best, making the Elohsians laugh and showing them how best to drink a smoky concoction from Wrigley's Pleasure Planet. Picard hung back and watched, smiling as Guinan held court. If anyone could make these people feel pleased about the Federation, it was she.

At one point, just as Geordi was relaxing, Luth walked over and with a conspiratorial wink said, "It is time to return the favor. You climbed all over my buildings; now I want to see what really makes this ship tick."

Still with mixed feelings, Geordi smiled and agreed, leading the Elohsian toward the nearest Jeffries tube. He idly wondered if the larger Elohsians might get stuck deep within the *Enterprise* and how that would go over with Daithin and Picard.

Data's tricorder sounded out of place amid the chittering sounds of native animal life-forms hidden deep in the verdant jungle. He was taking initial readings on the building that was hundreds of yards away from the research center. So far he had managed to gauge its building material, approximate age, and other basic facts. Built only in the last two years, Lan Mathli explained, it was specifically designed for experiments outside the center's normal range of activities. The seaweed project had begun early on and, with its success, became the predominant work done in the building.

Its boxlike shape was similar to the power conduit stations in the other cities they had visited, supporting the theory that their architecture was definitely more for function than design. It was at best one hundred meters wide and seventy-five meters long, with large front windows and a sloping roof that allowed rainwater to run off into pipes that took it away, perhaps somewhere to be stored. It had no outside decorations and was a drab monochrome so it mostly blended in with its environment. In some ways, Worf concluded, it would be an ideal supply depot for an army or even a bunker.

"I can understand the need for sunlight, but I do not

see why the back portion of the building is blacked out," Worf observed.

One of the researchers stepped forward and said, "It's not supposed to be."

With that, Worf withdrew his weapon and took on a defensive demeanor. After all, if the clues led them to this building and something was not as it should be, logic dictated caution would be prudent. "How recently was this building last inspected?" he asked Lan Mathli.

"I would have to check my records, but we usually make a perimeter walk once every six hours."

"Would your men have noticed this change in the structure?" Sela asked, now also holding her disruptor.

"I don't know."

Worf ignored Sela's dismissive sound and continued to lead the group quietly toward the building. Data adjusted his recording to biological readings and stood behind the others, scanning intently. "How many should be in the building at this time?"

The researcher that already volunteered information spoke up again, his voice noting surprise. "None today. We did our work there yesterday."

"Mr. Worf, my tricorder shows five people within that building. How do you recommend we proceed from here?"

"Allow me to be the first to enter, with Lan Mathli and . . . Commander Sela flanking. If they are hostile, we'll know immediately."

"If they have evidence to conceal, would not such an approach allow them time to destroy it?"

"A calculated risk," was all Worf would say.

He asked the researchers to remain where they were standing while he and the others made the first move. Withdrawing his own phaser, Data gestured for Worf to proceed as originally proposed, with the commander remaining in the rear.

The foursome moved closer to the building, and as they reached within four feet of the structure Worf was repelled by an electric discharge. He was merely stunned and knocked to the ground but then quickly regained his footing. Data immediately reopened the tricorder and adjusted the scans. "I did not take into consideration the possibility of a defense. There is a forcefield in place here."

"We don't use forcefields here," Lan Mathli said in astonishment.

"But we do," Sela offered. "As does the Federation. Data, you've found our prey."

Data shook his head. "Not yet. I have found a new problem but it may be quickly correctable. This is a fairly standard shield and easily circumvented. They obviously did not expect Starfleet or Romulans to discover their place of hiding." With nimble fingers Data set to work and within two minutes had programmed the small tricorder to emit a carrier wave pulse that would temporarily disrupt the field.

"Ready . . . now!" he called. The pulse was a bright violet against the shimmering electrical field, and all could see a tear form. As one, the four moved through the rip before the pulse ended and allowed the shield to regain stability.

Worf reacted quickly and smashed his way into the building, yelling for the people within to stay where they were. His cry was answered with a bolt of blue light cutting through the air and shattering the door trim by Worf's shoulder. The Klingon's phaser waved in the air before him as Lan Mathli and then Sela entered, their weapons also out and ready. From a rear corner shouts and shuffling feet were heard in the damp, humid room. The disruptor blast missed the four as each went diving under tables behind support pillars.

Taking rapid aim, Worf let out two bursts of phaser fire and knew he had made contact with something. A door was pushed back by the impact of the coherent beam of light and the second shot seemed to find a living target.

He looked to his left and saw the smile from Lan Mathli. "Nice shot, Worf."

Worf grunted and asked, "What are they firing?"

"I don't know. Nothing we have used in our battles even remotely matches that kind of energy." She crawled forward, gaining more of Worf's admiration.

Sela's disruptor fired next, also reaching a target, but in the process shattering a rear window. More matching, high-pitched blue bolts emitted from the room and those, too, shattered windows and light panels. This, in turn, set off the sprinkler system, dousing everyone with water coming down at high pressure. Sela shrieked in frustration and let off two more shots, at least one of which hit a shadowy figure in the rear area of the building.

Then, to Data's surprise, Sela launched herself forward, firing her disruptor rapidly, trying single-handedly to bring down the suspects. Her moves, he considered, were reckless but showed her warrior spirit on full display. Sela's lithe body moved quickly, covering ground and leaping over tables, avoiding the taller plants. However, she seemed not to heed the warning blasts that came from the back of the building. One such shot managed to clip a support beam, and the piece of metal twisted and bent. With a groan of tearing steel, the heavy piece tore free and started to fall toward the unsuspecting Sela.

Worf had perhaps two seconds to make his decision. He knew Data was too far away and Lan Mathli was pinned down in the rear by additional enemy gunfire. Sela was certainly going to be injured if not killed.

Without hesitation he leapt into the air, grabbed Sela's right arm, and yanked her down between two tables, letting the steel beam crash atop three other tables, shattering plants, stands, and recording equipment. He and Sela crumpled in a heap, getting even more soaked by a growing puddle of water. Bright eyes glared at Worf but he merely stared down at her.

"Why did you do that?" she asked, the hard edge in voice missing for a moment.

"I was assigned to work with you and that meant offering you my protection as well," Worf said stiffly. "Klingon honor, too, demands my behavior."

Sela stared at him oddly as he moved away from the Romulan, putting as much distance away from her as possible while still searching for a strategic position.

Worf noticed that Lan Mathli had used the brief interruption in the firefight to crouch and maneuver to a better position near the left side of the building. There, she was spraying off several rounds from her projectile weapon, all of which made loud cracking sounds, most unlike the high whine of a disruptor or phaser. No one would be able to emerge from the building while she was there.

Worf crept along the sidewall, inching his way toward the rear section, ignoring Data's low approach underneath the tables. Both would reach the rear about the same time, and it was important for both to act in tandem. As both grew closer to the rear of the building, Worf knelt low, moving slower, allowing Data to rendezvous with him. The synthezoid stopped his motion to listen to the back room. There was obviously no exit since there was still a lot of scrambling heard. Moans were also present, meaning people were hurt by flying glass or the return fire.

Dripping water continued to fall, enlarging small pools throughout the building. To complete this action without causing further injury, they would have to move quickly to contain the people, and hope Worf's formidable size would deter the even larger Elohsians.

Reaching the last row of tables, Data remained beneath, trying to catch Worf's eye. When he did, the android indicated he would go first and Worf should follow. The Klingon nodded slowly and then waited for Data's signal. A golden hand chopped the air, and Data sprang from beneath the table and rushed into the room, his phaser before him. Worf immediately followed, aiming his phaser in the opposite direction, intending to cover the entire room.

Within, two men lay on the ground, holding places on their bodies where they were hit. Their blood was mixing with the water, adding another hue to the room. Two other men were rapidly stuffing data disks and papers into a rectangular black box while the final person, a woman, took aim at Data. Before she could fire, though, Worf's phaser rang out and the woman crumpled.

Almost at that instant, the roof literally fell in.

During the firefight enough of the support beams were damaged or obliterated that the roof could no longer be held up, and it finally caved in. With it came sunlight and the sound of wildlife. The crash was deafening as pieces of roof crushed tables, experiments, and files. There was also a cry almost lost amid the cacophony.

Again without hesitation, Worf tossed pieces of stone behind him and worked his way down until he found Lan Mathli, nearly unconscious under the weight of the roof. She moaned softly and was bleeding profusely from her head and arms. Her left leg was twisted at entirely the wrong angle. As carefully as he could, Worf continued to remove debris and then picked up the woman warrior and carried her into the other room, which was unscathed.

Data had already placed the people inside under arrest and was securing the remaining information in a large black box. Worf barely took note of the situation as he laid Lan Mathli down and studied her injuries closely. Sela walked to the other side of the table and observed quietly for a moment before something caught her eye.

The Romulan walked over to a fallen weapon almost obscured by a chair, and knelt down to examine it. "It's a modified disruptor," she announced.

Data looked over at it, sparing it little more than a glance. "Consistent with a theory that is forming," he said and returned his attention to securing the box for transport.

"What do you mean?" she demanded.

"Commander, time does not allow me to go into an explanation. I would prefer that we vacate the building before it continues to fall apart." To punctuate the statement, more sounds of twisting material and shattering glass came from the main room. Everyone began working a little faster, including the annoyed but prudent Sela.

Worf had already called to the *Enterprise* and asked for Lan Mathli to be beamed directly to sickbay. He accompanied her, so it left Data and Sela alone to complete their search of the room. As the second officer rounded a corner, he stopped to study one of the men slumped against a wall.

"You are Waln, from the parliament," he announced.

Chapter Ten

WITHIN AN HOUR, there was bedlam in the parliament building. Picard sat back in Daithin's office and watched the tide of emotion build as accusations flew, safeguard officers sifted through documents, and parliamentary officials demanded instant answers to impossible questions. Larkin was holding his own, coordinating the information flow from his crowded office directly into Daithin's private room where Picard, Sela, and the premier awaited each new shred of evidence. As Picard maintained a relaxed pose in a deeply cushioned straight-back chair, Sela took the opposite approach and remained ramrod-straight against the wall, seemingly poised to spring. No one was saying much and Picard was just as content to await information and make no assumptions. He was confident that Data could make sense of the information found in the black box on that faraway continent that seemed so idyllic from orbit.

He paused to note that Sela, although still dripping wet, remained in command, regal, and still very attractive. She was so much her mother's daughter that he idly wondered what her father must have been like.

Those thoughts were banished when Data was admitted to the room by Larkin, who closed the door and remained within the office to hear the report from the Federation officers. Sela, Picard, and Daithin all edged a little closer, eager for the report which was about to be delivered.

Curiously, it was Larkin who spoke first. "We have obtained the identities of the four people with Waln on Delpine Dar. They are members of what they call The Assembly, a political group that exists to promote Eloh's isolation from other races."

"What?" Daithin cried. "How could we not know this . . . group exists? Have they done anything else to our people?"

"Apparently not," Data replied. "The Assembly's leader, a woman called Jasmia, swears the two incidents to date are all they have managed to accomplish."

Picard nodded, thankful that everyone else on Eloh would be spared further pain. Daithin seemed to echo the notion and nodded while Sela sat impassively.

"We discovered the materials required to make the ceramic casings for the firebombs plus an additional supply of the chemical compound," Data added. "Safeguard officers are continuing to study the disks we found, hoping it provides a complete list of their membership."

Sela stood up and announced, "Then the Romulans can be cleared of any wrongdoing."

"So it would seem," Daithin began to say. Picard was surprised by this since so many other questions remained unanswered. Still, Daithin was the leader and he would have to defer to the local authority.

"Not necessarily," Data said, stunning all. "You

see, Premier, by studying what we found today, I was able to understand the entire operation that much better. It answered some questions that bothered me after reviewing Commander La Forge's tricorder readings at the purification plant."

Sela's eyes closed to slits and she studied the android. "What do you mean?"

"The explosive that was used in the purification plant was something entirely different from that which destroyed part of this town," Data explained. Picard felt himself settling in for another lengthy explanation that would no doubt cast new light on the entire week's activities. He had to hand it to Sherlock Data for being indefatigable and adding things up where few others could.

"This, I suspect, was on purpose so no one could substantially link the two bombings beyond coincidence. We never did determine how the first explosive was set off. No piece of a timing mechanism was ever found despite a considerable amount of electrical material which managed to survive. Commander La Forge had correctly theorized that a signal had to be engaged to detonate the bomb, on a frequency not usually used on this planet so it could not be detected. Based on my studies of the remains, I believe they add up to a design activated by the low band frequencies used by Romulan communicators."

"What gives you that idea?" Sela demanded, her face reflecting her fury.

"When you used the silent signal last night, to return to the warbird, I made note of it with the tricorder."

"You were spying on me?" she demanded.

"Studying a potential adversary," Data replied calmly. "The signal matched my theoretical frequency for the detonation. Rebuilding the device under controlled conditions can prove that one way or the other."

"There are also the matters of one missing Romulan, and the technology being used to make the firebombs, and the disruptors we just captured," Worf added, seeming to enjoy annoying Sela despite their earlier close encounter.

"If there is enough evidence to suspect Romulan involvement in both incidents, Premier, I believe this bears further investigation," Picard said, sounding as sympathetic as possible to the leader.

Sela stalked the room and glared at Data. She nearly yelled when she said, "I thought we were allied in this, android!"

"We are," Data said.

"But you accuse me of terrorism!"

Data shook his head. "I do not accuse you, Commander, because you are not the responsible party. But the evidence clearly indicates a Romulan was involved in this."

Picard watched Sela stop in her tracks, still quietly dripping water from her thickly padded uniform, and pay attention to Data's reasoning. Her myriad emotions raced across her face, and the experienced captain suddenly found her difficult to read. He found himself enjoying watching her, intrigued by her very being.

"You are as determined as anyone to find the true culprits," Daithin said, sounding conciliatory. "Your work with Commander Data, I think, proves your sincerity. Just as you cannot blame all of Eloh for what has happened, I don't blame you for the action of another Romulan, if that is the truth."

Sela, barely mollified by the words, frostily replied, "Thank you, Premier. I will, of course, want to remain close to the investigation."

Daithin agreed and asked Larkin to oversee the interrogation of the prisoners, except Waln, who was to be brought to the office. Larkin left the room quickly, and then the premier addressed the remaining people.

"These are suddenly very difficult times, you must understand. I knew Waln a very long time, and will want to hear his words myself. You are free to remain at Parliament and consult on the investigations. We'll speak again later."

Picard knew a dismissal when he heard one, and led his people out of the office, Sela sullenly following behind them. Out in the hall, Picard found himself next to the Romulan and wasn't sure what to say. She seemed preoccupied by the implication of her people's complicity and appeared angry and volatile. The wrong statement could provoke a new round of hostilities, something he did not want at all. Instead, Picard turned to his officers.

"I appreciate your work, Mr. Data. You're free to return to the *Enterprise*. Please file your report with Commander Riker. I will remain here until we know what will happen next."

The officer acknowledged the directions and went out of the building with Worf to beam up without distraction. Sela watched them depart and Picard studied her, wondering what she would do with this newfound knowledge.

A burly safeguard, looking too big for his dark green uniform, walked into Daithin's office with Waln standing helplessly before him. The Elohsian premier thanked the guard and dismissed him, remaining standing and just looking at Waln.

"I'm in a very bad mood today, Waln," Daithin began. "I didn't sleep last night and I ache. I think it was the wound I received on the Jerinthian coast that bothers me the most."

Waln remained silent and Daithin stopped looking directly at him. He addressed a spot on the wall directly behind the old comrade. "We have served a long time in this building. Our careers go back even further, Waln. I still recall meeting you on the first shipload of troops from Hyanth. My own division needed the support and there you were, on the front lines, ready and willing to do whatever it took to regain my city. Since then, our children have grown up together and I thought I knew you, my friend. What can you say for yourself?"

Waln stood silent, looking out the window and seeming to ignore the words. He no longer looked like the proud statesman Daithin was used to seeing in Parliament day after day. Waln looked old and beaten. The realization reminded Daithin of his own recent thoughts about aging, and he recognized their time might be coming to a close together. He had to steer his people on a path and then step aside, letting a younger generation continue forward. The time was rapidly coming for Daithin to go home and reflect on a full career. It had been a proud one and a life that historians would approve of whenever they reviewed this era.

For his friend, no doubt history would be a harsh judge.

"How can I make you understand?" Waln asked in a sad, weary voice. "I agreed with you that the time had come to end the war. Not because of some possible new race of space beings, but because we had done enough damage to each other. War was being fought for no real reason anymore, and in the end we just seized those promises of a galactic future because it came at the right time.

"But I never wanted us to go from Eloh, jewel of our system, to Eloh, member of some other government, a game piece in someone else's plan. When Nefor started discussing these feelings at our table, I listened. It was my son and the others that first formed The Assembly—an answer to your overcelebrated unity. I considered that your course of action might be wrong, and Nefor convinced me of it. I . . . I began to attend Assembly meetings, listening to young firebrands discussing how our destiny should be left up to them, the people of tomorrow. We're old warriors and we're old thinkers. Their words rang true, Daithin, and I supported them fully."

"But to kill, Waln?" Daithin remained incredulous.

"We didn't intend for that to happen," Waln said. "We didn't know how destructive these weapons would be. The supplies we received didn't come with instructions, just words."

"Now we're getting to the crux of the matter. You obtained Romulan materials, Waln, meaning you had contact with them. Who? How? Did you hire the mercenary or did the Romulans? Was the Federation involved at all?"

Waln shook his head with fatigue. His eyes shut and he seemed to be having trouble controlling his emotions, which had always been close to the surface. "What difference does it make, Daithin? Something went horribly wrong and now my life is ruined." He seemed ready to cry, something, in all their years together, Daithin had never seen before. It made him feel very sad to see his friend crumble before him.

"You asked me why the rush." Daithin's new tack caused Waln to look directly at the premier.

"I am suffering from more than my aches, I fear. I am dying and I cannot let this world devolve back to bickering children. They are so close to reigniting the civil war, still unwilling to admit either side was wrong all these centuries. We deny ourselves a future. Our place is in the stars, Waln. We've suffered too long, and too hard, not to take our place out there. Will we be as powerful as our new neighbors? I don't know. But I do know I want a chance to improve conditions here, and to do that we as a people need help.

"Like it or not, Waln, *I* am going to make a recommendation and Parliament will cast a vote. We have no more time to examine the governments represented here. In days we will be aligning ourselves with one side or the other. I want to make an intelligent choice, one that will benefit our world." The leader of Eloh's parliament took a deep breath and leaned forward, looking Waln directly in the eye, and then whispered his plea. "Help me with the facts." Daithin then returned to his seat, silently watching his friend, feeling older by the moment.

Sela stood near Larkin's office, appearing like a cat ready to pounce on its prey. Her arms tightly crossed before her, Picard idly wondered what she would be like if she ever lowered her guard and relaxed. Instead, he turned his attentions toward Larkin, watching as the aide worked furiously, scribbling notes on a blotter, typing instructions into his computer, and assessing information while also shouting orders. If there was a real secret power on Eloh, it resided with Larkin. Daithin might guide the people on the big issues, he noted, but the little people like Larkin kept the planet moving.

Picard's reverie was interrupted when the premier came out of his office, holding a shaken Waln by the arm. Neither man looked happy, he noted, and a grimness masked Daithin's face. The imposing safeguard officer took Waln into the next building's security wing, and Daithin allowed himself a moment alone. He then turned to Sela, still leaning against a wall, and gestured for her to follow. The officer then beckoned toward Picard to do as well.

Once inside the office Daithin did not take his usual seat, but instead stared out of his window, hands clasped behind his back. Picard watched and a feeling of empathy washed over him. In just a matter of days, he had watched a man he had come to respect grow old. The great warrior was becoming an old man, and he found it an unpleasant picture.

"Waln has finally explained things to me," the premier began moments after the door closed. "It appears that the mercenary was brought here secretly, aboard the warbird, and deposited in that bunker your men found, Captain."

"Impossible!" Sela blurted.

Daithin patted the air with one hand and said with a voice that seemed drained of vitality, "Hear me out, Commander. He was the one to bring the bombs, detonation devices, signals, and so forth. I don't understand all the technology used, but that man did. The bunker was built by that isolationist group and it was all very well arranged. Waln says the mercenary was in the employ of a Romulan officer, one the man boasted of being well placed aboard the ship. I need Commander Sela to name that man."

Sela raged, "I know of no such officer that would be a party to this! Our standards of security are exacting, it would take one of my top three officers to manage such a feat." She stopped a moment, withdrew her own communicator, and signaled the *N'ventnar.*

Moments later, the figure of Plactus shimmered into view and he saluted his superior. Before the salute was complete, Sela launched into a terse explanation of the situation. Plactus did not display any emotion whatsoever during the explanation and Sela could not tell what the man was thinking. Picard and Daithin remained in the office, quietly letting the Romulan take charge.

"So, Plactus, can you tell me something of what happened aboard my ship?"

"Of course, Commander, I was responsible for the human being here."

Picard and Daithin shared looks of astonishment and Sela, glaring at the officer, demanded, "Explain yourself!"

"If you wish," he continued calmly. His composure was first-rate, she thought, watching him. "First, you should understand that what I did was not supposed to result in what eventually happened. Second, I want to formally state that I am with the Tal Shiar and my actions were done with approval." He removed the dreaded Tal Shiar symbol from a pocket and affixed it to his padded shoulder.

Sela watched, speechless and uncertain of what was to be revealed next.

Daithin leaned over and asked Picard, "What's that mean, this Tal Shiar?"

"The Tal Shiar is the Romulan Imperial Intelligence branch, which has no love for the military portion of the government. They have incredible influence throughout the Empire and work mainly through fear and an iron fist. They also trust no one."

"My orders," Plactus continued, "were to win Eloh by any means necessary. Our plan was to provide people with 'gifts' that would show them our strength and our sincerity. The faction I dealt with assured me that they had great influence within Parliament. I appear to have been misled."

"And why wasn't I told of this?"

Plactus changed his stance, allowing his pose to attain more authority, and he seemed to grow into this newly revealed position. "Because you, Commander, were bait. We knew of your history with the *Enterprise* and suspected Captain Picard would spend more time watching you than any of us. It gave us certain freedoms, such as placing the mercenary in position and smuggling down the 'gifts.'"

A pawn.

Picard did not expect the commander to have fallen so far, but there it was. He glanced surreptitiously her way, allowing her a little privacy to collect her dignity. Instead, she looked ready to rip Plactus apart with her bare hands. However, she stood paralyzed by this information. They could not have done worse, Picard mused, had they dressed her as a courtesan and beamed her directly to his quarters.

Everything she had done, he realized, to maintain the honor of the Romulan Empire and best Picard at his own game was actually a sideshow, meant to amuse Starfleet while the real work was done by a subcommander . . . no, Plactus, a Tal Shiar major.

"Plactus—Major Plactus I gather—what happened with the isolationist sect?" The question from Picard was asked quietly, probing for more information and obviously designed to allow Sela a chance to collect her thoughts.

Plactus gave him a cold smile. "Captain Picard, I have no reason to hide what has happened here and will be more than happy to explain everything to you. The people that contacted us after Premier Daithin's invitation indicated that they wielded considerable political power. The Tal Shiar decided that Eloh must be won over to the Romulan Empire. We felt that whatever enticements were asked for was worth the effort. Further, it was agreed that our involvement should remain anonymous. The mercenary was easily bought and used by our people. My aide, Centurion Telorn, secreted him about the *N'ventnar* and transported him to the planet well before your starship entered the system."

"Telorn is Tal Shiar? Is that why she has gone missing?" Sela asked, her voice quiet, reining in her anger.

"No, Commander. She was a loyal Romulan officer who recognized that my influence over her career would be more beneficial than yours," Plactus replied matter-of-factly. "She gave her life for the Empire, as any good soldier would."

"Who killed my officer?" Sela demanded, the fury once again threatening to unleash itself in unproductive ways.

"The isolationists did not like having the Federation looking into the firebombing, and I dispatched her to calm them down. A fight broke out and she died. In fact, Premier, I would very much like her body found and beamed aboard my ship."

"*My* ship!" Sela cried out. "*I* am the captain of the *N'ventnar* and don't *you* forget that. You've cost me much today. There will be plenty for us to discuss when this is concluded. You and your kin will not be pleased."

Major Plactus cocked a slanted eyebrow, obviously amused. "Interesting threat, Commander. It shall indeed be an interesting discussion."

Daithin stepped forward, trying to regain some command over the proceedings even though they appeared to be spiraling further out of control. "Major, I would very much like to know what happened. How were you duped, and by whom?"

"Good questions, Premier," replied the major, a touch of condescension creeping into his voice. "You

Elohsians are a craftier breed than I had given you credit for. I was lured to your world by a group called The Assembly and was allowed to arm this militant faction that passed itself off as allies. Instead, they would just as soon see my people hurl themselves into your sun, right after the *Enterprise.* They are a violent group, Premier, and must be brought under control before more of your own lives are lost."

"What happened to your mercenary, this man Stormcloud?" Picard inquired.

"The Assembly doesn't like anyone, nor does it trust anyone, Captain," Major Plactus replied. "I gather he was under surveillance and when your men began investigating the plant explosion, they killed him to ensure that their secret remained hidden. He, unlike Telorn, was eminently expendable."

"And before any more Romulans lose their lives, eh?" Picard asked, a satirical tone edging into his voice.

"Of course, Captain. I wish this matter to be concluded quickly and for the parliament to make a decision." Plactus stood still, looking self-satisfied and triumphant.

"How can you expect me to make any sort of recommendation given what I've learned today?" Daithin argued. "I don't know what to think. I do know this: I want everyone off my world. Right now. We'll try and find you your corpse, Major Plactus, but for the moment I wish you all to leave—now."

Recognizing that there would be no further discussion, the Federation and Romulan representatives returned to their respective ships. Daithin watched them vanish into the air, privately wishing he could do the same.

"What have I done to my people, Larkin?" he asked quietly.

"What you've always done," Larkin answered in a similar tone. "You thought this was best for our world, and so it seemed."

"How many lives have I cost us this week?"

"The count doesn't matter, you know. That's the past. We can bury our dead but now, my friend the Premier, what will you do tomorrow?"

"I don't know. I just don't know."

Chapter Eleven

"MY PEOPLE," Daithin began, "we have much to consider in a very short amount of time. After today's vote, our parliament will adjourn and our holiday may begin. With luck it will be peaceful; yes, peaceful after all we have endured these last few days. It'll be a terrible time to bury and remember our dead. But we have survived and prevailed, and we will do so again today. Our final presentations will be transmitted live throughout our unified world and the vote will take place only hours later. Listen carefully, my friends, for this is a day for history."

Picard heard the opening remarks only dimly, preferring to mentally review his notes and remarks. He already knew of the import behind the appearance this morning and did not need to be reminded. The past few days were tension-filled enough to leave him feeling in something less than peak condition. His mind was too often crowded with the random images of violence and accusations, and the haunting, cold smile of Commander Sela. He had to succeed, and to do so, draw upon his theatrical experience as a final fallback.

As when Sela spoke, the parliament was packed. It had taken the premier at least ten minutes to bring the meeting to order and launch into his own explanation of events by way of preamble. He was occasionally shouted down with questions, and the leader bravely answered all that he could. Gesturing toward Larkin, he had made the promise that the entire chronology of events would be posted on the world net before sundown. Also, the chief safeguards were rounding up the leaders of The Assembly, and they would be made to pay for their crimes against the people of Eloh.

Picard wondered, though, whether the very existence of an isolationist group would alter anyone's thinking. Larkin had explained that morning about shifting public opinion and how, according to Conductor Luth at the main computer center on Carinth Dar, people were reexamining their interest in space. This might then influence the parliament, which was scheduled to confer with their home sectors and vote the following morning. Within twenty-four hours, he realized, the planet's future would be decided, making the presentation now under way all the more critical.

Taking a very deep breath, Picard slowly let it out, pushed stray thoughts away, and rose to address the planet.

"I want to thank Premier Daithin for succinctly explaining yesterday's developments to you all," Picard finally began. "Eloh is seen by the Romulans as a great prize. A world that much closer to the United Federation of Planet's sphere of influence. It would be a lie to say that my government does not see this world the same way. If you are certain you want an intergalactic alliance, so be it. I will spend this morning

249

explaining the Federation to you and will answer your questions about our intentions. No gifts, no promises I can't keep, and certainly no more pyrotechnics." That last comment elicited a chuckle in the crowd and Picard was pleased to see that people were not being too high-strung about the session. An unamused Worf had personally overseen the security requirements and had chosen to remain nearby, just in case. Picard was just as glad to see Worf beam down with the injured, but recuperating, Lan Mathli. According to his security chief, she was an honorable fighter—quite high praise from the Klingon.

"We respect a planet's right to self-determination. Our principles allow member worlds to exercise their own laws, but we ask that member worlds subscribe to a core set of standard beliefs. For example, we respect the right of an individual to have free speech and a free expression of belief. Subjugation of any basic right is seen as contrary to the nature of the Federation charter."

Picard continued to explain about the Federation's history, its borders, and recent accomplishments. He recognized that technologically this world was far behind the Federation, but he also knew it was hungry to catch up. Also understanding their recent past, he made certain to emphasize Starfleet's role in planetary defense and its ability to respond swiftly to distress calls. He chose not to dwell on Starfleet's military skills or its clashes with the Romulans. Instead, he discussed the deepening alliance with the Klingon Empire which had stabilized the galactic peace for several decades. Such cooperation through peaceful means was a perfect example, in Picard's mind, of what the Federation was all about.

Looking out around the room, Picard chose not to

try and read the Parliament's reactions. Just as easily as they could be swayed by his words so, too, could they change their minds when Sela spoke next. Instead, he did allow himself to take several peeks at Sela herself.

She sat to the side, apart from the other Romulans who were clustered in the gallery. Attired in her formal outfit, Sela was composed but also riveted to Picard. Her gaze was impassive and his words seemed not to affect her one way or the other. On the other hand, not once did she look away. Could his words actually penetrate?

"Some of you have been on my ship, and others have attended the banquet in our honor," Picard continued. "My ship has representatives from thirteen different races aboard, including the only member of a recently recognized life-form." He was speaking about Data, for whom Picard proudly helped achieve such recognition from the Federation just a few years ago. "We cherish new life and new civilizations, those very words being the credo of my ship. The *Enterprise* is a proud name in Federation history and my crew is upholding those traditions of exploration and valor. Just being here and helping introduce ourselves to you is a significant honor."

The talk lasted a good forty-five minutes, and then the questions began. Some members of Parliament had read up on the information supplied to them by the Starfleet Diplomatic Corps, while others had obviously heard innuendo from the Romulans. Picard found himself being asked to defend the Federation's policies when it came to relations with "hostile" races such as the Tholians or the Romulans themselves. Again, he stole a glance toward Sela, who seemed to show disdain for his defense of Federation policies.

Her hatred was missing, and without it her blue eyes seemed changed, less energized—more human.

Some others were concerned about having to answer to a Federation charter with no say in its construction. One went so far as to question how a world in need of catching up could possibly be well represented within the Federation. Picard deftly handled each question, remaining calm and unflappable.

Larkin had explained to him that the parliament would conduct immediate polling of the people, with some hosting their own electronic forums. Opinion makers would be trying desperately to express their views and sway the people, who in turn would sway Parliament. The nature of a united Eloh was still very new, and the cacophony of politics was unsettling to Picard, who had witnessed more than his share of such matters in the past few days. He had also grown weary of politics and was pleased the entire affair was winding down.

When the last of the questions was answered, Picard took the moment to sum up his thoughts—his final official attempt to win the world. "I was not sure what to expect when I arrived on Eloh just a few days ago. Was this a world still at war with itself? Could this world have truly rebuilt itself in just a few short years? I ask myself similar questions each time I visit a new planet. I'll share something with you all: the answers are never the ones I expect. Never. The reason is that there are new things I had not previously considered or even dreamt about. Learning something new each time out, finding something wonderful about every place I have visited—those are the things that have driven me to explore space for nearly four decades.

"I want to show you that universe and share the

exploration with you. To do that, you need to be free enough to join me and sure enough of yourselves and your precious unity to step forward into a new era on Eloh. It cannot be done by you alone, not today. We can help you achieve that future so many of you have told me about. You want to find a place for yourselves in the galaxy, and I honestly believe that the Federation can point you in the right direction.

"I truly hope that we are allowed that singular honor. Thank you."

Picard finished and the room was absolutely silent. Moments ticked by and he noticed one pair of eyes after another looked past him toward the dais where Daithin sat prominently. Slowly, Picard turned his head and glanced up at the premier. To his surprise, those large eyes of Daithin's were welling up with tears. He had hoped to deliver stirring words, but certainly not something that emotional. But, just as he finished saying, he never quite knew what to expect on new worlds.

Daithin stood, smiling and gesturing to the crowd. One by one, the people stood, smiling at Picard and expressing their unified joy at his words. He had little doubt that he had given the speech his best effort and it was well met.

However, given the events of the preceding days, very quickly a nagging thought formed in the back of his mind. This may have been his best shot, but what if it was not good enough?

Sela had listened intently as Picard spoke. In her own mind, much of what he said was true and painted the Federation in the best possible light. She also privately scoffed at the gloss he put over the Starfleet's dealings with hostile races. The holier-than-thou Federation was a gathering of sheep, just grazing until the slaughter at Romulus's hand.

Picard was masterful, she admitted. In fact, it made her review her own preparations and find them wanting. After all, she had done so well the other day without extensive preparation she had presumed it would simply be a repeat performance. Yet, Picard's words reached her and made her rethink her position toward the *Enterprise* captain. Oh yes, he did cost her much back home, but his spirit, conviction, and sincerity also carried weight. She had listened and considered his words, saw his approach to the parliament and the cameras. There was no doubt this was a man convinced he had the most to offer. He did this selflessly, she realized, while she, in turn, wanted this world for her people and her career. And they were her people. In the end, that was going to count more than Picard's pretty words or his manner. The Federation abandoned her mother and they would pay, starting with losing Eloh.

"Our people can trace its history back only one thousand years," Sela said. "We certainly can't claim the same sense of perspective that Eloh can, and for that you can be thankful. History is a great teacher and lessons learned once can avoid problems in the future. The recently concluded conflict on Eloh means that future generations can learn to put aside differences and prosper."

Parliamentarians sat up straighter, some leaning in. Her words seemed to draw them closer and Sela noted Picard also leaned forward just a bit. She was going to give him a show.

"Whereas the conflict on Eloh could have destroyed your world, you had no alternative but to settle and unify. A millennium ago, we had a different choice.

My people abandoned Vulcan, set out into space to confront the great unknowns. We wanted a world where we could tame the environment and be in command as a race. That world, Romulus, stands as a beacon of light in a dim corner of the known galaxy. How I wish you could all see it. The world is beautiful and I can still remember the thrill I received the first time I was taken to see the firefalls of Gal Gath'thong.

"Our people grew as did our prosperity. We slowly started to spread that prosperity throughout our sector, settling Remus and forming the core of the Romulan Star Empire. People with like ideals and goals joined us and we grew powerful. That power meant invaders could be more easily repelled and our authority was respected. In time, the name Romulan stood for something, and we proudly stand behind the name today.

"I am deeply ashamed for the mark against my people, a mark made by an overeager officer who wanted this world more than he wanted his self-respect. You may trust me that no race—be it Romulan, Federation, or other—is perfect. Just as not every citizen of Eloh is pure-hearted nor is every citizen a cutthroat. Your place in time means that you are witnesses to something extraordinary. As you join the starfaring races of the galaxy be aware that each planet possesses a point of view, and at times those points of view come into conflict with one another. Such is the way between us and the Federation. We and they can offer you wonderful things, from protection to technology. You will have to ask yourselves a series of questions having to do with location, point of view, the future . . . all the things that will slowly lead you to a conclusion. With that, you may vote wisely."

Sela concluded with a few more conciliatory remarks and then she, too, took questions. Picard had sat back, openly amazed at Sela's oratory skills. That's just my first victory today, she decided. She was smug, knowing that she gave the speech of a career and crafted it in such a way that it would help the parliament ask itself the very questions required to lead them to the conclusion that Romulus was the better home.

The questions from the Elohsians were just as pointed for her as they were for Picard. There remained concern over occupying forces and restriction of Elohsian space travel. She deftly handled the questions with a touch of humor and tried hard to take a reading from the expressions of those assembled. It was tough to read them and the questions did seem a little harder-edged than she had hoped. When her time ended some ten minutes later, she could not tell for sure if she had carried the day.

James Kelly was completing his studies for the day when he noted the message light had blinked on. He immediately accessed his private mailbox and was shocked to see a message from Ensign Ro.

It said, "I seriously misjudged your desire to take me to the dance. I apologize for rejecting your invitation. But if it remains, I will gladly accept. Please meet me in my quarters tomorrow night to escort me."

Escort her! James was pretty certain he would get down on hands and knees and carry her to the event. Hands shot back through his unruly hair and he began to think about things to wear . . . a gift to bring . . . whether Riker had any other ideas now that he'd gotten this far . . . would there be enough time before tomorrow . . . would tomorrow ever get here soon enough?

* * *

Dawn came all too quickly for Picard. He had stayed up later than he had wanted. Upon returning to the *Enterprise*, the captain had invited his command staff to a private meal. He had found himself in need of companionship that was not fractious. The dinner went off exceedingly well and he had found himself deep in discussion with Crusher, La Forge, and even Worf until quite late. Still, it was a conversation and exchange of ideas that he cherished as he refined and sharpened the memory of that talk. Moving through a hurried morning routine that did not allow time for his ritual breakfast with Beverly, Picard grudgingly allowed concerns and speculation over Eloh to creep back into his consciousness.

Fighting to keep a troubled expression from his face, Picard all too quickly found himself on the transporter pad being beamed back down to Eloh, perhaps for the last time. As he shimmered in the light, Picard contemplated the scenery and envied Troi and La Forge the time they had to go exploring around this world. Next visit, he mused, he would allow those two to attend the meetings and let him explore the countryside.

Larkin was waiting for Picard at the accustomed beam-down spot, looking completely unruffled by the past five days' events or the coolness of the season. His officious manner and subdued mode of dress had also been unchanged, and Picard had come to expect nothing but efficiency from the colorless man. With a gesture, the adjutant allowed Picard to walk into the parliament building. As he complied, the captain noted that safeguard officers seemed to be in abundance: a wise precaution, no doubt.

"Have things calmed down yet?" Picard casually asked.

Larkin considered a moment. "It's not like it was

before the *N'ventnar* came into orbit but certainly better than yesterday."

"You don't necessarily like us being here, do you?"

Again Larkin paused and collected his thoughts. Looking down at Picard, the slightly taller man said, "I'm amazed at how quickly I grew used to having aliens walk among us. I just don't know if I want them telling us how to live our lives."

Picard gave him a concerned look. "I thought I had made it clear your destiny would be your own."

"So you say. So they say. Words, Captain. Yours and theirs. I've had my fill of them."

Larkin silently opened the door for the captain and then stepped aside. This was going to be a private session; just two people would first hear the decision. As Picard understood it, Parliament had debated the issues, polled their constituents through the computer networks, and then returned last night for a vote. The tallies were routed directly to Daithin's personal office computer, and he could either accept the decision of Parliament or veto it and make his own. Then, the results would be made public, along with the premier's verdict.

Picard could not tell by walking with Larkin which way the vote had gone—there was no overt change in his demeanor or that of the safeguards. The integrity of the vote seemed intact and he was getting anxious for the pronouncement.

Inside the office, Daithin immediately stood and greeted Picard with a broad smile, once again showing off well-maintained white teeth against the dark skin. "Sit, Captain, please. Commander Sela is just now beaming down. Marvelous device, you know, just marvelous. I'm very glad we'll be able to gain access to the technology."

Picard took his usual seat in the smallish office and glanced out the window. Already, an army of workers was clearing the rubble from the fire and rebuilding their city. They were certainly a hearty race of survivors and knew when it was time to argue and time to stop fighting and get down to work. This was a race that could easily adjust to new circumstances, and had to after decades of war. This was an admirable trait, and one that would make them eager participants in either government.

After refusing a hot drink, Picard and Daithin talked around the issue at stake and waited a few minutes before Larkin ushered Sela into the room. The door closed softly and the moment had finally arrived.

Picard glanced over at Sela as she took her seat, hands clasped over her lap. She seemed serene and totally in control over the situation. Her confidence was enormous and also appealing when studied in the abstract.

Daithin stood from his place behind the desk, looked down at the alien representatives before him, and sighed. "When we first invited you both to visit Eloh, I could never have imagined what was to happen. I am sorry that you, Commander, lost a valued officer to the subterfuge of Major Plactus. And Captain, I must apologize on behalf of my people for ever suspecting Commander La Forge. On the whole, both crews were exemplary and I was impressed by everyone's candor and willingness to cooperate.

"Our vote last night was an interesting exercise in terms of examining just how unified the people of Eloh had become. Most interesting, indeed, since I earlier suspected there might be a split vote along Populist and Dar lines. Surprising indeed, since that was not the case. In fact, the vote in some ways was also a vote on the unity to see if it could survive a global issue and one that affected everyone's future equally.

"We voted as one. As the first premier, that means my job is done. It has given me the confidence to announce my retirement at the end of my term and truly hand over the future to a new generation. My job is done . . ." He trailed off, realizing he had truly just made the decision and was surprised that he had confided in aliens before his family or friends.

Daithin took a moment to reorganize his thoughts and tried to hurry things along, aware two very anxious people were seated before him. Picard and Sela avoided looking at each other and their gazes rested uncomfortably on Daithin. "The vote and my decision are in concurrence, which pleases me. We have decided to ask for an alliance with the Romulan Empire."

Sela beamed. Picard frowned.

"May I ask, Premier, what led your world to such a decision?" Picard asked, keeping his voice neutral and hiding his shock.

"You've seen my people—the best of us still bickering over decades-old insults, or imagined slights to our particular clan. We need Unity!"

"Unity enforced at gunpoint?" Picard asked.

"Yes," Daithin said firmly. "Even that. Our integration came too fast—we have grown too dependent technologically. If the old rivalries were to surface again, it would hurl us back to the days when we were beating each other senseless with clubs."

Picard nodded. Part of what Daithin said was true—he knew that not just from his observations over the last week but from those of his officers as well.

The Romulans would give them nothing to question, would not encourage them to think for themselves in any matter. The Elohsians would be given a path to walk, and would not be allowed to deviate from it. Their Unity would be preserved.

But at what cost?

Picard looked at Daithin, and then at Sela.

"Despite the truth I sense in your words, Premier," Picard said, "I believe that there is much danger in what you begin here today. I will respect your decision —but I want you to know that if at any time, you have cause to reconsider, you have only to contact us."

"I appreciate that," Daithin said. He smiled. "I have great respect for you, Captain. You have dealt with me honestly and with great honor. While Romulans may feel aggressively toward you, I do not. May we each enjoy rich futures and may we never have to face each other across drawn battle lines."

A feeling of warmth grew in Picard as he stepped closer to say farewell to the premier. Philosophical differences aside, he had come to like Daithin and was sad to realize they would most likely never see each other again. "Thank you, Premier. I hope things work out for the best—for you and Eloh."

Sela who had remained in her chair during the exchange, now rose.

"Captain Picard, I can honestly say it's been a pleasure seeing you—this time." She smiled. "I am hereby officially informing you that Eloh is now a Romulan protectorate, and as such falls under the terms of the Federation/Romulan Non-Agression Pact of 2160. You and the *Enterprise* will have four hours to leave this system. After such time, your presence here will be considered a hostile act. And we will respond accordingly."

"Of that, I have no doubt, Commander," Picard nodded. "This round is yours."

"So it is, Captain Picard," she replied.

"No doubt our paths will cross again," he began.

"Surely. After all, I made certain the Romulan Senate was aware of how their Tal Shiar major was duped by a powerless faction on the planet and nearly cost me and them this world. He has been chastised by them and will soon be by me." The wicked gleam in her eye cast her face in a cruel light, which irritated Picard.

"Then you are a pawn no more," he commented.

"Yes. And this victory will certainly be the first step in a long process. Oh yes, Captain, you will be hearing from me again."

Not wanting to allow her the time to gloat, Picard merely turned and left the room. Passing a curious Larkin, Picard nodded a farewell and returned to the bright morning sunlight. There, he tapped his communicator and returned to the *Enterprise* without pausing to take a final look around this beautiful world. His final thoughts before the beam took him home were about how unspoiled the world seemed today and what it might look like when the Romulans were finished moving in.

Moments after stepping off the transporter platform he signaled he wanted to meet Counselor Troi and Commander Riker in his quarters. That in itself was a rarity but Picard did not feel like being among the crew right then. When the trio assembled, Troi immediately nodded sympathetically.

"They chose the Romulan Empire," Picard said softly. He took a seat and seemed to let his body go limp.

"Any orders?" Riker asked tentatively.

"Follow our plan and prepare to break orbit. Have the helm get us out of here in an orderly fashion."

"Aye, sir," the first officer said.

"Captain, should we postpone the Newcomers' Dance?" Troi looked hopeful and sympathetic at the same time: an interesting trick, Picard mused.

"I know you timed it assuming we were going to prevail today, Counselor, but we did not. Still, we shouldn't avoid our tradition, so proceed."

The officers decided to make a quiet retreat and set about their business, leaving the captain with his thoughts.

There was just enough time left for Ro to glance in the mirror and make sure she looked her very best. She didn't have much time for social amenities like dating and was unsure of how she wanted to proceed. Selecting an outfit was not difficult; her wardrobe was sparse when it came to off-duty attire, and even rarer was the outfit that matched the evening's planned events. She had chosen a deep emerald dress that had a very low scoop neck and a skirt that tapered into a diamond tip just above midthigh. It had a plunging back fitted into a sunburst clasp that glittered in the dim light. Her shoes were also emerald and made of a material that seemed periodically to absorb and then emit shimmering light. Her slender, callused hand readjusted a stray strand of hair and then she declared herself presentable.

The chronometer read 19:59 hours, and by now she knew her date was a most eager and punctual individual. With the final moments ticking away, she surveyed the room: lights low for mood, her furniture properly neat and organized. She mentally ticked off the final odds and ends required for the evening. Her arrangements with Guinan were secure and should be equally punctual.

"Computer, Vulcan études from the neoclassical period."

"Specify composer," the computer requested.

Ro made an annoyed face. "Random selection."

The computer whirred then complied, and odd-sounding instrumentation filtered through the cabin, completing the atmosphere she desired.

Finally, the clock ticked off twenty-hundred hours, and Ro took several deep breaths. This entire evening was a cautiously arranged affair and she wanted everything to go according to plan. If done right, things should improve tremendously for her. If not, she might have a horrible time explaining the situation to Riker—and that was not a conversation she wanted to have. Ever.

Her door buzzer sounded with its quiet electronic chirp and she invited her caller in.

James Kelly walked in, a small box in his right hand. He was decked out in a one-piece jumpsuit of cobalt blue, with a patch from his last home affixed to the right breast. His wide, thick black belt had a glittering bright red stone set in the buckle, and his shoes seemed low and comfortable. The hair that was usually soft and wavy was now slicked back with a spit curl dangling over the left eyebrow. He took three steps in, saw Ro, and exclaimed, "Holy Kolker!"

"Something wrong, James?" Ro asked, her voice modulated to be as inviting as possible.

"No, nothing wrong at all, Ensign. You look totally flawless."

She took a step toward him, flashing a smile which showed off perfect white teeth. He instinctively took a step back. "I think for tonight we can drop the 'Ensign.' Tonight, for you, I am Laren."

"Laren. Sure." He began to look alternately nervous and excited. Ro wasn't sure which way he would decide.

"Before we go, James, I want to thank you for agreeing to be my consort."

A puzzled expression appeared on his face. "Consort?"

"Why yes. I'm from Bajor, and there we have a very organized mating order. We're at the very beginning of this and I'm very excited. It's been a . . . long time."

James Kelly stared at Ro, taking in her appealing form, trying to comprehend her words. She watched, waiting for him to make a move and then countering with one of her own.

"Well, if that's what we're doing, uh . . . Laren, then what's next?"

Ro stepped back into her quarters and let a hand rest on a long, curved instrument made of polished wood with a metal attachment that flared into five sharp points. "Come in. We can be a few minutes late to the dance. After all, being first isn't necessarily being best." She tried to giggle, found it sounded as if she was gargling, and promptly gave up on this approach.

Kelly walked in and stared at the item she was casually stroking. He then seemed to notice other such instruments proudly displayed on walls and even over her bed.

"Bajorans are a passionate people, James. It's what fueled our desires while we fought to free ourselves from the Cardassians. Our rituals go back centuries and have never been violated. Mating among our people is a cause for celebration, but there are steps to be observed. Come closer, please."

Kelly took a hesitant step forward and Ro smiled. She hefted the instrument in her hand and extended it toward him. With now-sweaty hands, he hefted it and felt the weight of the wood and iron, ignoring the polished sharp edges or the fully detailed etchings on the handle. "Should someone challenge you for rights to my . . . passion," she explained, continuing her attempts to sound enticing, "this is what you will use to defend me. I've made sure holodeck four is preprogrammed and ready to run the Bajoran tournament. First blood wins."

She stood behind him, kissed the top of an ear, and paused. Kelly didn't move a muscle, nor did he drop the weapon and run as she had hoped.

"We'll go to the dance, of course, and then when it's over, return here. I'll boil us some Kevas wine and then we can retire for the night."

Kelly let out a contented sigh at the prospect. He'd gotten the hook and line, as it was explained to her once by Riker. Now for the sinker.

"Oh wait, I forgot," she began. "Before . . . that . . . we must experience the ceremony of flesh and blood."

"Flesh and blood," Kelly repeated.

"If you do not fight for my honor tonight, then protocol demands we undergo the ceremony. With a familial knife we will each cut off a small piece of our skin. We place the skin and the dripping blood into a chalice. Then we use sacred spices to mull the mixture and just before we consummate our prolonged relationship, we share the drink."

There was a full thirty seconds of silence in the room. Ro listened to Kelly's breathing increase in rate and patiently awaited his final reaction. Slowly, very slowly and carefully, Kelly lowered the weapon to her desk. Then, he took a few steps away from her and refused to meet her eyes.

"Is there more to life with a Bajoran?" he managed to ask.

Ro continued her act and took another step toward him, the smile still inviting. "Much. But you said yourself you're interested in xenology. Haven't you read up on Bajorans yet?"

"I didn't realize how different your people were from mine," he said, seeming to think quickly. "I'm still seventeen. I don't know if I'm ready for that prolonged a relationship. I'm really terribly sorry, Laren, er . . . Ensign, er . . . oh . . . but maybe this isn't for the best." He backed toward the door.

Ro stood her ground and watched, keeping her face from showing delight. "I respect your wishes and commend you on a wise choice before we were inextricably bound. I'll miss you."

"Sure. Right. I'll, er, miss our time, too. But you have your duties . . ." The door slid open, spilling bright light into the cabin.

"That I do."

"Right. I'll see you." He stepped backward and out into the corridor, allowing the door to close immediately.

Ro immediately broke into a genuine grin and then commanded, "Computer, abort music and full lights." As the room returned to normal, Ro's hand reached behind her and unclasped the dress. Letting it fall to her feet, Ro decided to go for her usual off-duty Bajoran look, remain in the room, and try and finish the Dixon Hill caper. After all, tonight she proved she had learned what it was like to be a doll or a tomato; now she wanted to learn whodunit.

But first, she thought, she had better return all the

weaponry to Worf with her thanks. Bajor may have its
own brand of armaments but nothing worked as well
as the weapons from a legendary warrior race.

Pleased with her night's work, Ro replayed Kelly's
reactions in her mind and let out a pleased chuckle.
This time it sounded just right.

Two hours later, the Newcomer's Dance was under
full swing. The holodeck was filled with civilians and
officers; the Federation Horns, a live band of veteran
crew members, played their hearts out, and Guinan
had a makeshift bar set up in a corner. Counselor Troi
had personally overseen the decorations and theme,
which was a simulation of a dance hall she grew up
near on Betazed. Everything was in bright tones and
the lighting was artfully designed so as not to create
any shadows.

Will Riker had just completed sitting in on a set
with the Federation Horns and was now enjoying a
drink with Troi. Both had considered the event a great
success and a relief from the tensions of the past few
days. One thing about being a civilian aboard the ship:
it meant remaining blissfully ignorant of most
nonshipboard activities.

Riker had just finished a bad joke involving a
Ferengi, a Klingon, and a Benzite, when the holodeck
doors parted and allowed Captain Picard inside the
festivities. He seemed dour to the first officer and no
doubt felt the pressures of the past few days more
keenly than anyone else on board. Riker also knew
that Picard welcomed having civilians aboard the
ships but personally disliked events such as this
dance. He was here because duty called for his presence. Riker then entertained the amusing idea of
Picard's also being here so as not to incur Troi's wrath.

"Number One, Counselor," Picard greeted them.

"Captain, I'm so glad you finally showed up," Troi said, looking lovely again in her off-the-shoulder bright blue gown. It was one of her favorite dresses, and Riker's, too, so he was always happy when she chose to wear it.

"Everyone seems to be having a good time," Picard noted, briefly surveying the room. People were dancing to the music, doing steps that must have been all the rage on a dozen different Federation worlds and new to the command crew.

Riker then noticed James Kelly slowly walk into the dance. He was alone, which surprised him. The slump of his shoulders indicated that their planning did not go well. He excused himself from Picard and ambled over toward the teen, a smile ready to greet him.

"Hello, James," he said.

Kelly looked up, surprised once again to have Riker notice him. "Hi, sir."

"No date, huh?"

"It didn't work out. There was too much of a commitment involved," he explained.

Riker looked thoughtful and confused. "Too much commitment for a dance?"

"Well, Ensign Ro had all these rituals . . ."

"Ro! This was all about you and Ensign Ro?" Riker was at once shocked and amused. His hand began stroking his beard to cover the smile he couldn't help show.

"Didn't you know, sir?"

"The woman's name never came up before, James. I have had a few other matters on my mind," Riker said sympathetically.

"It wasn't going to work, was it?"

"Ro is definitely not your speed," Riker said, still grinning. "I think I owe you an apology. I never would have encouraged you to pursue her had I known.

There are plenty of young women your age, James, and some must be here. Go ahead, you'll find someone. I'll be watching out for you, I promise."

"Okay. Sure." Kelly, still somewhat despondent, hesitatingly moved into the crowd.

To Riker's surprise, before the teen could go ten feet, Guinan was coming directly toward him, towing a young woman by hand. He watched the practiced hostess go to work.

"Hello, James Kelly. I've been waiting for you to get here, you know."

He barely looked at her, and certainly didn't notice the woman. "I didn't know. I'm sorry."

"No problem. You know, Counselor Troi has worked really hard to make this party work, and that means the guest list was carefully balanced. This is Elizabeth Seward, and she has been without a dance partner for at least fifteen minutes."

"Hi," he said, looking at the round-faced girl with shoulder-length brown hair. She was wearing a peach-colored outfit with a bright yellow belt and looked rather attractive. Riker watched the boy realize that this was a young woman far more attainable than Ro. He also thought he heard the teen mutter, "Flawless."

"I'm from Maryland, on Earth's North American continent," Elizabeth said.

Kelly broke into a long story about how he ended up aboard the *Enterprise,* and Guinan quietly slipped back into the crowd. She caught Riker's eye, gave him a wink, and then returned to the bar. Now Riker was sure he had seen everything. This was the woman who could stare down Q, make Worf sociable, and now was a matchmaker. He would never underestimate her skills again.

Riker scanned the room to see where the captain gone to, hoping he had not already departed. He had yet to meet all the newcomers and Riker thought now would be a good time to get his mind off Eloh. Instead, he watched as Picard seemed to complete a circuit of the room, nodding absently at crew members he knew such as Specialist Robin Leffler or Chief Rick Taylor. Then he began to make a beeline for the door.

The alert first officer followed him into the corridor and caught up with Picard at the turbolift. Silently they entered and Picard asked to be returned to the bridge.

"Gamma shift is running smoothly," Riker said, just to say something.

Picard nodded and seemed thoughtful. Looking up at his officer and friend, he finally said, "You're probably wondering what I have been thinking about these past hours.

"There are times, Will, when we presume too much of ourselves and our way of life. I think it is a flaw mankind has endured since civilization began. Earth history is filled with incidents where one society considered itself the perfect one and tried to subjugate others to their way of thinking. The Holy Crusades, the Second World War, the Eugenics Wars, and so on. I had thought we might have grown past that, but I see we did not.

"We came to this world and naturally presumed that since we had the most peaceful and benevolent of intentions we would be more desirable than a government hell-bent on conquest and a rigid way of life. My own arrogance let me think we would prevail and I never once considered that philosophically the Elohsians might prefer the Romulan way of life."

The lift stopped and deposited them on the rather quiet bridge. Lieutenant Michael Hagen rose from the center seat, but Picard patted the air and indicated he should remain on duty. With Riker, he strolled to the ready room and they took seats on the couch. The captain appeared lost in thought again.

Finally he broke the silence by saying, "Daithin had made the observation that he never could have predicted what was to happen when we were invited here. Nor could I have possibly foreseen what was to come. What a marvelous thing life is, constantly surprising us and rarely lulling us into a false sense of security."

"Isn't that what you like most about your career?" Riker inquired.

"Quite, Will. I said so to the parliament. Maybe they had enough surprises over the years and wanted something they could count on. It will be most curious to see what happens to this world in a decade."

"Where will we be then?" Riker asked, not sure of his own answer.

"I don't know. I imagine I will either remain as captain of this ship or settle down commanding some starbase. Certainly I don't want to be tied to Starfleet Command on Earth. That would be too predictable a life for me." He actually chuckled at the concept and Riker laughed along, knowing his distaste for the "good old boy" network that occasionally flared up during administrations. "Maybe one of the deep space stations since they remain closer to frontiers."

"Sounds nice," the younger commander said.

"One thing is certain, though," he said, more to himself than to Riker. The first officer looked at the captain and waited for a response, without prompting.

"Commander Sela is not one to be underestimated. Marvelous speech at the end, and she knew better than I how to play to the crowd. She did her job rather well this time and no doubt will parlay that so we will contend with her again. Maybe then I can find out if her claims are true."

Riker noted that Picard always seemed fascinated by the woman, but had not previously realized just how deep that feeling went. There was no question that they would cross paths again, he knew, and he speculated as to how the two commanders would fare when they next met. Picard was certainly the more resourceful leader, but Sela's bewitching looks and history would be exploited to her advantage.

"We'll see then, Captain," Riker replied. "But today, she's back there, on Eloh, and we're going somewhere new. We have much to do before arriving so I'm going to start on the quarterly personnel review."

Picard looked at him and Riker could tell that the captain was already putting his reverie about Eloh in the back of his mind somewhere, done mourning a mission gone sour. He was clearly returning to his duty mode. "No, Number One. Please go back to the party and enjoy your evening. The reports can wait till the morning."

"Very good, sir," Riker said, rising. "Remind me to tell you what happened aboard the ship while you were gone. You might enjoy one or two items."

"Indeed, Number One. I look forward to it." Picard also stood, tucking his duty jacket back in place, and then walked toward his desk ready to do something to get back to work.

Commander Riker left the ready room while Picard paused to glance out his windows. The stars streaked by as the ship continued to accelerate, leaving Eloh well behind. He watched for a moment, considered that each star held the promise of something new, something wonderful, and was content to take each such discovery one star at a time.